STONE GODDESS

THEA ATKINSON

Paperback ISBN: 978-1-0689100-5-0

CHAPTER 1

The man watching me was not human.

I woke to his sky blue gaze and somewhat attractively squashed nose to some alarm at first. I all but bolted upright from the sofa, but the familiarity of Maddox's jaw and almost irritable stance he held as he watched me made me fall back onto the cushions. He was a glorious being truth be told. Any woman would get her panties in a bunch of lust just looking at him, but I was too tired to bother to work up a lather because that would just take more precious energy in the end.

Fear and trembling took a lot of juice. And I'd already lost plenty of valuable energy over the last 24 hours.

I didn't know how he got in, or what he wanted, but the fact that he loomed over me while I slept with his arms crossed over that muscled chest while I lay completely unaware in a fit of dreams just seemed a normal state of affairs, all things considered.

"You remind me of a young Chris Isaak," I muttered as I closed my eyes again, shutting off his frown from my view. I'd had a hard night. I was not in the mood for him to be frowning at me. Especially when said frown and the fuzziness of coming awake managed to make him looked even sexier than he usually did.

"*Wicked Games*," I said, lifting a finger to the air and following it up with a second. "*Baby Did a Bad Bad Thing.*" I chuckled to myself, imagining him crooning those songs out. "Except you're much ruddier and much, much bigger than he is." I held my hands apart at shoulder length over my chest to indicate how wide. Then they grew too heavy to hold up and I let them fall again to my sides.

I felt his gaze burning my face and peeped open one eye. Yes, still frowning and looking decidedly glorious with auburn hair tied back even if the frown had begun to shift to the side of scowl.

I opened the other eye and out from beneath squinted eyelids the way a drunk in trouble might. "And apparently pissier," I tacked on at full sight of his demeanor.

His brow furrowed. The biceps twitched as he tapped his fingers on them.

"Yep," I mumbled. "Much, much pissier. Seriously. What man wouldn't want to look like Chris Isaak?"

He sighed heavily, withdrawing his arms from his chest to jam his hands into his trouser pockets.

He wore khakis, an unusual thing for him. The white T-shirt pulled taut over his chest in a way that would have most women sizing him up with their palms, just to be sure he wasn't made of sculpted stone. The thought of dozens of women running their hands over him just made me grouchy.

"What are you doing here?" I mumbled. "Anyone ever tell you monsters hide under the bed; they don't loom over a sofa while a gal is sleeping."

I'd known monsters before I met Maddox. It was just that they were all the human kind. My ex-lover, for example.

Scottie kept his people safe, but it was the way a cat keeps a mouse. His to play with. Once in, you had two choices: stay and always wait for the last playful cuff before the teeth bit down. Or become part of the paw that clawed at everything in its path. His specter would always be there, shadowing the sun and adding a deep chill to the rain no matter how long I was out from beneath his violent thumb.

A recent visit from him left a residue of negative energy in my apartment that reminded me of one important thing. No one ever escaped Scottie Lebans. Even if she'd sent him straight to hell on a merry-go-round ride courtesy of a magical stone.

It wasn't eight hours after I'd sent Scottie on his merry way with a stone capable of transporting him straight to Hell in his meaty fist. I hadn't stuck around to see the result, but I knew he'd end up touching it, and he'd end up meeting Lucifer the same way I had.

Alone and scared.

I was sure I'd regret the hasty decision at some point, but I was too exhausted right then to think about it much more than the effort it had taken to accomplish the deed in the first place.

Maddox blinked once before raking a hand through his hair. Then, seeming to realize he'd clubbed it back with a leather tie, he tugged at the short tail of it instead. He smelled of wood smoke the way he always seemed to. A hint of vanilla lifted from his T-shirt every time he moved. I inhaled that scent and felt it cocoon me.

A gal could do worse than wake to that face, really. Not that I wanted to admit that too loudly to my psyche. She might get ideas. And I was feeling languid, the way only a deep, comatose sleep can do. So it was particularly dangerous territory.

His knees popped as he sighed beneath his breath and squatted in front of me. He was so damn close and he smelled so damn good and if I was honest with myself, I just wanted to curl up in his embrace and pretend all the last few years had been a nasty dream. There had been no Scottie. No hell. No horrible fae who sent me scrambling on a goose chase that even the gods couldn't solve let alone a mortal woman in mortal fear of her life.

I pushed those thoughts aside as he cleared his throat, pulling my gaze to his mouth.

"I have a proposition for you," he said, not saying good morning, not indicating he felt embarrassed about catching me sleeping. Not the least bit guilty that he'd barged in uninvited and let me lie there for God knew how long while drooled and snored and twitched like a dog.

Closer to my eye level, I could make out the trace of ruddy stubble that dusted his jaw. My sleep weary body responded by sending me an image of that stubble tickling my thighs. I had to squeeze my eyes shut to make the image stop. I wasn't in the mood.

Whatever proposition he had, my body had already decided it was a yes. And that scared me.

I tried and failed to prop myself up to my elbows. I was still groggy and gave up, flopping back down to the cushion again. It smelled of oily hair and dirt. I winced, imagining just how filthy it must be. Not exactly seductress material. Probably a good thing; the last thing I needed was to complicate my life by getting involved with anyone, let alone a someone who wasn't even human.

My body could go screw itself.

"Not interested," I said and made to turn over.

His hands bore down on my bare legs, preventing me from moving, but not so rough that it bordered on violence. I stared up at him with a disinterested glare until he withdrew them, not right away, but leisurely, tickling the fine hairs on my ankle as he let go.

I'd been propositioned a few times in my adult life. Mostly, it came from men who knew nothing about Scottie Lebans or the stake he'd pounded into my psyche that claimed me as his. Those men who dared speak to me found out pretty quickly that I was a do not touch sort of gal—some of them far too late to save themselves a black eye or broken rib.

I'd learned that propositions were dangerous. Every single one of those poor sods who'd dared make a pass at me in the first place was testament to it.

"Well," Maddox said, no doubt because I just sat there gawking at him as I tried to shed the remnants of a comatose sleep. A whole host of unwanted memories, and a newly awakened desire I hadn't felt in years rode my spine as he eyed me. "You don't look the least bit curious."

"And you don't look the least bit like my ottoman," I mumbled, tasting the gummy film from the deep sleep in the corners of my mouth. "which should be the only thing I wake to in a locked apartment, so i guess we're even."

I rolled onto my side to see him better and feel less like a bug pinned to a corkboard. "How did you get in here, anyway?"

His expression didn't shift one bit. Nope. No guilt there at all for breaking in.

"Maybe I'm a dream," he said. "A wonderful, sensual, untouchable dream." He smirked, and damn if that grin didn't make my throat ache. I really needed to get up before I did something I'd regret.

A soft groan of exhaustion and desire escaped me. "I'm up, " said. "I just need a sec."

He canted his head at me. "You can have all the secs you want."

I gaped at him, unravelling the word sex from the pluralized abbreviation he'd used, and I decided he wasn't really trying to be coy. His owl-eyed expression was too naïve, and I was pretty sure I hadn't given myself away that I wanted him badly enough to imagine the proposition was sexual in nature.

Even knowing that, I wasn't sure why I was disappointed he wasn't offering. And that made me cranky. I thrust my elbow into the cushions for a bit of leverage in one more bid to get up.

"I'm not whatever the Hell it is you have in mind," I said. "But I've had a bit of a day."

My voice evinced a sort of nose-pinching gesture, one that indicated I had a headache or worse. Worse. Definitely worse. Each muscle in my body—even in long forgotten areas—shrieked its protest of moving.

"Take your time," he said, but he tapped his fingers against his biceps the way a man does when a woman has been shopping a little too long and left him standing outside the shop holding a handbag.

Things felt a little uneven with me lying down and him hovering over me, and I felt a bit queasy still. A trip to hell will do that to a gal. I let my eyes close just to ease the sensation of bed spins. Several seconds ticked by and I thought maybe he'd decided to leave me be, finally.

"Well?" Maddox said, his patience at an obvious end.

I wanted to say that the last proposition I'd entertained in this apartment had ended with me hitching a ride on the hell train. Such a delightful journey that I wanted to repeat it like I wanted to step into a blazing fire in my bare feet and wearing a grass skirt. Some places aren't worth visiting no matter how warm the climate. But I heaved a sigh, reluctant to let go the sleep that took away all that dread for a few hours, and managed to keep the comment to myself.

I blinked the weariness from my vision, deciding right then to take my damn time getting up. "I told you. Not interested."

Was it because of an innate streak of masochism that made me want to pull him close so that I could nuzzle in to his chest and just breathe in that comforting scent of vanilla and wood-smoke? Because nothing good could come from that. And only a masochist would go looking for that sort of thing after the night I'd had no matter how gorgeous he was.

As though he'd read my thoughts, his voice went all smoky and rasping, and I had the feeling he was doing it on purpose, damn him.

"Are you sure, Isabella?" he asked, my voice a rasp of pure sex on his lips. "It's a pretty scandalous proposition."

I swallowed down hard. Was he teasing me? I was so spent, I just wasn't sure. All I knew was that if I didn't get up soon, I was going to do something decidedly scandalous.

CHAPTER 2

No man offers a proposition but for the innuendo behind it that meant he was going to turn your ass into a plaything. That was one thing I'd learned from Scottie. Caution regarding offers from unscrupulous men should always be a gal's first reaction. So when Maddox grinned at me, pleased with himself for tempting me with an as-yet undeclared offer, I snorted at him.

"Come on," he said. "You're just the sort of woman who would be interested in what I have to offer."

"You mean a woman with a brain and a killer bod?" I said to cover up the flaming sensation that rode my cheeks. "Because the last woman I saw you with seemed more interested in sharing your ass than keeping you to herself."

The sass was just bravado. Carefully, meticulously cultivated after a decade of living with Scottie. Never let them see your interest, never look greedy.

"I think Kerri would be offended to hear you think she's nothing more than a sex kitten," he drawled. "She's the kind of goddess who takes herself very seriously."

"I saw how serious," I said, remembering her loud complaint outside the museum that he didn't satisfy her sexually. "Your bedroom skills obviously leave her wanting."

I looked him over. Teasing aside, the last few days had been hellish. Literally. I wasn't in much mood for jokes or teasing.

"So that's all you have for me?" I said. "No mention of where have you been, Isabella? What happened to you after the vampires attacked you?"

Yeah. I'd forgotten that in my post exhaustion rousement. I'd not just gone to Hell, I'd been chased there by vampires while he and Fayed held them at bay. Nice day. Good day. Wonderful reasons to be so exhausted. I stretched my legs out in front of me, resting my heels against the throw rug, and glared at him.

Maddox's russet eyebrows knit together at the mention of Fayed's sociopathic progeny who had tried to drain me right in front of him. When he rubbed his fingertips against his jaw, I could hear the faint rustle of that stubble.

"Well?" I said.

When it was clear he wasn't going to answer, I pushed to my feet and headed to my kitchenette. Now that I was awake, I felt much less inclined to be propositioned than I'd been half-asleep. I'd had enough already.

"Whatever your proposition is," I said, fumbling my way back to the original topic. "It's tone-deaf."

"Tone deaf," he said blandly, and I looked at him over my shoulder. His hands were stuffed into his khakis. He'd got to his feet, and he blinked at me as though he didn't understand what I was saying.

"Yes." I arched the kinks out of my back and aimed for the sink so I could wash down the dryness in my throat with a bit of water.

"This is the first time you see me since I left Fayed's, and you don't even ask how I'm doing? You just go straight to a proposition without checking to see if I'm all right? Well. No. Whatever it is, the answer is no."

I couldn't look at him anymore. We both knew the last time I'd seen him wasn't one of those fun-loving get together where you get together with friends and meet at a bar to knock back a few drinks or laugh over a few stupid jokes. The way normal people did. The way people completely oblivious of all the supernatural dimensions coiling around our own did.

No. The last time he'd seen me, he was holding a starving new vampire by the throat, holding her above his head while a cluster of her bloodthirsty brethren swarmed the bar. I was grateful that he'd given me the chance to run, but I'd have expected him to at least ask after my welfare.

I stared instead at the sink, focusing on the way the tap dribbled water at a rate that was about as enjoyable as jazz played by a three year old. I heard him scuffing to his feet along the throw carpet, but I didn't turn around right away. I couldn't. I didn't want to see that blank, emotionless expression he was so good at putting on over top of his features.

The sound of his footsteps stopped and in its wake came a heavy sigh.

"What makes you think my proposition doesn't include concern for your welfare?" he said from behind me.

I swept the cat from the sideboard where she was eying my uncovered butter dish and onto the floor. I noticed long, speckled trails cutting through the creamy surface of the butter and shot her a scolding look. She licked her nose and shook a back leg at me before sprinting toward my bedroom.

"First of all," I said, gathering my dignity and spinning on my heel to face him. "I don't remember inviting you in, and second of all: a man who's worried about someone doesn't proposition them before asking how they are doing."

I watched him watching me, no doubt trying to come up with some excuse to cover both bases.

He lifted one russet eyebrow. That adorably squashed nose wrinkled with annoyance—which I didn't expect.

"It's obvious how you're doing," he said. "You've been snoring there for the better part of an hour, drooling onto that ratty pillow."

He pointed at it with his elbow, and I couldn't help glancing at it. There was indeed a large wet spot on the seam, revealing the truth of his statement. I bristled, thinking he'd been standing there for over an hour. That I'd slept like a woman in a coma while he watched me.

It wasn't disquieting; it was terrifying. Anything could have happened while I was that out cold. The thief in me fought the urge to check every window latch immediately while the abused woman sagged as though she'd expected no less.

Because I couldn't squash either emotion, I fidgeted with the tap, trying to get it to stop dripping. It bled out water like scraped capillaries on a bended knee.

"You have no idea what I had to go through since I saw you last," I said.

"Really?" he said. "Like you know what I've been through, fighting off six blood thirsty vampires while you saunter home for a mid-morning nap?"

He raked his gaze from me to the floor beside the sofa. I tracked his gaze to a pile of leather and vinyl heaped into a bloody and stinking pile that I'd abandoned hours earlier. My heart clotted into a knot at sight of it. They'd been the clothes Lucifer made me wear in his boudoir and I had forgotten all about them until right that moment.

No doubt the sidhe who had decided I owed him and sent me to Hell in repayment left it for me when he'd closed the portal to his manse and cut me off from his protection. Maybe he thought I wanted it as a souvenir. I squeezed my eyes closed, wishing it away.

I'd left hell with that trashy fabric on my skin, and although I didn't judge some folks' penchant for S&M attire, I wouldn't ever look view the activity the same way again. My skin crawled at the thought of the leather against my flesh. My chest caved in at the notion of even touching the outfit long enough to toss it into the trash.

"No wonder you were sleeping so soundly," Maddox said, interrupting my recollection of that awful journey. "You were plum tuckered out from all that fun."

His voice sounded tight as a nun's wimple, but the accusation in his tone was clear.

"Just what do you think I was doing?" I demanded. "You know I owed the sidhe. You're the one who sent me home to repay the favor."

"Looks like you paid him back in spades," he drawled, and I noted he wouldn't look again at the heap of leather and zippers with its hood and fish-like tail.

Instead, his gaze seemed pinned to my throat where I knew my heartbeat was pounding an internal tattoo onto my skin.

I peered down at the sagging T-shirt I'd pulled on after I'd sent Scottie packing. The fabric gaped at the collar, exposing a fair bit of skin, and I knew if I looked beneath the material, several bruises would have bloomed all over the flesh the shirt covered.

The after effects of trying to fight off Lucifer's advances. The sidhe hadn't healed them when he'd given me the choice to leave the apartment he was no longer glamoring. He'd given me a bugout bag, a pair of pants and a top, but he'd not erased the evidence of Lucifer's assault. My throat choked up.

If I'd have been anywhere near that pile of disgusting material, I'd have flung it in Maddox's face. It was insulting enough to see it there, but after the things I'd endured in Hell to get Kassie and myself back home, his inference that I'd enjoyed a nice romp in bed with a fae seemed a bridge too far.

"You broke into my apartment to insult me?" I said, hating the trembling in my voice. "Just moments ago, you said you had a proposition for me. Is that what you have in mind? To make me feel like a prostitute?"

First off," he said. "Your door was wide open, not exactly a Brinks safe up in here." He planted his feet wide enough from each other on the floor that a hurricane wouldn't have toppled him. "I figured under the circumstances we left it at, that you might be under some threat and took it upon myself to barge in to make sure you were alright."

He said it with all the reasonable tone of a man explaining logic, but the word barge came out as a curse.

"Well, I'm just fine," I said, but it was a lie.

I was rested, but I was most definitely not fine. I had the feeling I'd be suffering night terrors for the next ten years, I was so not fine.

He toed the pile of leather with his boot and scowled down at it, oblivious to the precipice I was clinging to. "And second," he went on. "How do you know I didn't check you over while you were sleeping to be sure you were okay? I've been watching you snore on that disgusting sofa for the last hour and could pretty much tell by the way you were drooling over the cushion that whatever you escaped after you left Fayed's — safely, I might add because of me—didn't seem to keep you from enjoying a nice nap."

I wiped my arm across my mouth to mop up any residual wetness. I had the feeling it was caked there in the corners and he was letting me wear the dross out of spite. I had a tenuous hold on my emotions. My grip on the edge of the counter behind me was tight enough to whiten my knuckles. I sucked in a breath, more to calm down than anything else.

I forced myself to remember he had no idea what I'd gone through after I'd fled the bar. He'd held back those vampires so I could retreat and run to the sidhe in the hopes of saving Kassie. Something we both wanted because the teenager was a pitiful thing in the clutches of Lucifer and needed our help.

Except she wasn't a teenager at all. She turned out to be the Morrigan of all things. A triad goddess who had renounced her powers and was as impotent as a man with a new vasectomy. And yet, she was the reason I'd managed to escape hell.

Nothing was what it seemed anymore. I felt like I was swaying on my feet despite the tight grip I had on the counter.

Maddox's long legs devoured the distance between us. He loomed over me, his eyes all pupils and furrowed brow. "What is wrong with you, Isabella?" he said.

I snapped my gaze up to his, the words tumbling out before I could stop them.

"What's wrong with me?" I blurted. "What's wrong is that I just went to Hell and back, that's what."

It sounded like a gasp even to my ears. I had to clamp my hands over my mouth so I didn't start to cry. I hated crying. And I was horribly close to it. So close I could hear the tears in my tone.

When he saw me as I must have looked, terrified, with a stare the size of a goggle-eyed lemur, his hand balled up next to his thigh. He shoved it into his pocket and took that last step toward me that gave him the reach he needed to touch my cheek.

I had the horrible feeling he was about to crush me in a pitying hug.

I couldn't take that. I didn't want it.

"Don't," I said. "Don't you dare touch me."

Maddox blinked, and I thought I saw his throat convulse. I might have decided he had a heart after all, one that could be broken by an unkind tone, but the cat streaked out from the crack in the doorway and launched herself at him with a hiss.

Like some sort of feline ninja, she bounced off the chair and propelled herself at his shoulders, reaching up with a paw and scratching him across the neck. Then she squalled and ran up the stairs to the empty third level. I watched her on the top tread, staring down at us with a glassy glare.

"Devil cat," he said and laid a palm against the scratch. I doubted it had drawn blood, but it had to smart.

"Maybe she recognizes a devil when she sees one," I said, grateful to the beast for distracting Maddox from my out-burst. "The sidhe warlord had quite a different effect on her," I told him, drawing out the distraction, knowing following a shift in conversation didn't just put distance around a regret-ful outburst, it pretty much buried it.

He murmured something in a language I didn't recognize and pulled his hand away to check for blood. When he swung his gaze to mine, all trace of pity was gone. In its place was the guarded, composed expression, one I felt more comfortable with.

"Fae have an affinity for nature and all its creatures...what I am? Not so much."

"And what are you?" I said.

He just smiled. "I'm someone you can trust, Isabella. Someone who needs you."

"Needs me?" I said.

He nodded. "Well, not you so much as what you have."

I had a lot of things. A sore body. An aching soul. Maybe a few hundred dollars stashed in a bug out bag that could get me nowhere great in no time flat.

"What do you need from me that you can't get for yourself?" I asked.

"The Lilith Stone."

The Lilith Stone.

There we were, right back to the topic I didn't want to discuss. It had been the instrument of my descent to Hell, tossed blissfully at me by the sidhe, Colin, as a means to trick me into touching it.

In catching it, I'd found myself transported by its magic to a copper tub the size of a pool in a realm I couldn't have taken a bus, ferry, or plane to. Lucifer's own bath, it turned out. So what I knew of the stone was painfully little: that it could transport its holder in and out of that hellish boudoir at a touch.

I'd had a narrow escape. I didn't relish reminiscing about it, but that wasn't why I couldn't let on to Maddox that I knew about the stone. I'd given it to Scottie as insurance. He kept the valuable asset while I gathered necessary intel on how it could be used as a weapon by some powerful people I was working with.

At least, that's what I told him.

I was running a long con on a man who thought take-out pizza was too long a wait.

Letting on I knew about the stone to Maddox would risk my freedom, and I'd worked too hard—conned too hard—for it.

I flicked a crumb from the counter the way someone might do if they were ignorant but curious. Stared casually out the window over my sink. I could see that the sun had already set behind the buildings and it was growing gloomy in the room. I flicked on the switch over the basin, and the LED light cast a blueish glow over the sink.

"This Lilith Stone?" I said. "Is it anything like Lilith Fair?"

I dragged my gaze from the light switch to my wrist as though to check the time. "Because I think you're a decade too late for that."

His shoes squeaked as he advanced on me. "Don't be coy, Isabella," he said in a gravelly voice that I instantly recognized as a threat. "I know you have it."

CHAPTER 3

I knew the sound of a man about to lose his cool. My body knew it even more acutely than my mind. I turned and crossed my arms protectively over my chest as I leaned against the counter as I faced him. A waft of sleep sweat crept up my nose at my motion, and I was weary again just thinking about what I'd gone through. Survival requires a level of endurance sometimes that can rival a triathlete.

I didn't think more than eight hours had passed since I'd escaped from Hell. The thought of just crawling into my bed in my T-shirt sounded about right. I wanted to sleep for days. Apparently, it wasn't an option as Maddox laid his palm down on the sideboard on either side of me, leaning in as though he wanted to cage me there until I got flustered and gave up my secrets.

He obviously misjudged me.

"I need a shot," I said. "Want one?"

I wasn't sure at first that he'd let me go, but when I edged sideways, he lifted his arm, drawbridge style and let me pass. I pulled open a cupboard door. Several bags of opened chips grinned back at me. A jar of pickles.

No booze, though. I knew better than to check my fridge. I didn't have a carton of milk or a bottle of orange juice. I'd not been shopping in forever. My stomach gurgled, thinking about how long it had been since I'd eaten. Water would have to suffice.

"What I want is for you to answer me." His biceps flexed and moved, drawing my eye from the sparse cupboard. "Tell the truth."

I pulled down a glass from the shelf beside the fridge so I could avoid his searing gaze. I bumped past him to run the tap till it was frigid before sticking the glass beneath.

"What makes you think I'd lie?"

I watched the water foam to the top and run over the rim into the basin, where a small pile of dirty dishes had been left. I'd been in the middle of doing them, I remembered, when all the trouble with Scottie and the sidhe had begun. I hated doing dishes, but in retrospect, that hellish duty would have been preferable.

Maddox reached toward the top of the stove and plucked the pepper shaker from its spot. He spun it about to face forward with three deft fingers and swapped it out for the salt shaker. Then he lobbed an accusatory glance at me because the salt was all gobbed on the top. He thumbed the grains away and brushed them on his pants.

"Maybe you don't know what the Lilith stone is called, but you have it," he said.

"Never heard of it," I said and took a long draft of the cool water.

It braced me, lifting gooseflesh to the back of my neck, and I eyed him over the rim.

He pushed the spice shakers toward the back of the range and advanced on me to stand no more than an inch away. I had to look up at him and realized the back of my head hurt. Everything hurt, to be honest. Just standing there felt like agony.

"I tripped over your bug out bag on my way in," he said. "Half-empty can of pepper spray. Pistol. But no stone. So where did you stash it?"

He was close enough to me that he could track the back of his fingers along my arm to my elbow, and he did. I wondered if he'd sensed my earlier lust and was using it now to fluster me.

"You have it here somewhere, Isabella. You're not a good liar. It's not yours to keep. It was stolen from a sect of monks from the fifth world who would very much like it back."

"How many damn worlds are there, anyway?" I said, catching my breath at his touch. Damn, he was something. All danger and rugged good looks stuffed into a dress shirt and jacket that was groaning to be yanked open. Just exactly the kind of man who got me into a world of hurt in the first place.

"Nine," he said, and his palm whispered against my elbow. "As far as we know."

I edged away from him and backed into the sideboard.

"Don't—" I started to say until those fingers clamped down a little too roughly. My throat closed up again. Panic started to open up a tight bud in my chest.

"I know you have it, Kitten," he said. "The smell of it is all over you. It's all over the apartment."

I shook him off because if I waited one more second, that bud of fear would bloom and then I might end up just sobbing till I couldn't breathe.

"That stink is sweat," I said. "A girl gets a little overheated when she has to fight for her life."

I put a safe distance between us. Close enough to the fridge, I yanked it open and noticed a heel of a bagel sitting on the top shelf in its bag. The cream cheese container sat beside it, book ended with an opened can of beer I must have left in there weeks earlier.

I pulled out all three, hugging the bagel and cream cheese to my breast as I upended the can. As barricades, they weren't great, but I felt better with them between us.

With one eye on him, I tossed the empty toward the trashcan.

It circled the lip before falling to the floor with a metallic thunk.

His gaze narrowed to two small slits.

"In Hell," he said, drawing both words out the way you do when you're finally putting two and two together.

"Yes," I admitted. "Hell."

He poked his tongue into the corner of his mouth, thinking.

"Well?" I said. "Cat got your tongue? I just told you I went to Hell. I almost died there. Almost ended up putting curtains on a cozy bedroom made of hellfire and brimstone. In fact, by my count, I told you twice and you don't seem the least bit concerned."

He reached down and plucked the can from the floor and dropped it where it belonged then shoved his hands into his pockets. His fists bulged against the material.

"To Hell," he said, narrowing his gaze to suspicious slits. "Literally?"

"Would I lie about something like that?" I said. "The sidhe warlord. Colin. He sent me."

It took several moments before his shoulders sagged and he dropped his gaze to his feet. I watched the transformation with interest because I didn't expect him to look so guilty. I mean, I wanted him to hurt, sure, but he wasn't responsible for me facing down Satan. That was all the fae's doing.

"I'm sorry, Isabella," he said. "I'm being an obtuse bastard."

I lifted my eyebrow at the word.

"That better damn well mean you're being insensitive," I said, because after all the huff I'd put up, it would make his apology seem worthless if I just passed it over.

But I was flustered at his reaction, so I plopped the stale bagel down into the toaster and plunged the lever just so I could turn away for a moment. Once I smelled the yeasty scent of warm bread, I lifted my gaze to his again, feeling more braced.

He laid his palm down on the sideboard and tracked with his gaze the flush I knew was rising from my chest to my face.

"Tell me," he said and leaned one hip against the cupboards. "I want to hear about it."

I took my time peeling the back the top of the cream cheese container so I could gather my thoughts. The last thing I wanted was to think about the trip to Hell and the monster that owned a menagerie full of souls he used for his pleasure.

Even so, I had to tell him. I had to tell someone. Keeping it bottled up wasn't going to do me any good, and I'd insinuated he needed to ask. I couldn't back out now.

"It was the sidhe warlord," I said, recoiling at the layer of mold on one side.

If he noticed my reaction, he remained stoic and patient. He waited till I spun the container around so the mold faced the other direction. Having started, I found it difficult to continue, so I pulled a knife from the drawer and aimed it at the container.

I tore my gaze away from the green fuzz and lifted it to his face.

"Colin. He sent me to Hell to pull Kassie out. Just like we thought, she was in there, trapped."

The rest of the story came easier. In between scraping cheese from the untainted half of the tub, and spreading it over a burnt bagel, I explained how Kassie had re-assembled herself into the Morrigan long enough to rescue me, leaving out the part about the stone that she had used to do so, the stone I'd pawned off on Scottie because I knew fate would end up taking out the man I didn't have the power to finish.

At least I hoped so.

Maddox listened quietly, grimacing as I crunched down into the bagel. His eyes flicked toward the cream cheese tub and I thought I saw him swallow convulsively.

"See?" he said. "Your admission that you went to Hell for Kassie...That's how I know you have the stone," he said. "That's one of its powers."

"One?"

He nodded slowly, as though he'd said too much. "It's an amazing relic, actually."

"Well, I don't have it," I said. I wasn't lying, and knowing I wasn't lent the confidence to stare him down, I headed toward the sofa. Standing there in a T-shirt and not much else was making me antsy.

"I'll pay you," he said, halting my steps mid journey.

"Not interested," I said around a mouthful of bagel. I wasn't about to tell him it wouldn't matter. I wasn't about to visit Scottie to get the thing back unless it was for enough cash that I could buy my way back out again.

I chewed the piece of bread while I flopped down on the cushions and threw one arm over the back of the sofa.

He canted his head at me, indicating he didn't believe me.

"It's not something a human should play with, Isabella," he said. "You're best to just give it to me. Scratch that," he said.

"I'll pay you for it. Right now. I have a thousand dollars on me."

He dug through his pockets and I eyed him through narrow eyes at mention of payment. I had a tribute coming up for Scottie as part of my sabbatical deal, the only thing I could think of to keep him from dragging me off with him to a future that involved showing his goons how much control he had over me.

If the man didn't open the little velvet pouch out of curiosity, I'd need a good deal of cash to keep that hard bargained for independence.

"Just how valuable is it?" I said.

His search of his pockets stalled. Green eyes flashed and narrowed suspiciously.

"I thought you didn't have it."

"I don't."

He waved his hand. "Like I said, its scent is all over you. There's no sense pretending when I know better, so let's just cut to what's important to you. I'll pay. To keep you safe if nothing else. It's really nothing to mess with."

He hitched himself onto the counter and I watched the play of muscles in his chest work beneath his T-shirt as I chewed and his fists clenched and unclenched against the countertop.

I ignored his mention of me smelling like magic because after I'd seen the things he could do, I didn't doubt he had some weird affinity for magical relics. It explained why he owned the Shadow Bazaar and why he had a network of pawn shops in his arsenal to fuel the sale and bargaining of those kinds of things.

"So," I said, "How much will you pay for this artifact, assuming I can retrieve it for you?"

"Ah, there's my greedy kitten," he said.

Let him think greed motivated me. What did it matter to me? Except it did. I had already decided I wasn't going to run anymore. I was facing my demons head on. But it wasn't enough. My particular demon required cash to let me stay rooted without being torn up in the most vicious manner imaginable.

I tossed the last half of the bagel onto a side counter when a hint of mold struck my palate.

He grimaced and nudged it further away from him, pushing it far enough that it mashed up against the toaster.

"You don't have to retrieve it," he said. "It's too dangerous. Just tell me where it is."

"Believe me," I said. "After that experience, I wouldn't touch the thing with a forty-foot pole and a hand made of iron."

He grinned. "Not for all the tea in China?"

"Not for all the gold in El Dorado."

"There is no money in El Dorado," he said. "It's just a tale the mothmen tell to lure humans."

I had no idea what a mothman was, or that they lured humans at all and it intrigued me. "What do they lure them for?"

He lifted a hand. "Don't ask."

He was right. I didn't want to know. Stick to the stone and the possibility of payment. Especially payment I didn't have to see Scottie to get.

I did know where it was. At least, theoretically. That meant I had the upper hand. An easy score. Instead of telling him and letting him wrest it from Scottie's clutches himself for free, I could earn a tidy tribute and pay the bastard with his own insurance. Supposing he was still on Terra Firma anyway.

I stretched, letting my arms climb above my head.

"I know better than to mess with the stone, but if I can get my non-literal hands on it, I'd want at least 20K."

"I'll give you 20K just for telling me where it is," he countered.

It was generous and I knew it. It was safer than facing Scottie, and I could get at least one quarter's tribute. But if it was that easy, then I could do better.

Besides: if Scottie was still on this earthly plane, then that stone was safe in its pouch. Ready to be pilfered. If it wasn't, then no amount of money was going to change that.

"I can get it and have it to you by tomorrow night. " I tugged my shirt down once I realized the stretch had pulled the hem up over my hips. "For that, I'll need forty thousand."

His jaw seesawed back and forth and he sighed.

"I don't like it," he said. "But if you can have it in my hand by tomorrow midnight, I'll pay you what you ask. If you can't, you agree to tell me where it is and I pay nothing."

"Will I have to go to the Shadow Bazaar?" I asked.

He shook his head. "I'll come to you. Just like now."

"But you'll knock this time, right?" I said, imagining finding him hovering over my bedside and fearing what I might do if he caught me half asleep.

He stuck his fingers in the air like a boy scout, and he stiffened his back formally.

"I will only enter uninvited if I think you're being assaulted, beaten to a pulp, or eating another moldy bagel," he said.

I stuck my hand out.

"Deal."

I gripped his hand with the kind of firm handshake I'd always imagined deal-makers used, but when his palm met mine two of his fingers trailed around to my wrist, tickling the skin there, turning it into something entirely different.

His gaze touched down on my mouth at the same time his fingers brushed the inside of my wrist.

I hated the way my cheeks flamed as he eyed me, obviously waiting to see what my reaction might be.

"That wasn't an invitation," I said and pulled my hand away before I ended up lassoed to his chest by a lust I couldn't seem to manage this close.

He grinned. "Guess that means I need to leave," he said.

I watched him spin on his heel and head for the door. He back-kicked the bug-out bag further into the room and deftly avoided the cat's leap from the stairs. She landed with a soft thud on the tiles behind his back as the door closed.

She yowled at me when he'd left.

"I agree," I said, but I felt a disquieting niggle of uncertainty.

It was one thing to agree to a heist, quite another to plan to steal from a mobster.

And stealing from Scottie was a death sentence.

CHAPTER 4

A foolish girl might decide to charm Scottie out of his wares. I'd certainly been a bit foolish in my day, but recent events had smartened me up a bit. At least, I hoped they had. I couldn't just stroll into Scottie's hotel room and steal the stone out from under his careful gaze.

No. I needed a ruse.

And I needed protection.

Fayed would provide both, if he was amenable. I had no reason to believe he'd help me, except for the guilt he might feel that his progeny, Ismé the sociopathic vampire, had tried to kill me.

I dressed in my most comfortable yoga pants and a clean T-shirt, pulling a light jacket over my shoulders in case the overcast sky opened up to rain.

The cat eyed me with a baleful look. No doubt she was getting a bit of PTSD from being shuffled off unexpectedly to other realms whenever I left her alone.

I had no idea what had happened to her the first time, but I doubted she'd been hard-pressed in her visit to the fourth world with the sidhe. She had acted toward the warlord as though she wanted to become a living stole wrapped around his neck to keep him warm at nights.

Personally, I hoped the bastard froze to death.

"You'll be fine," I muttered to her when she followed me to the door. "Just go shred some socks. I left a new pair on the floor of my bedroom just for you."

I had indeed left a pair of socks to occupy her time, but they'd been old ones, not new. I wasn't about to lay out a pair of fresh white Mirena (TM) socks for her to tear to bits. I'd lost too many good ones already. Although how she managed to dig them out from my dresser drawer was a mystery. I figured if I baited her, she might leave my good ones alone.

She yowled at me and I stooped to rub her ears. She let me get one good pet in before she batted at my wrist, tired, already, of my attentions.

I took the hint and toed her toward my bedroom then slipped on a pair of running shoes. I slung my workout bag over my shoulder, complete with all the preparatory things I needed for an evening jaunt in the city: one pistol, a full can of pepper spray, and a burner phone.

The Rot Gut Tavern was on the seedier end of the more nefarious parts of the district. The quickest route was along the waterfront, and a gal did not travel that way without a good deal of courage and a hell of a lot of backup.

I took an Uber straight from my apartment steps: one lovely side effect of having made a deal with Scottie. I didn't need to spend unnecessary time and energy walking three blocks and backtracking before heading where I wanted.

I momentarily reveled in that fact as I watched my building fade from sight in the rear view mirror. The bricks looked warm in the orange light of the setting sun.

The tavern itself was a sort of mish mash. The bar took up most of the wall, with tables along the sides of the walls. Fayed had carefully placed wooden kegs propped up here and there as impromptu tables, and the windows--what there were of them--were painted black so no natural light entered.

There were three doors that I knew of. One was the front, one in the back alley, and one that led to a part of the bar reserved for the basement and where he presumably let rooms for the day.

Now that I knew Fayed was a vampire, and that his bar was a sort of hostel for all sorts of night creatures looking for a safe place to spend their days, I was careful about keeping the room within easy sight as I panned the bar for him.

I kept the exits in easy proximity, never getting trapped between a chair and a table. I'd once come to this bar happily oblivious to the supernatural dangers.

Regular human dangers, I was prepared for, and used the bar as a sort of sanctuary. No easy prey type of woman would be caught dead in there, so I assumed my acceptance had come from my brazen unaccompanied visits.

I'd had no idea Fayed was holding the clientele at bay for my sake.

He stood at his usual post, in intense conversation with a rather beefy looking woman. She had the look of a body builder, but her hair was braided back and her profile revealed delicate features.

"Hey, Fayed," I said, careful to stay close to the end of the bar closest to the exit. A quick pan showed only three other patrons and while I wasn't ready to relax, I did feel a little more safe.

Fayed swung his gaze at the sound of my voice and his own went dark and guarded.

"I told you never to come back here, Isabella," he said, and the woman spun on her stool to eye me. She glanced down at my shoes before running her gaze up my yoga pants and jacket, then she dismissed me with a sniff.

I supposed I deserved that. He had told me not to come back because it was dangerous, but I imagined the dark glare had more to do with the fact that to save me, Kassie had sacrificed his progeny to Lucifer.

I held up my hands, showing my peaceful intentions.

"Just stopping in for a drink," I said and pulled my workout bag in front of me to show him I'd been doing thirsty work. "Yours is the only place in the district I trust."

He harrumphed and signaled for me to cozy up to the bar. His gaze trailed over to the patrons in the room and I imagined he wasn't keen on them noticing me.

"Sit here," he said. "One drink. Then you're outta here."

His mocha skin seemed unusually flushed and the eyes I knew to be a mossy green had all but filled up with his pupils. He leaned in close to the woman he'd been speaking to and said something under his breath. She shoved a twenty dollar bill at him across the bar.

"Red ale," she said, giving me a sidelong look. She was sizing me up, I realized, trying to figure out what kind of creature I was. What had he said about me, I wondered.

I grinned at her but she sucked her teeth and turned away. Fayed placed a short tumbler in front of her filled with reddish fluid that had the slightest bit of viscosity. The red ale, I gathered, was blood watered down with beer. I tried not to gag.

She took it from the bar and with a hateful glare, headed for the back room.

I pushed onto the stool nearest him but still within easy access to the door. A gal couldn't be too careful in places where *otherworlders* congregated even if the manager of the place was a friendly.

"Her knickers are in a knot," I said.

"She doesn't wear knickers," he said. "Iron girded panties, more like it."

He gave her a long look and while I didn't take him for being attracted to a muscled female, he certainly looked as though they'd shared time together.

"Do tell me," I said. "I never once thought about the mating habits of the rarely seen otherworlder." I flicked at a crumb. "Might make a great reality show," I said. "Lifestyles of the dead and deadly."

He canted his head at me. "You came to poke fun," he said and I quickly backtracked, holding up my hands in surrender and assuring him I didn't want to make trouble.

"What is this term," he said.

"Reality Show?" I fluttered my fingers over my drink, swatting away a fly attracted to the aroma of liquor. "It's a new kind of television--"

"Otherworlder," he said. "What's that?"

My eyebrows drew together. "Seriously?" I said. "It's you." I twirled my finger in a circle in front of him. "You and your ilk. All you things that aren't human."

"Ah," he laid both palms down on the bar-top on either side of my drink. "We call ourselves Kindred. You might want to do the same unless you want one of our 'ilk' to decide they need a bit of flesh and bone for dinner."

He pushed the glass sideways so that I had to grab for it.

"Now," he said. "What brings you here, really?"

"I left in a bit of a rush last time," I said.

"Indeed."

He wasn't going to make this easy, it seemed. I expected a bit more from him, being that he'd told me never to come back because it wasn't safe, but he didn't offer more than the single triangle his eyebrow made over his left eye.

"I thought I should repay you for all your help."

He made a noncommittal sound deep in his throat.

"A repayment of the getaway money I gave you might help," he said.

I shifted on the stool, remembering that he had given me a load of cash, expecting me to quit the city.

"I can get that back to you," I said. "Plus a few more bucks in your pocket. All it will cost is a bit of your time."

"What I need is information," he said. "I don't need a few more bucks."

"What about a few thousand more bucks?"

He rocked back on his heels then leaned his forearms on the bar, easing in close enough that I could smell the coppery tang of blood on his cheeks. I tried to lean away without offending him.

"Where would a girl who was running from a bad situation all of a sudden come into a few thousand dollars?"

I explained the predicament with Scottie, starting with the night I'd run from him in my pajamas, and ending with the way Alvin broke into my apartment on Scottie's orders and put a decent beating on me.

In between, I stuffed in the parts of the story that held the deal I'd made with Scottie for him to grant me what we termed, a sabbatical.

"I have to pay tribute to him once a quarter until I have divested all the intel out of my weapons contact," I said, putting air quotes around the weapons contact.

"He sounds like a douche-bag," Fayed said and reached under the bar for my favorite liquor.

The Rot Gut, named for the tavern, was a mix of leftovers from the various bottles and had a crystal of absinthe at the bottom. Patrons could order the Rot Gut but they paid extra for the crystal and it wasn't cheap.

I declined with a shake of my head. I wanted to be focused.

"He is a douche," I said. "But there were times when he wasn't. Indeed, there were times he was sweet and affectionate; they just grew more sporadic and less frequent as the years went on."

Fayed grunted. "I've heard that song before," he said. "A dozen women's counselors have heard it too, I bet. You need to break that piece inside you that pines for the times he was a good guy. He's not a good guy. No good guy would do those things to another human being."

"Says the vampire," I said and he shrugged.

"I've done some awful things in my blood-life, but we're not talking about vampires or near immortals," he said. "I was talking about mortal men. Human beings are born with a soul. They have consciences. All sorts of roadmaps for how to behave and moral compasses to keep them going in the right direction. I'm old, but not so old I don't remember that."

He reached over the bar to run his thumb along my cheekbone. "Any man who could order this delicate bone structure to be broken is no man. He's an animal. Get rid of him."

"That's what I'm doing," I said and rested my palm against his hand. His skin was cool but in a way that made me feel tingly. "It's why I'm here."

He curled his fist over my hand and squeezed before letting go. "You want me to kill him?"

CHAPTER 5

I let go a nervous laugh, half expecting he was joking, but he looked serious. The wide pupils in his mossy green eyes pinched down to pinpricks, and I thought I saw a glint of fangs peek out from beneath his full lips.

"No," I said. "That would make me no better than he is."

It would be easier, I knew, to finish off the Scottie threat with his body in the morgue, but I had never enjoyed the violence I'd witnessed at his hand. He was a bastard, but he was human. A life with a soul no matter how black it had grown.

It was one thing to leave Scottie to his own fate by deciding whether he trusted me enough to check the stone in the velvet pouch was what I said it was, but it was another to snuff out his life.

"I just can't," I said. "Best to leave him to his own fate, whatever it is he decides."

I leaned back on my stool, fleeting a glance at the exit when I heard the door open, but I couldn't see who came in.

Fayed pressed a cool glass against my fingers.

Water.

I nodded at him in thanks.

"Speaking of fate," he said, clearing his throat, and I grasped that whatever was making his jump onto such an awkward segue meant that he had been biding his time before I came back to the tavern.

He might not have wanted me to come, but now that I was here, he planned to make the most of it.

"Yes," I said, carefully.

"Have you seen her?" he said. "The Morrigan, I mean."

I had. I chewed my lip. The last thing I wanted to do was admit I had seen The Morrigan. Fayed had been pretty territorial and fatherly over his new progeny and if he knew Kassie as the Morrigan had bartered her soul for mine, I wasn't sure how he might take it. He was a friend. A good one. One I had come to rely on.

I couldn't risk that.

"I don't know where she is," I said, offering the truth instead of an answer to his question. After the Morrigan had renounced her powers again, I'd not seen any aspect of her. He could take that at face value.

He sighed. "I was hoping you'd say you had."

He eyed me, and I thought he was trying very hard to get me to meet his gaze, but I couldn't. The tip of his nose let me look at him without the risk of him seeing the guilt in my eyes.

"Why?" I said. "What do you need her for?"

"She came here, the triad aspect, and she took my progeny."

There was a hard edge to his voice and I was relieved I'd not confessed any more than I had.

"I can't have a naive newborn out there all vulnerable and exposed."

I traced a water stain on the bar. It seemed Fayed had some pretty rose-colored impressions of the sociopath who had in her days stolen possession of a woman's body to bait a vampire into making her.

"I wouldn't exactly say she's naive," I said, daring to offer at least some of the truth that Ismé had a pretty nefarious past. Maybe it would help him forget his paternal blindness.

"What is that supposed to mean," he said.

I shrugged. "How well did you know her before you turned her?"

I tapped my finger in the water that dribbled down my glass to pool onto the bar.

"Maybe she had issues. Maybe her past wasn't quite so linear."

I knew she had issues. I'd been privy to a horrible blow by blow replay of her life, death, rebirth, and consequent death by vampire, finally. Namely, Fayed. Her past was stained the way blueberries ruined your teeth.

He stiffened. "I made her," he said. "I'm responsible for her. I won't let her hurt herself or others."

I wanted to say, too late, but I touched his hand instead, distracting him from his single-minded defense of the vampire. Going down that line of conversation would only open up other, more risky questions.

"She did try to kill me, Fayed," I said.

"That was just newborn hunger," he said as though distracted and then changed the subject, expertly rounding it back to me.

"So then," he said. "What is it you need from me if not the final drink?"

"Your muscle. Your presence."

"How so?"

"Scottie has something that if I steal, will bring in a few thousand dollars. Enough to pay my first tribute."

"And you want me to steal it?"

I shook my head. I'd thought about it the whole way over. If Scottie was still in this realm, it would prove he trusted me enough to not open the pouch and touch the stone. If he wasn't, then he'd handled it and gone straight to Hell.

I had no doubt that if he entertained any small doubt about my sincerity, he would ignore them, because under it all, he wanted to trust me. It was the reason he'd agreed to give me the sabbatical.

"He doesn't know what he has," I said to Fayed. "In fact, I'm certain he hasn't even seen it."

Fayed looked over his shoulder toward the door as more patrons funneled in. I could see he was getting antsy about me being there.

"So you're thinking that if you steal it, he won't know."

"I'm thinking I can replace the item with a different one. But I need access. And I need to introduce you as a contact from the weapons intel to solidify his trust."

"And because he can't kill me, I'm your muscle."

I grinned. "Exactly. If things go wrong, you can muscle me out."

"I can do better," he said, leaning in and catching my eye.

I felt a warm flush all over, as though he'd poured warm, scented oil over my head and it was coating my skin. When he spoke it was in a hushed tone that reminded me of smoldering ashes and long languid drinks of Irish coffee.

"Kiss me," he said. "Deep and slow. As though the world turned on our desire."

It was a sudden shift in direction, and there was no pre-amble or touch to ignite such a bald order. I didn't need to wrap my arms around his neck to kiss him, but I did. And why I pulled him to me and planted my mouth against his,

I couldn't understand. All I knew was I felt compelled to do it.

When his lips brushed against mine, I opened to him and savored his taste. It put me in mind of toasted marshmallows and chocolate.

A slide show of images shuttered through my mind, some sexual, some frightening. I saw things of Fayed I knew I would want to forget later.

I might have kissed him for hours if I hadn't felt the prick of something sharp against my tongue. I tasted blood and recoiled.

I stared at him, my hands still around his neck, but feeling as though someone had just thrown a bucket of ice water over my back.

"What in the Hell?" I said.

I jerked away, my closed fist swung in an arc that grazed his ear.

He chuckled darkly. "Compulsion," he said. "One of our greatest weapons."

I scrubbed my mouth with the back of my hand. "You could have just told me."

He shrugged. "I'm not so benevolent as that," he said. "Make no mistake, vampires let mortals live for a reason."

"And the reason I'm alive is because you want me to owe you."

"You're alive because you amuse me," he said.

"But will you help me?"

He swiped the corner of my mouth with his thumb and I was shocked to see a smear of blood against the pad of skin. He stuck it in his mouth and grinned around it.

"I think I just answered your question."

He leaned away from the bar and, as I blinked stupidly, a ruckus at the door made me turn.

The sight of a slight woman with a short pixie cut left me gaping in disbelief. I knew that woman, if woman was indeed the right word.

I believe Fayed and Maddox had both called her a fae. Finn the dark sorcerer had used the word assassin.

Whatever term she preferred for herself, she was the one who hunted me down to retrieve the rune tile I'd accidentally stolen from Finn.

She'd attacked this very bar in an effort to kill me.

And now she was looking straight at me.

CHAPTER 6

I felt Fayed stiffen beside me. She'd torn his bar up pretty good last time in her search for me, but she'd also come in lights blazing back then. This time, she entered as though on cat's paws, soft and leisurely, with an arrogance that reminded me of my own rescued pet no doubt shredding my best socks in my absence.

She paused in the doorway in an eerily reminiscent posture to the one she'd exhibited before. Feet splayed shoulder width apart, her diminutive size doing its best to fill as much space as possible. I got the feeling in those moments it was her normal stance. Always wanting to look bigger than she was.

This time, however, instead of blasting the bar with destructive volleys of fae magic, she swung her gaze around the room in patient scrutiny.

Her combat fatigues had been replaced by what must have been a sort of dress uniform in the fae realm. It glinted off the lights in shifting colors as though it had invisible Bedazzle rhinestones sewn in. One moment it was red, the next a pale yellow, the next a sea foam green.

She looked stunning, to be honest, just in a terrifying way.

No one seemed to notice her except me and Fayed.

"That can't be good," he muttered.

"How comforting," I whispered back. I was already edging sideways, slipping my right cheek off the stool in an effort to slip away unnoticed.

I braced myself to duck under it or dodge to the side.

Recognition lit the assassin's expression and a slow smile spread across her features.

I stared back at her, my lips pressed together as my brain flooded with stimuli. I had a shot glass in front of me for a weapon, a vampire at my side. Two exits behind me, one that led to an alleyway.

I didn't have to run. I didn't want to.

"Come on, bitch," I whispered. "I see you."

A smirk played on her lips. She'd heard me all right.

She tipped her fingers to her forehead in salute and those black eyes of hers trailed down my body, inspecting me. Foe or friend, she was thinking and I tittered out a chuckle to think anyone could be considered cozy enough to an assassin to be considered a friend at all.

A thin eyebrow lifted above her right eye at my nervous laugh and then she lifted her palm toward me. A flare of purple light filled her palm and roiled into a ball about the size of a potato. I flinched involuntarily but the light remained nestled in her hand.

It grew brighter, shifting colors.

She was giving me a good show of her power, letting me really see it and give me time to know exactly what kind of magic would hurl itself at me.

My pistol was nestled nicely in my workout bag on the stool beside me. I'd be damned if she'd let fly while I sat there doing nothing. With slow movements, I slipped my fingers into the gap in the zipper but found only my can of pepper spray.

Fayed must have sensed my heartbeat had shifted into overdrive. He clenched my wrist and held it down against my side. All while the ball of light grew bigger and brighter. I hissed out a bracing breath.

"Hold off," he muttered. "Look." He jerked his chin toward the muscled woman from earlier who had gone rigid in her seat.

"She's here for her."

A chair scraped back as Kelly veered away from me and headed toward the back of the bar, where a beefy looking man with hair down to his shoulder blades had noticed her finally and was hustling his way along the back wall, presumably to safety.

Her freshly shined lace-up combat boots beat a path along the wooden floorboards.

The woman lifted her gaze from the glass she was nursing and landed on Kelly.

"Shit," she said.

The light crackled as it left Kelly's palm and streaked across the room. It slammed into the chair, splintering it into a dozen sharp pieces that spread like shrapnel. The long-haired dude grunted in surprised pain as a piece stuck in his bicep.

"For fuck's sake," Fayed bit out.

Time decided to spin back into normal countdown. Chaos erupted around me. The surly creatures in the room launched themselves behind tables or threw weaker men in front of them to protect themselves.

One, a broad-shouldered man with a mullet and hairy arms shifted into a bat the size of a vulture and shot up to the ceiling where he clung by his feet to a light fixture.

A chair sailed across the room, splintered from the blast that shot from Kelly's hands.

I had time to realize that the woman, obviously another fae, was fighting back. What was truly astounding was that she was meeting Kelly's blasts of light with pools of inky blackness. It was like watching someone throw out the contents of a bucket of molten tar.

When they met, the black swallowed up Kelly's light, sending sparks out sideways.

Kelly cursed, then squared her shoulders at her opponent, shaking out her hands.

"You want the full Monty?" she said with a laugh. "So be it."

A white stream of light erupted from her hands and hurtled toward the other woman. I folded myself into the smallest ball I could as I lunged sideways. I needed cover. The last thing I wanted was to get stuck in the cross fire.

When their magics met, a swirling mass of color punched through the fabric of air in the room. It actually looked for one microsecond, as though we could see into another realm.

"What the Hell?" I said.

The woman leapt behind a table as another volley of short bursts erupted from the stream, each of them forming what looked like pinwheels of energy. They slammed into the table and chairs all around the woman and I had to dodge a chair leg that had broken off and splintered just in time to avoid it embedding in my stomach.

Fayed's hands clutched my shoulders so fiercely his fingers dug into my skin beneath my shirt. He yanked me without mercy over the bar. I slid awkwardly on the surface, my legs splaying to the sides before I landed on my shoulder and butted up against the lowest shelf that lined his back wall.

Bottles clinked together and one, a clear crystal bottle filled with a viscous red liquid broke. Clots slid over the floor, making me gag.

"I thought she was a vampire," I said, remembering the bigger woman's order of blood ale.

"Hybrid," he said. "An abomination in the fourth world. This is going to get ugly."

Something snapped in the room like a live wire striking metal. The room lit up with white light and Fayed groaned in agony as he buried his face in his forearms to avoid the brightness. I smelled burning hair.

I was blinded for a moment as chaos overtook the bar. I felt Fayed's hands roaming my back, seeking assurance I was alright.

"I'm fine," I muttered out. "I'm fine."

The light fizzled back to the easy gloom of a dingy bar and I stared wide eyed at him.

His pupils had all but obliterated the beautiful green of his irises. No doubt he'd gone into some sort of preternatural mode, letting in as much light as possible so he could take process every detail.

"You need to get out of here, Isabella," he said as another streak of light sizzled into the shelves and shattered several bottles. Liquor poured down over me, and I was thankful it only smelled of alcohol.

"I'm guessing Kelly is winning," I said.

"She always wins," he said. "Trouble is, I'm not in the mood to let my bar get ransacked. Again."

A strange look crossed his expression.

"And I think I might have just found my answer to the Kassie question," he mused. "If I can get her to talk, that is."

He pushed himself to his feet and hauled me along with him. I could see the hybrid bobbing and weaving to avoid the onslaught of volleys Kelly threw her way.

She weaved past a blast that turned the television into a sizzling mass of smoking electronics, then ran toward the bar. Kelly chuckled and took aim again.

Fayed pushed me over the counter again and toward the door, urgency laced into the way he shoved my backside as I crawled over the surface.

A blast struck the edge of the bar, sending debris flying.

He swore out loud.

"Dammit all," he growled, giving me one final push that sent me reeling toward the floor with all the gracefulness of a baboon dancing Swan Lake.

"But wait," I said, stumbling over several pieces of broken table once my feet landed on the floor. "What about my proposition?"

Kelly shouted something at her quarry that sounded like run while you can and I caught sight of the hybrid grabbing for a bowl of peanuts that no one ever seemed to touch. The nuts rained down on her and the bowl went flying, thrust an even greater distance by a wave of black that made it smack against Kelly's ear.

The assassin ducked aside in time to avoid the black wave that swallowed up the outdated pinball machine against the wall.

"Fuck," Fayed said. "I had high score on that thing."

I clutched his sleeve, noting with some anxiety that his fangs had punched out and that his eyes had gone washed in red now instead of just pupil-filled.

"Fayed," I said, prodding him. "Answer me."

"Midnight," he said. "I have a feeling this will take most of the night."

I fled for the exit, fully intending to leave this uproar to the supernatural creatures that created it.

Closing the door on the chaos behind me magnified that sense that everything had got out of control again. I amped up my need to do something. The adrenaline soaked into my tissues, reminding me that a life spinning like a pinwheel and shooting sparks off in every direction was not a life at all. It was Catherine Wheel firework.

I had to stop the spinning. Or at least become the center instead of one of the sparks.

If I sold the stone to Maddox, I would continue to be in Scottie's debt, rendering unto that Caesar tribute after tribute. But at least, I'd have perhaps two tributes in the bag.

Scottie thought he had in his possession a key to the most powerful weapon that the government had created. He was going big time, as far as he was concerned, and if he truly had a weapon element in his possession that could propel him into Caesar type territory, he wouldn't muck with it.

Fayed would be my 'contact', the proof I was completing my side of the bargain by weaseling out information that could net Scottie a massive fortune in extortion.

If Scottie trusted me, I continued the sabbatical.

The only issue was if the warrior in Scottie overrode the part of Scottie that wanted to trust me. If he decided he wanted to know what it could do, he'd find himself slammed into a world where he was the spark and not the center.

Every one of those scenarios was in my favor as far as I was concerned. It was only the percentage that was in question.

There was only one cog in the machine that could spin the wheel out of control.

Scottie might have seen the stone.

I knew the heft and weight and still had a good idea of what it looked like.

I couldn't count on Scottie not having simply plopped it out of its protective pouch and examining it without laying a finger on it.

He might even have had someone else handle it.

That meant I needed a reasonable facsimile to replace it if I planned to steal it.

I didn't flee the bar so much as sauntered down the dark street, taking the time to walk beneath the streetlights because at the end of it all, this was the seediest part of the city. Nothing lured the criminal element so much as timidness.

The evening air had taken on a chill that had me shivering in my light jacket. I pulled the collar up and hunkered down into it, sealing the heat into my core.

Several rats scurried from my step as I passed an overflowing dumpster that smelled of sour milk and rotten meat. I pulled my workout bag in front of me and slipped my hand in to find the pistol within its depths. My palm rested against the butt, ready to yank it out if I needed to.

A gunshot rang out several blocks away and I tightened my grip automatically.

The sooner I was out of the area, the better and ran down my list of contacts in my head. A pawnshop would be the most likely place to find a cuckoo's egg.

I didn't know of any in this part of town.

Well. There was one.

The Pawntoon. Errol's shop, where he collected and sold everything from military accoutrements to geodes.

I shivered not because of the chill, but because Errol was an incubus with limited powers. I wasn't sure why some of his powers had been taken away but I was certain I didn't want to know what could be black enough that a demon could have his powers revoked. I didn't even know it was possible.

I just knew he was a weakened incubus and that I'd black-mailed him by using the knowledge that he was luring children into his shop and selling them in the Shadow Bazaar. Those innocents went to a witch who supplied vampire bleeder dens.

All under Maddox's nose.

While I'd love to see what would happen to a powerless incubus in a jail cell, I had my doubts it would actually 'take' and instead kept the threat of discovery hanging over him instead. One thing I'd learned from Scottie that had proved useful over the years was that information and threat was more powerful than action at times. Much like the power of desire versus climax.

One could be exploited; the other was the currency.

Errol had so far abided by the bargain as far as I knew, but I'd not been in his shop since and the thought of his disgustingly greasy porn star face made my stomach roil.

I sighed and turned left at the next street corner because who was I kidding? If there was a substitute for a supernatural hunk of rock, it would be in that shop.

I just had to face a lecherous incubus to get my hands on it.

CHAPTER 7

Errol's shop smelled of sugar and cinnamon and the yeasty sweetness of donuts as I pushed open the door. The bell above it rang out with an obnoxious clarity that made me wince as I stepped inside. Like Pavlov's dog, my psyche and muscle memory stored the events of my last visit and reacted to the chime above the door in a way that made my skin crawl.

A man entered the main shop from behind a beaded curtain at the sound of the bell. He was busy polishing some fist-sized bauble and was responding to the clamor almost automatically, bustling behind his counter without looking up to see who had entered his shop.

I peered around the room, wondering if I had somehow entered the wrong store. Errol's shop should have had a candy counter at the front and aisles filled with military paraphernalia and trinkets.

There were still shelves with military artifacts like helmets and bayonets and maps and the like over by the farthest wall, but the area immediately around the counter and doorway looked more like an old fashioned coffee shop than a place to pawn unwanted goods.

It might have been the wrong shop, but I'd checked the sign on entry. I'd been to the location a dozen times; I knew

I knew I'd not gone in the wrong door. Besides: there was no mistaking that beaded curtain.

He'd nearly dragged me through it last visit, intent on assaulting me.

This was the right shop, alright. It was just the wrong guy.

I expected a greasier version of Ron Jeremy, but the man who lifted his gaze from the strange looking object gave me a charming, if not disarming smile, looked more like Colin Farrell.

"Is Errol in?" I asked, lingering at the doorway.

A smirk crossed the man's face and I knew in that moment, who it was.

Errol. The incubus had found some way to shed his nasty looking skin and fit into a more alluring one.

My mind reeled back to our last encounter. I'd threatened to turn him in to the police and instead of being upset, he'd seemed entirely too pleased with himself. I'd been too interested in getting out of his shop and staying the hell away to care why.

He must have made a deal greater than the one he'd made with me, one that no doubt included a return of some of those lost powers.

"What bargain did you make to get that face?" I asked him, halting just inside the door and letting it fall closed behind me.

"Immortal bargains are for immortal creatures," he said with a lifted eyebrow. Meaning, none of my business.

I gripped the pepper spray can from inside the workout bag and strolled in with a determination not to let him make me nervous. I needed the upper hand. There was only one way to get it.

Remind him of what I had over him.

When I'd been in the Shadow Bazaar, I'd discovered that he lured children into his shop with candy before shipping them off to a witch in the bazaar.

The only reason he was still free and clear to run his shop was because I had blackmailed him with that information. He'd been closer to human than demon, and he seemed afraid of incarceration.

I used that anxiety to my own advantage.

Or at least I thought I did.

I'd got a dirty bit of glamour out of the deal that ended up sending me to Hell.

"I'm not here to turn you in," I said.

"Not here to turn me on, either, it seems," he said with a note of sadness.

"Got me," I said, with a tone that indicated if they were free, my hands would be up. "But I meant what I said. I'm not here to turn you in."

He laid the flat of his palm on the glass counter by the register and leaned in as though his hips were mating with the cupboards on his side.

"There's nothing to turn me in for anyway," he said, letting that black eyed gaze of his travel the length of my legs in the yoga pants and stopped at the crotch. I ran my hand over my hips to break his stare.

He slowly lifted his eyes to mine.

"So," I said. "You've changed to baiting kids with donuts?"

I waved my hand in the direction of the individual baking machine that filled out the left corner of the shop. It had a distinct look of carnival confectionery.

"What did you do with the candy stand?" I said.

"Gone. Replaced because of our arrangement," he said and licked his lips. He might look like Colin Farrell, but there, in that movement, the greasy porn star was back. I shuddered, pulling the workout bag closer to my chest.

"Where's your boots?" His gaze flicked to the running shoes I wore before lifting again to my face. "And your wig?"

I'd come here so often in various disguises--one of them being a dominatrix type outfit--I didn't think he'd have put all of those aliases together.

He crooked his finger at me, inviting me closer.

"Come closer, little mortal; I don't bite."

I didn't like the way I was drawn to him but I couldn't help myself. There was something about those black eyes of his. He smelled very much like cinnamon sugar. His skin even looked dusted with it.

"So now you lure people with a different type of sugar before you abduct them?" I said and found that the closer I got, the closer I wanted to get.

He shook his head in denial and scraped through his black hair with his free hand as he came out from behind his counter. I noted he kept the one on the counter lying there, and I wondered what he might have close at hand behind the counter that he might want to pull on me.

I pulled the workout bag closer over my chest protectively.

"No kids," he said. "Evelina is long gone and with her my market for saleable goods."

He hitched a hip along the counter and crossed one ankle over the other as he watched me approach. I narrowed my gaze at him, trying to figure out why I didn't find him so repulsive anymore. It wasn't just the handsome face, either.

He dusted his shirt off and ran his palm down along his thigh.

"Are you sure you don't want a taste this time?" he said. "You might find the offer a bit more attractive now."

"You're still the same greasy demon underneath all that charm," I said but I didn't even sound convincing to my ear.

"Eve found a demon well worth her trouble," he said.

"A snake in gilded scales is still a snake."

I stopped several feet away at the corner of the counter, what I thought was a safe distance given I had no idea what kind of powers an incubus might have besides being irresistible. I promised myself a good bit of time on my laptop and Google after all this was over.

His smile slid over his face like a bead of oil.

"You could be missing the time of a lifetime. Or several lifetimes," he sighed.

"I regret I've got but one life to give for my sanity," I said and ran a finger along the glass counter.

I'd never paid much attention to what was beneath the glass before, but I could swear it wasn't icing frosted donut holes and confectionery like it was now.

I canted my head at him.

"What's with all the sweets?"

"Do you really want to know?"

I found it harder and harder to pull my gaze from his. I shook my head, more to dislodge my eyes from his than to argue.

"No," I said. "So long as it's not to lure children to their demise, it's all good."

"Oh, it's very good."

He finally pushed off from the counter, obviously thinking he wasn't going to get far with his charm if he hadn't pulled me in by now. I silently wondered just how much of his power he'd re-acquired or even if there was more to an incubus's power than mere charm.

I watched him move behind his display case and splay his arms out sideways, his fingers tented over the glass.

"So," he said. "What are you in for tonight, Ms. Hush if not a taste of the Divine?"

I squinted at him, wary and startled. I'd not told him my name. Not ever.

"How is it you know my name?" I said.

He canted his head to the side. "Your friend Colin told me. It's time we dealt on honest terms, is it not?"

"You mean Chu-chulain," I said and watched as he smiled broadly, interested that I'd figured it out. "Did you know that bastard would want repayment for a favor you collected on?"

He shrugged. "The fae of every breed and world likes to be repaid. It's common knowledge." He paused for effect. "At least for Kindred."

"Yes, well, I'm not one to pay more than the value of an item," I said and he chuckled softly to himself, lifting the hairs on my arms.

"Bastard," I said. "You knew he'd want to keep me in his eternal debt."

"The fae and their ilk love being owed," he said. "At least now you know that and you aren't too worse for the wear, now are you?"

I pressed my lips together. It was useless arguing and it was getting far too late. Maddox had told me once that most pawns and dealers in major cities worked for or were supernatural factions. Dealing with Errol, at least I knew what I was working with.

"I need something that looks old and weapony," I said. "Do you have something like that?"

He ran his palm along the counter thoughtfully, scrubbing with his thumb at a smudge. "Old and weapony. Interesting."

"And it needs to look very much like a rock and fit in a velvet pouch about so big." I spread my fingers apart to indicate the size. "And I need the pouch."

As I described what the stone looked like in as much detail as I could remember, he leaned forward onto his forearms on the counter.

"And you came to my little shop for those things," he murmured as his black eyes rested on my mouth. "I'm flattered."

"Don't be," I said. "You were closest."

I was careful to make it sound as though I'd walk out at any moment and find a more useful place. I was fully aware his shop was more of a front for his Shadow Bazaar interests than to find prodigal supernatural artifacts, but every salesman is a salesman.

What I didn't know was whether he would call my bluff. Because demons were demons.

His fingers walked toward me for several inches before tapping down on the glass.

"I might have something that fits the bill."

I tried not to lean forward and follow the track of those fingers, tried not to show interest.

"Those donuts will only assault my digestion," I said. "Come up with something better."

He chuckled and it sounded like warm oil. "Oh hush," he said, inflecting a tone of double entendre as he invoked my surname. "Look closer."

I craned forward to peer into the display case. What I'd thought were all donuts were a mish mash of items. A grenade shaped like a penis lay snuggled against a land mine formed into a vagina.

"What the hell?" I said, feeling my face color.

He laughed harder.

"You see something you want," he said.

I snapped my gaze to his. "Disgusting little bastard," I said. "Are they donuts or explosives?"

"You tell me."

I looked again and the explosives were nothing but banal looking stones. Grey and speckled, they could have been ostrich eggs or beach stones.

"Stop it," I said because I knew somehow he was manipulating reality. "Show me something real."

He sighed with great disappointment. "You've ceased to be fun, Ms. Hush. I liked you better when you were masquerading as a dominatrix."

"What makes you think I was masquerading?"

He shrugged. "It was fun for a while to pretend a tiny human woman might flog the living moonlight out of me, but that aura of yours doesn't shift change with a change of clothes or a few wigs."

I tried not to smile at the thought of all the times I dressed for him, thinking it had somehow greased his inclination to deal. Apparently, it had, just not the way I'd thought.

I propped my hand on my hip. "Don't try to pretend now that you weren't going to assault me a few weeks ago."

He laid a shamed hand against his chest. "I would never deny it," he said. "Although I must admit, it would have been very pleasant to reminisce of better days with you."

"Better days?" I argued. "You nearly raped me."

His lips pressed together primly. "Hardly raped. I didn't even get my fly undone before the monk came."

"Intent and opportunity are the same in my book."

I hadn't forgotten my near miss, but I had to admit, I was warming up to him, and I didn't like it one bit.

He cocked his head to the side and a lock of black curl dipped into his eye. He raked it back impatiently, as though he weren't used to his hair being as lush as it was.

"Are you interested in rectifying our missed encounter?" he asked.

I laid my hand on the glass over one of the beach stones, willing it to turn back into a donut. "Hell, no," I said. "A gal doesn't jump onto the grill once she's sizzled on the frying pan."

He followed my gaze to the display case. "You must be hungry," he said, "to be speaking in terms of food."

He reached in and his hand moved over several large stones and then, as though pondering the best choice, wavered over a clutch of smaller ones. When he withdrew his hand, he had a small donut hole pinched in his fingers. Powdered sugar dusted his knuckles.

He laid it on the counter, obviously thinking I was too skittish to take it directly from him. Then he rolled it, warbling toward me.

"It's safe," he said. "Part of my rehabilitation."

"Donuts are your penance? I must be down the rabbit hole."

He lifted his sugary fingers to the air, waggling them in front of me with a crooked eyebrow. When I shook my head, he stuck them, one at a time, into his mouth and sucked on them. Those black eyes locked on mine greedily.

"I don't barter children anymore." He sighed. "Too risky."

He looked at me pointedly because we both knew I was to blame for that. "But adults, well...they are a different story altogether."

"You entrap policemen?" I said, stuffing the donut into my mouth and chewing.

It was delightful. All cinnamon and sweetness, just a hint of nutmeg and sour cream. I resolved to buy donuts to go along with a carton of milk.

"Think of it as an entrance fee," he said and the bright light went out in his eyes and his expression fell to one of blank expectation.

I had time to wish I'd just shot myself in the foot and saved myself the trouble before he snagged my elbow and my knees turned to water.

"Come along," he said and tugged me along with him toward the beaded curtain.

I had got close enough to the beaded curtain before to see that inside was a chamber filled with sexually deviant supplies. He had told me it also contained a portal to the Shadow Bazaar, which was how he'd transport the children he lured in.

I barely escaped that last time, and then, only because of Maddox.

There was no way I was going to let Errol drag me in there now.

Except none of my muscles seemed to want to obey my brain. In fact, my legs seemed all too eager to let him lead me.

"Take your hands off me," I said, thinking I was struggling but was gaining ground toward the curtain. "Let me go."

"Don't be ridiculous, Ms. Hush," he said. "You ate the donut; now you must pay."

Chapter 8

The incubus sent a chilly look at me as he looked at me over his shoulder. "Don't be a baby. No one in there is the least bit interested in a mortal woman." his gaze traveled my body from hair to heel in an assessing glance. "At least not for what you're thinking."

He caught my eye and something like a film slid over his corneas. It put me in mind of the ticking over a bird's eye. It was gone as quickly as it came, and when he blinked again, there was no sign of it, just an inky blackness to his pupils that seemed far bigger than before.

It should have creeped me out, but I followed him silently, drawn to the set of his shoulders as he flipped aside the curtain and held it open for me. I swung my gaze left and right, feeling a dread sort of fear that the darkness in the room held untold horrors.

It was my own fault I was here.

"Don't be afraid, Ms. Hush," he said next to my ear. His breath moved my hair and smelled of cotton floss and straw-berries. I imagined evenings in front of a fire, with a lover hanging over me, trailing berries along my bare skin.

I turned to him in a daze and he nuzzled my cheek with his chin. I couldn't feel the tiniest hint of stubble. It was as though his skin was smooth granite.

His hand went to the small of my back. The heat from his palm sang up my spine.

He guided me ever so gently but firmly further into the room. I was aware of a dozen sets of eyes on me, but couldn't for the life of me identify whether the onlookers were male, female, or even human.

Each time I tried to make out what they looked like, a wash of heat wave shuddered over them and I lost focus.

It hurt, to be honest, and I began to think it best I not try to get a good look at them.

Besides.

I imagined I wouldn't want to know.

With each step deeper into the chamber, the fog of darkness receded and I was better able to see the surroundings. I'd been given a peek of his back room before, and I expected a dank closet sized room, with a blazing portal ringed in fire, impatient to send me to the Shadow Bazaar.

There was no blazing portal or torture chamber awaiting me beyond the curtain.

It was like a speakeasy in there.

Crystal glasses hung from wooden racks in the ceiling over what I could loosely term as a bar. Loosely, because the counter wasn't made of wood or granite, but some sort of ivory surface with mottles of brownish color.

The railing itself looked to be made of tanned hide of some kind instead of oak slats. Bottles of different colored liquid lined the wall behind it.

I shuddered involuntarily, even if I couldn't bring myself to back out again through the curtain. Some part of my brain whispered danger, but my body didn't want to obey.

Beings of all sorts hung around it, and if I strained to make them out, I could see that some of them were humanoid and some seemed in transition from one thing to another.

I caught sight of something with bat-like wings with talon tips. One patron, a wolfish looking man caught sight of me and licked his lips.

A headache stung the back of my brow and I resolved to stop trying to work out what kinds of creatures they were.

They're human, I told myself. *Just regular guys and gals out on the town.*

The headache evaporated.

"That's it," Errol said. "There's the ticket."

I stared at him numbly. An image tried to nudge forward of a grimy room and a beat up armoire, replacing the speakeasy setting.

"This was a grimy back room last time I was here," I said.

"Just a bit of incubus glamor," he retorted. "Last time you tempted me, I only had a trace of my skills and magic. Residual power, if you will."

"So this is what's real?" I asked and caught his eye. The ticking closed down over his eye without his lids moving.

He extended his arm to indicate the breadth of the room. "This is closer to real."

His mouth formed into a smile that was both secretive and victorious. "You came at just the right time. I'm having a meet and greet."

I didn't know what sort of meet and greet an incubus would put on or why, but everyone in the room seemed to be having a good time. Glasses clinked together and a dull roar of conversation just barely disguised a lower, more thrumming sort of moaning that could have been pain or pleasure.

I shuffled backward, not sure I wanted to know any more than that.

"No worries, Ms. Hush," he said. "It's just an evening of drinks with friends."

He pressed the small of my back gently, guiding me deeper into the room. My feet felt heavier with each step. Though I could see more clearly, each inch into the chamber seemed to rob more and more of my muscle command.

"Just drinks?" I heard myself say and he nuzzled my ear with his lips.

"Drinks and snacks."

Snacks. I expected pretzel bowls or hors d'oeuvre trays and I found myself wondering what sort of snacks might whet the appetites of Errol's clientele.

In fact, I wondered what sort of clientele he catered to at all.

The headache bit into my skull again and I sucked in a breath.

"See anything you like?" he said. "I've had to up my presence after my power decline. It was a long fifty years, but now I'm feeling very much like myself again."

He tipped an imaginary hat to me and clicked his heels.

"All thanks to your creative persuasion. Had you not forced my hand, I might not have had the chance to barter the Coalition for the return of my baser powers."

As he prattled on about still working on getting all his magics back, I wondered what sort of things Errol might have done to offend a coalition of demons.

I swung my gaze about the room, searching for evidence of how bad it might be.

Speakeasy was the best description I could come up with, since it did seem a bit clandestine. The energy in the room was anxious and frenetic. The humanoid creatures kept a keen eye on me and the door at first but when they saw I was with Errol, they went back to whatever had them occupied.

The closest bar no doubt fulfilled the same function as lingerie did in a sex shop. Teasing the patron forward, easing the more squeamish of buyers into a sense of normalcy before going hard core.

"The pawn shop is for my human customers," he whispered as though I'd spoken out loud. "But now that I have nearly all my powers back--thanks to you--I decided to celebrate my return with a few prodigal fair weather friends."

Someone brushed past me, carrying a tray. I reached out almost automatically for it, half expecting my palm to meet a glass. I recoiled when my fingers brushed against soft fur. A set of tiny teeth bit down into my finger and, shocked, I blinked at what I'd assumed was a tray of drinks.

The server was balancing a board filled with newborn kittens.

"What the hell?" I said. "Your guests eat cats?"

He plucked one from the tray and passed it to me. It mewled loudly as he crushed it against my chest. The soft little head burrowed against my neck.

"Don't be silly," he said. "I wouldn't acquaint with anything that would ingest all that fur. Those breeds are too aggressive to be of use to me."

He jerked his chin toward a patron who plucked another tiny thing from the tray and brought it belly first to his mouth. "I just invited the ones who enjoy the soft underbelly."

I gagged as I watched the creature bite down and suckle and the kitten in my grasp meowed loudly in response to me tightening my grip involuntarily.

I looked at the thing crushed against my chest and swallowed hard. All these poor innocent kittens. It was disgusting.

He nudged me with his elbow, no doubt because he saw my reaction.

"Don't be too put out. Kittens are a delicacy, and even though cats breed like rabbits, they're nowhere near as prolific as rats. Most of the breeds that frequent the ninth world subsist on rodents unless they can find stray felines. Not impossible, mind you," he said, peering at me. "Just less convenient," he went on. "And I so wanted to put on a good show. I had to find half a dozen pregnant feral cats just to provide five trays."

He waved his hand in front of his face. "An ordeal, I can tell you. Now come along. I want you to meet someone."

"You're a monster," I said and let the kitten squeeze closer to my armpit where it no doubt felt heat and warmth and protection beckoning to it.

He shrugged. "Demon, actually. Now do you want that stone or not?"

Part of me wanted to tell him and his buddies to go fuck themselves, but I imagined he would enjoy that. Then I remembered the donuts and stones in the display case and wondered if maybe he wasn't testing me somehow, showing me versions of reality to see how far he could trust me.

I grit my teeth and let him tug me further into the room. The place smelled of musk and sweat and sweet things all at the same time. A waitress plucked the kitten by its scruff when it poked its head out from above my armpit and passed it to a nearby patron.

Glamor or not, I wasn't going to let that poor thing suffer the fate of its kin. I didn't care what sort of test it was. I thought of my cat at home and how she had faced down a sizable rat the day I'd rescued her.

Without thinking, I reached out toward the waitress's ponytail. Her hair felt like steel wool in my hands. I prayed it wasn't a wig and yanked.

Hard.

She yowled and arched backward into the pain and I kicked her feet out from beneath her. She fell onto her backside, the tray upending and kittens ran everywhere. Mine, the tiniest one with a tuft of orange atop a gray head streaked for the beaded curtain. Several were smart enough to follow before the waitress managed to scramble to her knees and scoop for the runaways.

She looked terrified and I glanced at Errol whose eyes were nothing but narrowed slits. A couple of patrons leapt for the scattering animals and collected them the way a contestant in a money booth grapples for dollar bills.

"You should be ashamed of yourself," I yelled at the server.

I kicked the tray from her grasp again and it clamored to the floor. Whatever kittens she'd rescued ran in every direction.

"Seriously?" I said. "Find your humanity, woman."

She looked up at me and flashed a mouthful of fangs. She hissed the way a badger might and I startled.

Errol caught me.

"Please, Ms. Hush," he said. "You have more important things to consider this evening than a few kittens. You wanted a specific stone. I know who can make it for you. He's very good and he happens to be here tonight. We can discuss the payment later."

He waved his hand toward the back of the room where just through the murky shadows another bar hunkered against a wall. I noticed another cluster of patrons huddled around it.

That bar had naked women and men standing against a raised dais all in a row. There had to be a dozen of them in all shapes and sizes, their wrists bound above them by a chain dangling from the ceiling.

At first I thought them decoration of a sort, but when a cloaked patron pointed at a petite blonde, the bartender pulled a sharp knife from a drawer and sliced off a bit of skin from her thigh. He handed it to the patron who tilted his head back and dangled it over his open mouth.

First kittens, now this.

"No," I said. "I can't do this."

"Do you want the introduction or not?" He hissed in my ear. "People are beginning to stare."

I gave him a hard look but squared off my shoulders. I should have waited for Fayed, but it was too late now. Retreat at this point would be fruitless and ludicrous.

"Alright," I said. "Take me to him."

We were weaving our way toward a shadowy corner of the room, brushing past servers. Each time I got a chance, I bumped hard into them as though I was a drunken mortal being led to her doom. Kittens spilled everywhere, and I smiled to myself as the servers scrambled to get them back into place.

"Admirable," Errol said once. "But if you keep it up, I might not be able to take the time to escort you, and that would not be to your advantage."

I behaved then, and all but went still until someone touched the back of my neck.

CHAPTER 9

Chills went down my spine at the touch. I swung around, ready to throw a punch at whatever had touched me. It was relief to see the willowy Kerri standing there.

She extended her hand to Errol who took it like the most genteel of aristocrats.

"I know this little mortal," she purred and snuggled up next to him. She turned her green-eyed gaze to mine. "You know all the best people, Errol," she said.

He all but preened at the compliment.

"You're Maddox's prize folly," she said, turning to me.

I imagined she had mispronounced filly and started to tell her I was no one's prize anything but in one movement, she managed to extricate me from Errol's grip and guide me far enough away that I felt my head clear.

Someone offered me a drink. I tried hard to emblazon the features of this someone on my memory but all I knew was a smiling face, rows of teeth, and laughter. I felt as though I was stumbling along, blithely smiling in response to comments I would never remember.

I blinked at her as Errol spoke.

"She's here to see Absalom," Errol said to her.

Her features closed down like a shutter over a window.

"You're an evil little thing," she said to Errol.

"A moment ago I knew all the best people," he said. "It's her idea, not mine."

I looked from one to the other, confused. What Kerri would even be doing here was a mystery.

"Be wary," she said. "A mortal is no match for an alchemist like Absalom. Do you want me to accompany you?"

Errol rankled. "She has me."

Her silvery eyebrow raised a notch. "You need me," she said. "Come. Errol can interpret, and I'll be your muscle."

"There's really no need," Errol said but she cut him off.

"This mortal helped me get something precious returned to me. I'd be happy to help."

I couldn't imagine this tall lithe woman being any kind of muscle, but I nodded silently at her and let her go in front of us.

In an alcove toward the left, a corded off area was swathed in ambient light. Torches lined the wall and gave off a cool glow that radiated like heat across the expanse, and yet the light was flameless.

As we approached, the headache that had plagued me off and on upon entry cleared. I guessed whatever magic Errol was managing to keep me from seeing his patrons clearly wasn't interested in cloaking either Kerri or the man we approached.

Absalom looked very human and if he was an immortal, he was ancient. He had long wavy hair with streaks of silver shot through in a way most women would have paid dearly to achieve.

He reclined on a lounge the color of watermelon flesh with a server who sported short nubs of horns behind her ears. She was offering him a tray of what looked like regular old human chocolates.

I breathed a sigh of relief. Chocolates I could handle.

I watched him pluck one bon bon from the tray and pop it into his mouth. He chewed discreetly, behind his hand and then waved her away.

Then his eyes landed on Errol, Kerri, and I heading his way. He sat up and brushed the front of his lounge jacket.

Sparks flew off in several directions as he flicked his hands sideways. He wore something on his hand that was the source of those sparks. I couldn't decide if it was a glove or a web of rings attached to his fingers.

"He doesn't look so bad," I muttered.

"Looks are deceiving, little Isabella," Kerri said. "Remember that. He's a shapeshifter of a very rare breed."

When we drew close enough to see individual features, I realized he had a scar over his top lip as though he had been born with a cleft and got it repaired. Kerri whispered in my ear that I needed to keep my eyes downcast.

"In fact," she said. "You're far too assertive looking for anyone in here. I've been glared at already by several demons. So keep your eyes down."

My gaze shot downward to my toes from the sheer hum of threat in the warning. I only knew we were immediately in front of Absalom when Errol introduced me. He tugged me sideways and I stumbled, catching a hold of him to steady myself.

Kerri sidled next to me, looming over me by at least a head and shoulders.

"This human is looking for an alchemist to create a stone for her. An amber one with a ruby embedded in its centre," he said. "About yay big."

I didn't look up, but I imagined his hands were held slightly apart indicate the size.

"Not just that –" I started to say, but Errol stomped down on my foot. Kerri pinched my elbow. I presumed I wasn't supposed to speak at all. He leaned close to me when I tugged on his arm.

I whispered the other thing I wanted, the thing that was going to help me take my life back. He caught my eye as he leaned away and I drilled him with my gaze. I meant business. An alchemist? Surely he could do better than fashion a replica.

"My human forgets herself," Errol said to Absalom. "She knows I'm supposed to speak for her, but she's anxious."

"And what does this human want with this stone?" he said, but it seemed very clear that he already knew.

"I believe she also wants it imbued with some sort of magic."

"Yes," Absalom said, his gaze flicking to mine. "I expect that's why you sought an alchemist."

He grazed me with his scrutiny and for a second I thought I felt ants crawling up my spine.

"What sort of magic?" Absalom said, waving his fingers in front of his face as though to show off the special effects of sparks swirling in pinwheel pattern. I chewed down on my lip, seeing it as a sign.

"The human wants it charmed with just enough magic to make the owner believe he's being repaid whatever he asks of her." Errol said.

He grunted. "That sort of magic doesn't come cheap," he said.

There was a pause while I felt his eyes on me. Tension bit through the air and I had the feeling he was doing more than just studying me. He was seeing through me, pulling strands of energy back through and tying me up in a neat package that he planned to store in a safe somewhere.

"It doesn't look like it's flush with cash."

He didn't sound impressed.

Kerri stiffened beside me. "It has done me certain favors," she said. "I believe it's capable," she said.

He murmured deep in his throat. "Then perhaps it can be of service."

I wanted dearly to speak up and Kerri must have felt my intention because she laid her lips against my ear.

"You don't come this far and make demands, Isabella," she said. "You simply agree to the terms. Now be quiet while they work it out."

I said nothing but kept my eyes downcast. Long moments passed but eventually Errol tugged me backward.

"Tell it I am amenable." Absalom said and something else shivered in the undercurrents of his voice. Desire, maybe? Anticipation? "Give it my terms."

I peeked upward to see Kerri's eyes widened, and though none of them spoke, I felt as though some sort of conversation had happened without me. The next thing I knew, Errol was tugging me along backward through the meet and greet.

This time it seemed as though the waves of crowd parted to leave an open path for my retreat.

I pushed through the curtain the way a drowning woman pushes through the surface of water.

I gasped.

I swung on Errol. "What the hell was that?" I said. "What did I just agree to?"

CHAPTER 10

Errol rushed me through the curtain and toward the front door, leaving Kerri gaping at me before getting closed off from view by a dozen patrons as the beads swished closed again. I resisted, trying to pull Errol's hands off me and make him face me.

He was strong and held me in a viselike grip by the elbows as he pushed me out the door. I struggled. As much as I wanted to leave this place, I wasn't going without knowing exactly what I had agreed to.

I snapped my arm backward, the crook of my elbow slamming into his chest. I felt his sharp intake of breath as he obviously didn't expect me to attack.

I retracted my arm, fully intending to snap backwards again.

He gave me a shake. "All right, Ms. Hush," he said. "You're right. I do have to tell you, just not in here."

He looked around and over his shoulder as though he thought he was being watched.

"Outside," he hissed.

He twisted the lock on the door, running his hand down along the seam of door frame where it met the door and several clicking sounds echoed through the air. Invisible dead bolts, obviously. Supernatural ones that no human could see or break through.

I rounded on him when we met the outside air. The honking of horns and raucous noise of traffic washed over me and a breeze tugged at my hair. Sweet clarity engulfed me the way a room must feel after being swept of cobwebs.

I looked over his shoulder to the inside of his shop. I'd left my workout bag and weapons on his counter. I tried to shoulder my way past him, making for my stuff because there was no way I was leaving it here only to have to come back for it.

He placed his arm over the door, barring my way.

I peeled into him with an angry look.

"My bag," I said, pointing over his head toward the interior of the shop. "I left it in there."

He pressed his back against the door, no doubt because he expected me to push past him.

"Leave it be," he said.

He looked like he wanted to check over his shoulder to be sure it was still there but didn't dare let me out of his sight. "I'll have Cherise bring it out."

I crossed my arms over my chest, splaying my feet on the sidewalk. I caught scent of something sweet and gummy and glared at him.

"Stop that shit," I said, narrowing my eyes into irritated slits. "I know what you're doing."

He sighed. "As you wish." The ticking flicked down over his irises. "Most women love the smell of caramel."

So I was right. Part of that seduction was a pheromone. What I wondered was whether it was keyed to the individual, like a codex.

"I'm more of a tequila gal," I said and thought I saw a flicker of amusement cross his expression. No doubt he measured each woman's desire and matched the pheromone scent to something deeply embedded within an individual's psyche.

"So?" I demanded. "What have I got myself into?"

I wanted my life back. Though I had no problem executing a heist, and less problem taking on less than honest activities, I wanted a choice in them. I wanted to know exactly what that entailed.

He wafted toward me, bringing the smell of rotten fish and garbage from the dumpster to my nose. The neon sign overhead, blinked and went out as though someone had struck a switch.

He watched my face intently, and I imagined he wanted to gauge my reaction to the reality of scents around me instead of his unique blend of manipulation and fragrance.

"Well?" I tapped my foot on the asphalt, determined to reveal nothing.

He swallowed, nervously, I thought.

"Oh, come on," I said. "You're a demon. Surely it can't be all that bad."

My bravado was disappearing in the face of his anxiety.

"It's not that the job is impossible for a woman like you," he said carefully. "Just that it puts me in rather...a pickle."

"What do you have to do with any of it except for the introduction?"

"Because he knows that in exactly three night's time, I've arranged for a sort of soirée."

He crossed his arms over his chest defensively, daring me with a double licking of that membrane over his eyes, and I get the feeling that soirée was a euphemism for something decidedly more hedonistic.

"And?"

"And you're going to steal something for him from one of the guests, and that puts me in the worst position possible. My party? My responsibility."

"Then maybe I'll just go as a server."

I thought of all the little kitten entrées and even though my bravado was creeping back, I didn't think I could do it.

He shook his head. "The soirée isn't quite the same as what you saw tonight."

The sound of his voice made me swallow down hard. "Then what exactly is it?"

He spread his arms out to the side, laying his palms flat against either side of the door frame. A rustling sound and squealing to my left indicated one of the many rats had just run into one of the mother cats.

"I'm not exactly flush with power anymore," he said canting his head toward me. "Only about half juiced."

"What did I agree to?" I insisted. I didn't give a flying fig how much power he had or not.

"I'm an incubus," he said. "What in the name of Hades do you think is going to go on in there."

It slowly dawned on me with horror exactly what he was talking about. An orgy of sorts. I imagined all manner of beast and man entangled in the worst of deviant activities and swayed a bit on my feet. I clutched my throat in reflex.

"Exactly," he said with a nod as his eyes flickered over my neck. "You got it. But it's not humans who are on the S list. In fact, any mortal in attendance must be escorted."

"Escorted?"

He nodded again. But this time there was a glint in his eye that made me want to slap his face for some reason.

"You will be my pet for the night," he whispered.

I gagged deep in my throat. "Pet?" I said incredulously. "I'm no one's pet. I belong to no one."

"How else will you get in?" He sounded irritated at my hesitation. "I can't entrust you to any other, knowing the sort of clientele who will be helping me regain some juice and now there's no question that you must attend. Absalom is quite decided now."

"No," I said, cutting my hand across the air in front of me. "I won't go as a pet."

I imagined leashes and muzzles and decided that no matter how badly I wanted to steal the stone from Scottie, it wasn't worth that kind of degradation or danger.

He lifted a black eyebrow. "How badly do you want that stone and how badly do you want it magiced? There aren't a lot of alchemists with the power to imbue an inanimate object with the kind of charms you're after."

I stomped my foot and my fingers bit into my palm as I curled my fist.

"Not badly enough to let you touch me."

I was walking away, trying to rack my brains for another avenue to get the stone from Scottie, shiest it onto Maddox and get my pay, when Errol's smooth voice stopped me.

"He agreed to your request," Errol called out before I made it four feet away. "Velvet pouch, replica stone, and magic, all for that one price."

I spun on my heel. He was still standing in the door frame, but the light above him had taken to flickering in time with my heartbeat. I caught sight of a girl I assumed was Cherise clutching my workout bag over her head just beyond the door.

"What price? Serving myself up for a supernatural orgy?" I spat out.

His brow furrowed. "You won't be participating unless you want to, pet. All he wants is for you steal some little thing for him. He said he's not met any human in all his centuries worthy of doing so."

I knew the extra was an add-on from Errol as a means to charm me into agreeing. I wondered what he'd get if I agreed. But I supposed it didn't matter.

The answer to my troubles was right in reach but I needed to have the stone to Maddox by tomorrow. The timing just wasn't right.

Unless I could stall him.

"Doesn't matter," I said. "If he can't deliver tonight, I can't help him."

He sidled closer, all sense of the strange compulsion I felt for him gone.

"You came to me, Ms. Hush," he said. "I would say you owe me something just for the introduction. It's not every mortal who peeks behind the curtain and comes away unscathed."

"I wouldn't say I'm unscathed," I said, thinking about the things I'd seen, but in truth, I'd seen worse. Scottie's lifestyle put me in direct optic and visceral view of some pretty nasty things. "And I doubt that was a real peek behind the curtain."

He grinned and the neon light buzzed back to full life over his head. It sizzled and reshaped itself into the words: you owe me.

His advance on me was slow and languid and I had the feeling my feet were mired in tar. All those times I'd been in his shop, submitting myself to his revolting advances in order to unload ill-gotten gains, he'd been nothing but a disgusting man.

Now he was something much more compelling. His every pore wafted pheromones that I registered as all the things I loved: strawberries, manly soap and sweat. I'd been a woman resisting revolting advances then. Now I was a human before a demon who fed on sexual energy. I needed to be wary.

I managed to back up a step and he outright laughed.

"You're a strong little thing," he said. "But how strong will you be when I'm back to full flush and find your home with no more than a thought? You all swaddled in your bedclothes, dreaming dreams of lust and adventure. Makes for a prime opportunity for a demon like me."

He was right. I'd rather pay up with a chance of getting what I needed from the alchemist than pay up and get nothing.

"What are the specifics?" I said and mentally noted that if I agreed, I'd have to reschedule Fayed and stall Maddox. I pinched the bridge of my nose. Things were getting too complicated already. Too many fingers in the safe.

"You lure the target within reach of the Fire Gate. I don't need to explain how. You'll figure something out and I'm sure the circumstances will provide all the opportunity you need." He flashed me a lecherous grin.

"How will I know the target?"

He ran his hands down over his face with a sweeping motion that encompassed his entire body. Where his hand touched morphed with shivers of light and flesh into a different form. He grew taller. Older. What had once been a youngish Colin Farrell doppelgänger became more of a Sean Connery. At least the target was handsome. It might not be too difficult to show enough interest to lure him long enough to steal whatever it was Absalom wanted.

"And the object?" I said. "What will I be lifting?"

Tentacles of light played over him and he morphed slowly back into the Colin Farrell look alike. He propped his hands on his hips.

"Once it's within reach of the gate, it reacts with the magic and lights up. You'll know it when you see it."

I narrowed my eyes at him. "I don't have to go in?"

He shook his head as the door cracked open about two inches. Cherise began stuffing my bag through the crack and I winced, thinking she was going to splinter the pepper spray can.

"And then what?" I wasn't used to such vagueness and I didn't want to have to come back.

"Who do I deliver it to? "And how do I get my pay?"

"He said all you'll have to do is toss it through the gate. Don't worry," he said. "Your payment will be secured."

"Not good enough," I said. "I want insurance."

He nodded. "He thought you might. The stone will be ready upon entry to the soiree. I'll have Cherise pass it to you. The magic will be supplied on your delivery of the item."

"Three nights from now," I repeated.

He nodded and reached beneath his armpit to pull my bag through. He yanked the last bit of leather from Cherise's hand and tossed it to me.

"Cherise has slipped a costume in your bag. Wear it. I like my pets to have a certain flair."

He spun on his heel before throwing another command over his shoulder. "And make sure to wear the thigh high boots and the wig. I like the blonde one."

Bastard, I thought as I slung the bag over my shoulder. He'd just guaranteed I'd do neither.

It all seemed too easy. All except for the gate part. I didn't want to get within three feet of it at all.

I'd had a bad experience with the Blood Gate and the Shadow Bazaar altogether. The last thing I wanted was to get sucked in to it. And although Maddox was the owner of the bazaar, it was a huge bit of property with stalls and buildings that stretched for a mile in every direction.

There was no telling where I might land or end up and even if I could count on him to help me if I found myself in there.

"Three nights. Midnight." Errol saluted me with a click of his heels then spun and disappeared through the crack in the door. It was only later that I realized he shouldn't have been able to fit.

And it was only on my way home that I gathered that little detour to Errol's shop might have cost me my meeting with Fayed. It was already 1130. Time had warped and frayed and left me standing out on the front step of my apartment building.

I climbed the steps with legs heavy from weariness. I'd lost time in Errol's shop, and I hoped Fayed was inside the porch waiting for me.

Someone was waiting for me alright, but it wasn't Fayed.

Chapter 11

I knew just by looking at him that the man waiting for me wasn't one of the Kindred who had somehow spelled himself into my apartment. He was real. Mortal. A living and breathing human man who had picked my lock and was now stretched out on my sofa, ankles crossed, his filthy sneakers creating mud stains of epic proportions on the arm of the sofa.

My first instinct should have been fear, but after meeting with Errol and nearly getting blasted by Kelly, just seeing those blotches of mud from God knew where in a city of asphalt, I felt more annoyed than anything.

Really. It was getting to be too much. What did a chick have to do to keep her home sacrosanct? Kick some ass, that's what. Obviously, there was no substitute for brute force in this case.

"I'm getting pretty sick of people breaking into my apartment," I said and slammed the door shut behind me.

I jammed my hand into the gaping zipper of my workout bag and dug around.

I didn't care what met my fingers first: pepper spray or pistol would do.

He wanted to break in? He was going to pay the consequences.

He unfolded himself from my sofa with such leisure, I suspected he wasn't just there for the crown jewels. I might not know who he was, but I knew who sent him. He was new, like Alvin had been, acquired by Scottie sometime after I'd left.

"He's getting lax in his protocols," I said to the guy. "Doesn't seem to care who he hires now."

A brief flash of confusion sullied his otherwise bland expression. He was long and wiry. His grey Metallica T-shirt stretched across pectoral muscles that flexed and squeezed beneath the fabric.

He was impatient to show off that muscle, if the one-size too small for him T-shirt was any indication. Not just some scrawny wharf rat then. Someone lean but hard-bodied.

Well, I was small and fast.

I waited till he scuffed his running shoes against the carpet the way a bull does before charging, and then I pulled the pistol.

He paused. Filthy skid marks bore into the pile of the area rug. The edge of his T-shirt pulled up at the navel and showed a glint of black metal.

"Not the smartest move," he said, eyeing the muzzle.

My eye went to the object tucked in his jeans. Not a gun, I knew, but what was it? Too big to be a phone. Too hard to be a notebook.

He cracked his neck back and forth as if he'd got stiff lying on my half sized sofa.

"I didn't break in," he said, going back to my original complaint.

I waved the Ruger at him.

"I don't give a flying fig whether you were teleported in from the Starship Enterprise. This is my damn house."

He crossed his arms over his chest and flexed his pecs at me.

"Your landlord was all too willing to believe I was another one of your johns."

My landlord was happy to pretend I was a prostitute because it annoyed his neighbors, but I didn't really think he believed it.

"Fuck you," I said.

He pulled a cigarette package from the front pocket of his jeans. It was crumpled and squashed and I couldn't believe the cigarette he slipped from the fold was still as pristine as if it had just left the factory.

"Just how many men do you have traipsing in and out of here?" he said, laying it on his bottom lip. He patted himself down, distracted. "Got a light, darlin?"

I blinked at him. "No," I said. "Now get the fuck out of here." For extra emphasis, I disengaged the safety. It wasn't loaded but he'd not know that.

He smiled, showing a cracked tooth in the front of his mouth. The cigarette rolled toward it.

I could already feel my hand shaking as it wrapped around the pistol. My gun was for show, not use. I'd seen too much killing to want to do some of my own.

"I have a hard time believing my landlord would let you in," I said and edged toward the kitchen counter. I wasn't comfortable with my back to the door now that I knew my apartment had been violated.

"He would if he saw this," he said and started to reach behind his back.

I stiffened and my finger tightened on the trigger, a reflex that told me had it really been loaded, he'd have been bleeding by now.

He held his hands up in surrender.

"No worries, darlin'," he said. "The only weapon I have is here in my crotch." He chuckled at that as my eye ran back to his waistband. "I promise I won't draw on you, pardner."

Without waiting for me to assent or not, he reached behind his back to pull out a pair of panties and my long blonde wig, which no doubt had been tucked into the waistband of his jeans.

I knew my landlord had seen me in the wig on more than on occasion. He'd been happy about it, in fact, believing the neighbors would be infuriated by a prostitute doing business in their district. And since he was an older man, curmudgeon or not, he no doubt he took one look at the panties and bolted for the door, embarrassment riding his heels like a cockroach running for cover.

I jerked my chin at my intruder's crotch.

"You must not have much in those pants if you can jam all that in there," I said.

The guy flicked the cigarette to the floor and closed the distance between us in less than four strides.

I stabbed the muzzle toward him and he chuckled.

"It's not a knife, darlin'," he said. "The boss forget to give you lessons when he gave you that pea shooter?"

He drilled into me with his gaze, no doubt trying to decide whether or not I had the stuffing to pull the trigger.

I knew what was going on behind that crystal blue gaze. I'd seen it play out plenty of times with Scottie. Will a criminal take the chance of having the police poke about if they fired a weapon and scared the locals with the noise? If the answer was yes, was there a chance of survival afterwards?

I did some quick calculations, and I watched as he saw me add up the obvious: I didn't have a silencer. I couldn't heft him if I shot him and had to dispose of his body.

And I couldn't call the cops.

The fact that it wasn't loaded meant nothing to that equation.

He put his hand down on my wrist. Two fingers curled toward my pulse. I felt it hammer against the fleshy pad of his index finger.

"Let's talk like civilized robbers," he said.

"I've got nothing to say to a piss ant like you," I said. "You touch me, and Scottie will hear."

"Who do you think sent me?" he said.

"Scottie and I have an agreement," I said but I lowered the Ruger. "Now get out."

"Scottie won't be happy if I return without bringing him what he sent me to fetch."

"Fuck you." I wrenched away from him, and shoved the pistol back into the workout bag. So maybe that was useless and he knew it. I still had the pepper spray. I rummaged around inside, searching for the can.

I had it in my hand and was pulling it toward the zipper when a jolt of pain shot through my arm. His fingers dug into the inside of my triceps with his thumb. I gasped and fell backwards, my body trying to escape the pain, but he twisted my wrist and punched into the muscle.

I sagged forward. He danced away before I could recover and the spray can fizzled out into the interior of the bag, sending a waft of spicy heat up through the zipper.

I coughed and dropped the bag. Whatever threat he posed, it wasn't as great as the incapacitation of pepper spray misting my bare eyes. I ran for the sink to wash my hands and lave out my eyelids. My throat burned like hell fire.

I half expected him to take advantage of my vulnerability to grab me from behind, which he did. I didn't truly care until his forearm blocked my throat.

"You're gonna be a good girl, now, eh?" he said. "Do what you're told?"

His free hand roamed down my ribcage to find my buttocks. He cupped one cheek and slapped it playfully. I might have thought that was all he'd do, but then I felt that same hand slip between my legs. He kicked my feet apart with his.

"At first, I wasn't so sure why he was willing to wait," he said. "But then, I can see you might be worth it after all."

Water ran down my face to pool at my clavicle. I told my heartbeat to calm the hell down. He wouldn't rape me. He couldn't. Because if he did, he'd have to kill me. And even then, Scottie would hunt him till he could enjoy a long week's leisure of making him pay.

"Too bad," I said with more calm in my voice than I felt. "Waiting was what he signed up for."

I felt something press into the tender spot between my legs.

"You know what this is, darlin'?" he whispered against my ear as he pressed the object deeper into my flesh. "Top of the line stunner. Multiple settings. No reloading."

My entire body went cold. I didn't even dare swallow for Pete's sake. I'd never been Tasered, but I'd seen it plenty. The thought of a jolt of electricity riding my nerves like a filthy hobo on a freight car was bad enough, but the idea of multiple barbs sticking into my crotch?

I near fainted from the thought.

He flung me sideways and I fell against the wall and sank onto the floor in an awkward splay of arms and legs. The garbage can skittered out from its place when I knocked it with my hand and a beer can leaked its last yeasty bit of fluid.

He loomed over me, the stunner in his hand.

"He just wants to remind you how important it is for you to get the information you agreed on."

So Scottie was still on the mortal plane, then. At least I knew now he hadn't touched the stone. But he wasn't happy having to wait. I should have known a man like Scottie wouldn't just sit idly by twiddling his thumbs while I searched out Intel that could change his life for the better.

He would try to prod me into doing it faster. Six months sabbatical? If Scottie counted time at all, it was in dog years. I added up that I probably only really had six days.

He leaned over and touched the stunner to my thigh. No barbs punctured my skin but the jolt slammed up my back. I arched backward painfully. I gasped.

"Lowest setting," he said and moved to touch my chest.

"Alright, alright." I tried to hold up my hands in surrender, but snapping bits of pain cracked into my shoulder muscles. I ended up being able to do no more than lift them waist tight.

"You got some sort of hard on for that device?" I grit out from between clenched teeth.

I finally managed enough strength to push myself onto my knees, but as if to prove me correct, he jammed the stunner into my rib cage.

My legs shot out from beneath me and I fell on my opposite side. I kicked at the air, unable to stop the muscle spasms for several moments while he stood there watching me. My teeth closed over my tongue, sending biting tears to my eyes.

He pulled another cigarette from the package and laid it on his lip, canted his head to the side. He was enjoying the torture, the bastard. Alvin had been a brute but he'd not taken such cold and calculated interest in my harm.

I knew right then what I should have already known. I couldn't trust Scottie. He'd agreed to let me loose for a short time because it suited him, but he was not keen on waiting.

All of the things I thought I'd known about my ex, shivered down my spine.

I'd been too complacent. Too kind. Far too willing to believe that he would feel some shred of decency because it was me he was cowing and not one of his goons or a stranger who owed him money.

I'd wanted to let Scottie choose his own fate and that was a mistake born of the young Isabella.

I couldn't make that mistake again.

The guy delivered one final jolt and waited until I finished spasming on the floor. I didn't realize I had drooled onto my chest until he leaned over me and wiped at the spittle from my chin.

He cupped me behind my head and lifted me almost gingerly to my feet. I staggered, weaving back and forth as the room came into focus. All of my muscles were nothing but sopping wet teabags.

He held me aloft by my waist as he dragged me toward the sofa. Whispered words of what should have been comfort fell from his lips, but they had the opposite effect, making my nerves jangle and my skin tremble against the muscles.

I couldn't do much more than whimper as he threw me onto the cushions.

I sank into the arm of the sofa. I felt more like a cloth doll than a human being. I watched him strip off his shirt and saw exactly how lean muscled he was. Whatever he did to work out built sinew and flexibility instead of hard boned muscle.

He wiped his face with his shirt, obviously sweating from the exertion of bringing me to heel.

His expression was lecherous and the thought that he might actually rape me fleeted across my mind.

"Touch me and Scottie will know all about it," I said.

"Touch you?" He said. "I wouldn't dream of it. My tastes lend to a little more masculine. But you do make a man hot."

A second shadow moved from somewhere past his shoulder and my eyes went automatically to seek out its source. It shifted and moved and grew into a shape that was far more massive than he was.

Someone else was in the room.

And that someone looked pissed.

Chapter 12

Maddox came out of the shadows as though he had been lit by a movie camera. One broad arm snaked around the back of the thug's throat and yanked the man, kicking, backwards off his feet.

His foot hit the lamp and sent it sailing cord's length across the floor where stuttered out sheets of light for two seconds before the lightbulb smashed into a noisy pop.

I threw myself forward, landing on the floor with my cheek grazing the filthy area rug just out of reach of splinters of glass.

I caught sight of the thug's dirty sneakers and had enough time to ascertain that the mud he'd tracked in was a nice mix of fine sand and potting soil. His left foot spasmed against the floor as Maddox crouched over him.

He gave me a long look before turning back to the thug and splaying his fingers over his face.

The intruder yelped and spasmed as though he was being throttled from within.

I didn't feel the least bit of pity.

I knew what Maddox was doing to him. I'd seen it before when he'd turned all the pain Alvin had inflicted on me back into his own body. It had killed Alvin, and while I'd been terrified of Maddox afterward, I'd since suspected that Alvin suffered more than just the results of the beating he'd given me.

He might in actuality have taken back all of the pain he'd inflicted on others.

I hoped this bastard had just as long a history of hurting people.

Despite the obvious pain the man was in, he did his best to roll over and scrabble to his knees. He somehow found a runner's lunge and squirreled out of Maddox's grip. His chest heaved as he faced Maddox, all muscles on the ready to bolt for the door.

Maddox stood and stared him down, projecting a furious enough sense of command with his mere posture that the man stilled at his feet.

"Touch her again--harm anyone--and you'll die."

I swung my gaze to the intruder. He clutched his head between both hands, squeezing as though he was still in pain. His eyes bulged as they took in Maddox's face, and I had no doubt the man believed every single word Maddox said.

But it wasn't enough.

The stunner was abandoned to the carpet and I reached for it, some part of me enraged and hurt and wanting to relieve my own misery at the expense of someone else's pain.

Maddox kicked it out of my reach toward the intruder.

"Go on," he said. "Pick it up."

The man gained his feet but turned from the stunner. He shook his head then peered at me with a vacant expression.

He weaved on his feet and stared down at the stunner then back to me again. He seemed to be working out what the connection was. Maddox toed the stunner back toward him, where it lodged against the man's sneaker.

"I told you to pick it up," Maddox said.

His voice reminded me of a cold pool of water at the end of a churning waterfall. The depths of the fury were unplumbed and unknown and I wouldn't have dipped my toe in if it meant my very soul.

The man's eyes locked on Maddox as he stooped and reached for the weapon. He got no more than one inch from it before he flinched as though someone had stabbed him.

He staggered on his feet. He grabbed his head again.

"What the fuck?" he said and hunched over into a standing fetal position.

"That's your intent," Maddox said. "Nasty bit of stuff, isn't it?"

He closed the short distance between himself and the thug and laid his hand on a quivering shoulder.

"You'll find for some reason that whatever you do to others from here on out will return to you two fold," he said. "If you're a cunning sort, you'll use that intent to improve your orgasms, but I doubt you're that smart."

He hunkered down to peer up into the thug's face as though he wanted to comfort him, and yet the words, the tone, even the look on his face were far from it. In fact, I felt the dead weight of it all press down on my shoulders like an oppressive heat.

"Get out," he said.

The man didn't wait one more second. He fell back on his heels in his haste to about face and when he fled to the door, he fumbled with the doorknob for several seconds before remembering that it should turn right.

He was gone without closing the door. I heard his footsteps pounding down the steps and disappear down the sidewalk.

Maddox plucked the stunner from the floor and that was the moment my cat chose to shoot out from beneath the sofa and deliver a series of rapid swipes to his wrist before tearing off toward my bedroom in a yowling streak of fur.

"Now you decide to protect me, you foolish thing," I said.

I immediately grappled for Maddox's hand, smearing a drop of blood across his wrist. His pulse thrummed against the pad of my thumb in an even rhythm, skipped a beat, and then sped up. I cradled his injured wrist in my hand and ran my finger over three long scratches, assessing how deep they might be.

"Superficial," I said against a tightness in my throat.

"She has impeccable timing if not ridiculous standards," he said.

I thought he was going to pull away from me because the tension in his entire body was electric enough to power a potato to light, but instead, he placed his other hand on top and his thumb ran absently along the lines of my wrist.

If this was a human man and the circumstances were normal, I might consider that touch an intimate act, one that preluded a kiss. I even lifted my chin out of reflex and a compulsion that my skin and tissues remembered from years of conditioning.

I felt my face flush with heat. I had to admit I liked his hands on me. There were calluses at the base of his fingers, rough ones that nibbled at my skin in a delicious way. I felt caught in that moment, like a hare in a trap. I could barely breathe for the sudden lust that prickled down my spine.

I'd always chased the wrong sort of man: dangerous types of men.

He'd just shown me again how dangerous he was. Far more dangerous than Scottie.

I hated that my body responded to him the way water runs into a gunnel. Because I wasn't that woman anymore.

I would put it down to weariness. Falling into bad habits. I was aching and sore and weak and my response to the adrenaline of being hurt was just a confusing muddle of past conditioning and the fragrance of him.

His gaze landed on the column of my throat and I fancied he watched my pulse tattoo an imprint from the inside. It sped up as his glance lingered there, seeming to savor the motion the way a thirsty man takes in a condensed glass of water.

So he felt it too, no doubt. That fight or flight adrenaline channeled into the drive to find satiation in something just as primal.

I swallowed down hard, knowing it all for what it was.

Instinct and years of bad choices. And I'd stop all that right now.

"You didn't have to do that," I said.

"What?" he said. "Let you roll around on the floor while some thug Tasers you? Not my style."

His voice sounded thick and throaty despite the sass of the words. He cleared his throat and pulled his hand from mine, then raked his fingers through his hair. A wisp clung to his lashes and he scraped it back behind his ear.

I thought I felt my fingers twitch, imagining myself doing it for him and I cupped my elbows in my hands to disguise how badly I fought the reflexive desire to run my own fingers up into that mass of thickness and grip it at the roots.

The whole affair must have unnerved him the way it did me because he put several paces between the two of us. He halted at the doorframe that bordered the foyer and living space, leaning against the jamb with one foot crossed over the other at the ankle with a casualness that his tense shoulders warred with.

He crossed his arms but I noted that both hands were fists against his biceps.

"What the hell was that?" I said. "That business of doing unto others? Who the hell are you?"

"Batman," he said, swinging his gaze to mine.

"Very funny," I said, but the humor did at least release the coiled tension in my stomach.

I realized then, just how sore I was. I sagged on my feet. My muscles felt like liquid fire everywhere the electricity had sizzled down my skin.

I rubbed my triceps, trying to smooth out the ache in the muscles.

"You didn't answer my question," I said.

"Maybe there's no good answer you'll want to hear," he said.

"I've heard plenty of awful things over the last few weeks."

I didn't say I'd asked the question but was terrified of hearing he might just be one of those awful things.

I gave up trying to smooth out the wrinkles in my muscles and collapsed backward onto the couch, my legs splayed out in front of me with my heels propped against the carpet.

I leaned backward, soaking in how good it felt to be on a soft cushion. I refused to look at the mess of dirt the bastard had left me to clean up.

Maddox eyed me silently for a long moment before he approached me. He stopped short at the armchair and his knees popped when he sunk into it. Dust motes climbed to the ceiling in the lamplight. I watched them swirl between us for a moment, afraid to speak.

"Good thing we had our deal," he said. "Or else I might not have come by in time."

I looked up at him. "Deal?"

He tapped his finger against his temple. "Remember the one we made yesterday? You get me the Lilith stone, and I pay you for your trouble?"

Yesterday. So I'd been in Errol's shop much longer than I'd thought. A full day had passed and now Maddox made no mention of what he'd just done to Scottie's thug.

No mention of the way he had to have seen my pulse speed up at his touch. Just back to that deal. One I didn't want to talk about at the moment. Things were complicated enough as it was.

I imagined Fayed waiting for me for nothing.

I chewed on my bottom lip, letting my eyelids close because it felt so good to pretend the best thing for me was sleep.

"Isabella?" he said. "You do have the stone?"

I said nothing.

"That's obviously why your friendly gentleman was here, am I right?"

I peeked from beneath shuttered lashes to see him wave at the dust in the air with a grimace of displeasure. When his gaze landed on me again, it was so intense that it dragged my eyelids up the rest of the way.

"You stole the stone like we agreed," he prompted. "And he decided to retrieve it from you? Where is it? In your bedroom?"

He cast a wary look toward the bedroom door and I wasn't sure if it was fear of the cat or fear of how dirty he thought it might be in there.

I shook my head and stared down at my feet. I hadn't bothered to take off my sneakers and I'd walked in a few puddles on my way home. I'd blamed my intruder for muddy marks on my sofa and here I'd rubbed in a good deal of brackish water to get it all good and grimy. There were smudges all over the carpet leading back to the door.

"Isabella?"

I stared him down with a direct look finally. There was no point in being coy. I knew I wasn't going to give him the stone even if I did manage to break into Scottie's hotel room. Somewhere between clamping down on my tongue and nearly wetting myself, I'd decided to let Scottie have the damn thing.

Eventually, he would open the pouch and handle the stone. Problem over.

The money was no longer a motivator. I could earn cash a dozen ways. I had one chance to get rid of Scottie for real. The fury was already building behind my heart, seizing it in a bitter grasp and squeezing slowly enough that I felt my shoulders drawing together.

How could he do that to me? How could he send Alvin to hurt me and then that weaselly thug?

He deserved to go to hell.

Literally.

"There's been a hiccup," I said.

His brow furrowed and the steely eyes shuttered down.

"I don't like the sound of hiccup."

I shrugged. "Would you prefer a horn blast in your ear? Maybe the sound of a train rushing by? I have some dishes I could throw against the wall."

"You made a bargain," he said and got up to loom over me, his arms crossed again. This time his fists were pumping open and closed. I watched them for some time before he spoke.

"You have to honor your end," he said.

He didn't mention the things he'd done to that intruder. He wouldn't. And I wouldn't either. I refused to add it to the equation because it might mean I'd rethink my decision.

And I didn't plan to.

He must have read the resistance in my eyes because he pushed off from the door jamb in one motion and splayed his feet, shooting me a suspicious look.

"You said if you couldn't deliver, that you would tell me where it was and I'd get it myself."

I laughed out loud. "Good luck trying to get anything out of Scottie."

He made a sound low in his throat that indicated he didn't think he'd have too much trouble.

I swung my gaze to his.

"You might be big and immortal, or whatever the hell you are, but there's no way you can get past Scottie and all his security and then break into the safe that he undoubtedly has that damned stone stored in."

He rocked back on his heels then strode toward me, crouching beside the sofa with his arms propped on his knees. He really was a big man; even squatted down, he loomed over me. I clutched the edge of the sofa, a reflex borne of a decade of uncertainty.

I'd lost count of the times Scottie had harmed someone who insulted or threatened me.

But it was never about me. It was about someone insulting his possession. And at the end of the day, he treated that possession any old way he wanted. He alone had the power, the right, to hurt me.

Maddox's gaze dragged down to my fingers and a strange mix of emotions melded into his jawline. He swallowed and trailed my tight muscles all the way back to my shoulder.

"I'm not going to hurt you," he said.

I thought he would reach out for me. I flinched.

He went so still I couldn't see his chest expand as he breathed.

Chapter 13

He wouldn't hurt me. I had to tell myself that twice before I believed it.

I released my breath through my nose, made an effort to let my fingers release the claw-like grip on the cushions. Only when I laid them flat on my stomach did he speak again.

"I gave you your chance," he said before climbing back to his feet. He stood over me with his arms crossed as he rocked back on his heels. "Don't underestimate me. I can and will do whatever it takes to retrieve the stone from your lover."

He said lover the way someone would say the word excrement.

"He's not my lover," I said, and he sighed with impatience.

Gone was the compassionate expression and tolerant attitude. I thought the speedy shift was just a bit too quick and it sparked something within that felt akin to hurt.

"You think you can lay your hands on a dozen men at once like you did to that thug?" I shook my head. "Dream on. I'm not sure how susceptible you are to automatic weapons, or even short range pistols."

"You'd be surprised," he mumbled.

"What are you?" I said but it was a moot point by then. I wasn't budging.

"It's not yours to decide, Isabella. I'll retrieve it with or without you."

"You're assuming it's still on this plane or in this world or whatever the hell you non-human things call us."

He pressed his lips together.

"We non-human things call you ninth-worlders. Some of us call you food. Some of us call you drink. And some of us call you damned stupid."

At that he pulled his dress shirt up on the side to reveal an angry looking symbol emblazoned on his skin. It looked like a red worm trying to burrow itself into his body and stretched for three inches downward before veering upward again at an angle as it tried to corner three dots.

He might have been branded except the mark was raised and not seared in.

I shuddered at how angry looking it was, how obviously painful.

"See this?" he said. "This tells me it's here in this world. I smell it in your apartment, on your skin. This tells me it's been activated and recently."

"So big deal. You knew that already. It's how Colin sent me to Hell."

I sat up, dangling my feet over the sofa and planting my hands on my knees. What was the worst that could happen? Scottie got out of my hair?

I shoved aside the painful recollections of the things Lucifer had done to me in his lair, of the things he'd done to others. They skittered over my memory like cockroaches, and if I thought too long on them, they built nests in my psyche.

I pushed aside the annoying thought that no one deserved that kind of pain. Not even Scottie.

But I didn't want to think that far. I just wanted Scottie gone.

"Isabella, it's important that we retrieve it, and not just because my client paid me to. Because you don't know what it can do."

"The hell I don't." I slid from the sofa and weaved my way to the refrigerator, planning on a nice pull of sour milk to get him out of my hair.

He snagged my elbow as I passed him. "No," he said. "You really don't."

The look on his face scared me. Not because I was afraid he'd hurt me, but because he looked afraid.

"That stone has been missing for centuries," he said. "Once it hit the ninth world again, this tracking rune transformed. It used to be a quaint black tattoo."

I looked it over, trying to ignore the heart-achingly sinewy look to the abs he exposed because the scar was disconcerting to see standing like an angry red weal on his skin.

"I was charged with finding it," he said. "This mark is the contract."

"Who charged you," I demanded. It sounded so mysterious, not just a deal struck for a few bucks. "You never told me that. I would think that detail would be important to a partner."

"Don't you trust me?"

"I don't trust anyone anymore," I said. "Too risky. You want my help, at least tell me why I should just let you traipse over to where it might be and let me lose out on thousands of dollars and put my head in a noose at the same time."

He sighed. "Because the stone isn't just called the Lilith Stone for nothing. It's called the Lilith Stone because she is trapped inside it."

"You've got to be kidding." I yanked at his shirt when he didn't let it drop and gave him a shove.

He sighed. "I'm giving you that detail now," he said. "An eon ago, a caste of monks forged the stone from Lilith's own blood and infused it with magic – and cursed her in the process. Her essence is trapped inside."

I remembered the ethereals in Lucifer's boudoir and in what he'd called his menagerie. He'd been able to release them at will to entertain him. What he called entertainment was nothing but horrific suffering.

I brought an image of the stone to mind, recalled its red globule like an insect trapped in amber. I'd thought it was blood. But what if it was the essence of a demon?

I knew Maddox was telling the truth. What I didn't know was whether it would change my decision.

"So they zapped her into stone like God did Lot's wife and then what? Left it in some jewellery box somewhere? Skipped it across a lake?"

I pulled open the refrigerator door and yanked out a milk carton. One shake proved it empty. I tossed it into the trash, then faced him with my hand propped on the open door.

I thought of the sidhe who used it to send me to hell for his own benefit. Whatever kind of monks they were, they were a wee bit lax about their job.

"If it was so valuable, they shouldn't have let just anyone have it."

"In fact," I argued. "Maybe they should have tossed it into a lake. It worked for King Arthur."

"Arthur was never a king," he said. "Just a lying braggart. Besides," he said. "The stone had the greatest security. It was mounted into an amulet and worn only by the stone master for safekeeping."

"Until someone stole it, of course," I murmured, imagining a thief like myself coming across a trinket so obviously valuable that it was never taken off. What self-respecting robber would let that go?

"So I'd rethink the whole idea of greatest security."

That one hit a nerve, I could see. He positively bristled at the comment.

"And so once it went missing they told you all this so you would know what you were looking for?"

I glared at him as he sat there, his hand absently running along his ribcage, tracing the mark over his shirt.

"Well?" I said. "How much are they paying you?"

He leveled me with a direct stare. "Enough."

"I thought Lilith was some religious fantasy."

He nodded. "That's what humans were trained to think. She was a creation of incredible power at one point."

I didn't know much about the woman, except the lore that permeated the Internet and entertainment.

"You may have noticed that for all my brass, I'm pretty small and I hear she eats children. So if your clients worship a demon that might find me tasty, you can forget it."

He chuckled. "You're not that small, Isabella and you most definitely do not look like a child." His gaze blazed a trail down my throat to the small hollow where my heartbeat thrummed.

I shrugged and closed the fridge in favor of dropping into the chair. My legs were too tired to hold me up and my brain was feeling decidedly squishy.

"You don't understand," he said. "The monks don't worship her. And the stone is not able to release her energy. Anyone who could do that is long gone."

There was a strange note of wistfulness in his tone but it came and went with a flash of a smile that wasn't the least bit sincere but a whole heck of a lot distracting. I wished he wasn't so damned handsome. It put me off my game.

"'Gone', you said." I made my fingers do the poof thing in the air. "Like the stone, eh? These monks don't have a great track record."

He ignored that remark even if he did look put out by it.

"It's not just a portal," he said. "It's a key and a threshold all in one. It can send someone to hell or pull them back out again. It's forged with hell flame and her blood and it can do so much more than just act as a portal. "

"Unless it can make me some dinner, I have no interest," I lied.

"I don't need you to get it back, Isabella," he said. "I just want you to understand what you're shielding. It needs an owner. One that can be its keeper. If a being is sent to Hell and back on its conduit, something changes in the stone. It begins to look for its keeper. If the same creature can survive such a trip, and remains in possession long enough, the stone automatically endows its keeper with immortality so it can be protected."

He paused for unnecessary effect because my mind was already swimming.

If it's in possession long enough.

I gaped at him.

"Oh my God," I said, blinking at the sheer magnitude of the possibility. "I'm immortal?"

He shook his head. "Have you walked in front of a bus lately?"

He tried not to smile at the absurdity and when he knew he failed, he perched on the sofa arm, lifting a shredded sock from the floor with the toes of his shoes.

"The sidhe warlord had it for centuries," I said testing and feeling the weight of the statement. Centuries sounded about right to me for a reward of such import.

Maddox nodded. "Yes," he said slowly. "And he is immortal."

"I thought Lucifer did that. Made him immortal, I mean."

He shook his head. "Lucifer lies. That stone gave Colin his immortality and it doesn't just wear off when the possession goes away."

"So," I said. "Just how much time are we talking?"

He gave me a queer look. "It isn't much, Kitten."

"In dog years, or people years?" I said, a slight unease climbing my back. "Please tell me it's people years."

He pressed his lips together in a way that indicated neither was right.

I felt my heart start to race. Scottie had that stone. While it would be amazing, ever so amazing, for that SOB to land himself in Hell accidentally, I couldn't, simply couldn't, risk him finding a way out and holding onto the stone.

Because then Scottie would be immortal.

And he would be my hell for eternity.

CHAPTER 14

I hung over my knees as I considered the scope of the problem. I couldn't risk Scottie touching that stone and I couldn't live under his threat any longer. There didn't seem to be a great answer that didn't involve me still in the cross hairs.

I lifted my head and watched Maddox pinch the sock at the heel and let it dangle from his fingers. He flung it toward the bedroom door where the cat merely glared out at it.

"How much time are we talking?" I said.

He gave me a distracted glance, all the while keeping his attention on the cat.

"Let's just say if a mortal man has it, better sooner than later."

I thought about Absalom at the speakeasy and his offer to make me a replica for the right price. And of course, Errol would want his cut. I wasn't foolish enough to think he was doing it for philanthropic reasons.

But was it even worth the risk of returning to that back room? I measured my options carefully in those moments. There was no telling what types of things Scottie would get up to if he became immortal. And if he was possessive now as a human, how much more persistent would he be if his own demise was no longer an issue?

I couldn't let Scottie live forever. Not just for me, but for all those nameless girls he would con, the victims he would hurt, the lives he would snuff out.

At least this way, I'd have Maddox's help. And since he knew far more about the otherworld than I did, I'd be foolish not to use him.

"I have a plan to retrieve it," I said and Maddox rose from his perch. He propped his elbow on one arm and ran his fingers down his chin, stroking an imaginary beard. I thought I could hear stubble rustling against his skin.

"Are you telling me you tried to honor our bargain?" he said.

I nodded. "I told you; there was a hiccup. We can't just storm at Scottie and grab something he considers his."

"Why not?" he said and I gave him a sour look meant to give him all he needed to know about the state of the man he wanted to con.

"Scottie is not fool enough to let someone just take what he believes is his."

Maddox centered his gaze directly at me intently enough that I licked my lips nervously. "That stone shouldn't be in his hands."

"Yes," I said. "But I can't just waltz in there and take it. I have to make him think he still has it."

"Poppycock," he said and if I hadn't been so focused on the issue of stealing from Scottie, I would have laughed at his archaic terminology.

Instead, I began pacing, wincing as I stepped on a bit of gravel from my visitor's boots and remembered the feel of my nerves wringing out like wet rags

"Maybe you don't have to live in this world, but I do."

He shrugged, as though to indicate he saw no issue with the reasoning. I ignored his nonchalance. One thing I was beginning to understand about Kindred, was that they didn't live by, or worry much about human concerns.

"We'll need a replica," I said.

"There is no replica of the stone," he said and rubbed his chin.

I took a deep breath. Now was the moment to spring my plans on him if ever there was one.

"I met someone who claims he can make one."

He canted his head at me. "Met someone? And what kinds of circles do you frequent that you would find someone able to re-create something like the Lilith stone."

His tone wasn't exactly accusatory, but his posture was. Maybe disclosure wasn't such a good idea.

I shrugged. "Artistic ones?"

He smirked at me. "You were planning to shyster me weren't you? That's a dangerous proposition, Kitten, you should know that."

I shrugged. "Not shyster, just play."

He sat on the sofa and pulled me down next to him. He felt all too warm beside me, the scent of wood smoke and whiskey all but swaddling me in some miasma that wasn't entirely unpleasant.

I almost wanted to cuddle up next to it but the flat of his palm spread over the back of my shoulders in a way that felt too much like a man about to smack an offending piece of meat out of someone's airway.

I sucked in a breath and let the story exhale in a rush. I told him about my short visit to Errol's shop and Absalom's offer, omitting the details that might make him predisposed to dissuade me.

"I don't know an Absalom," he said. "But alchemists don't do anything for free."

"Never said he would do it for free."

"Careful, Isabella. Most Kindred are not the philanthropic type."

"Errol is having a soiree in three days," I said, checking my watch. "Do you think Scottie will enter the land of the always living by then?"

Maddox grunted at the subtle threat, but he acquiesced. "A few days shouldn't be too much of a problem, but I can't guarantee after that."

"Good," I said. "Because I have a date," I said. "Errol."

"The hell you are. I'm not sure you know what he is--"

"Of course I do," I said. "All the more reason for him to escort me. It's his soiree. I couldn't be safer. And I have to be escorted, apparently. By a Kindred."

He grazed my face with an angry look. "I'll do just fine as your Kindred escort," he said. "He can argue it with me, but I'm taking you."

I thought of the time Maddox had found me negotiating with Errol and ended up saving me from the incubus's unwanted advances. It hadn't gone especially well.

"It's invitation only," I said. "And I doubt Errol will want you there."

"I know what pushes Errol's buttons," he said. "He wants to keep his portal into the Shadow Bazaar open. He'll let me in. Besides," he said and clipped his hooked finger beneath my chin, turning me to face him as though he needed me to see the deadly serious expression on his face.

"You have no idea what the fire gate looks like. How will you know you've found the portal?"

"All the bloody smoke and flames," I said and he chuckled.

"So like a ninth worlder," he said. "No imagination."

He leaned back on the sofa, pulling me with him. He crossed one leg over the other, bouncing his foot in the air.

It was so casually intimate that I leaned against him, enjoying the sense of planning. It was always my favorite part of a heist or lift. Those moments when the only boundaries are the lines your imagination chose to color within.

"Let's assume you're right," he said. "Let's say you locate Absalom's target and find the gate. How will you get through it?"

"Weren't you listening?" I said. "Errol told me I just had to toss it through."

He chuckled darkly to himself.

"What?" I said.

"That comment just proves you have no imagination. One doesn't just 'toss' an object through the Fire Gate."

He tutted beneath his breath, muttering about mortals and their ignorance. I nearly chewed the tip of my tongue off to keep from chewing him out. I waited without a modicum of patience for him to finish his private rant before I declared I didn't need him at all.

The arm that surrounded me brushed down my arm as though he thought I was cold.

"You've never been to one of these soirees," he said with a chiding tone. "I don't think you'll be ready for what you'll see there. Face it, Kitten," he said. "You need me."

I swung my gaze to his, scoping out a hint of tease. Maybe it wouldn't be so bad having him at my side instead of Errol.

"Then it's a date," I said and stuck my hand out to shake.

He didn't take my hand right away. Instead he stared down at it, measuring what it might mean for him to ally himself in an honorable manner with a woman he obviously thought had none.

"Shake," I said. "I'm good as my word."

I looked at his hand, so close to mine and slipped my palm against his. The skin was calloused in places and silken in others. All over, it was warm and large.

"I don't need imagination to conjure how bad this event might be," I admitted. "I saw things in the speakeasy that made my stomach churn."

"If you didn't outright run in sheer terror, then you didn't see half," he said.

"Doesn't matter. I have to do this."

"Brava," he said.

His thumb ran along my wrist, bringing a shiver to the base of my spine. I eased my eyes closed, mentally flogging myself for enjoying it so much.

I ended up talking too fast, rambling, to cover up my nerves.

"Errol gave me an outfit to wear."

His eyes hooded thoughtfully.

"I imagine," he said. "So have you looked at this outfit?"

A specter of a smile played at the corner of his mouth, tugging the formidable line into something playful. My face heated up.

"You haven't," he said and sighed.

"What do I care?" I said, recalling the dominatrix outfit I used to visit the shop incognito on occasion. "What's the worst it could be?"

His eyes trailed to the heap of leather from Lucifer's boudoir that still lay on the floor beside the sofa. I shivered and he pulled me close. I felt his lips against my hair and his warm breath cascaded down my neck.

"Maybe it won't be that bad," he murmured. "I mean, what kind of pet would an incubus require a mortal to be dressed as anyway?"

There was a note of teasing in his voice, but even so, I jerked away just enough to dislodge his lips from the top of my head. He looked faintly amused as he peered down at me.

"Pet?" I said.

He nodded. "Errol was always known for his soirees. They were...legendary."

A dimple showed in his cheek and I knew he was playing with me. At least I thought he was until he ran his thumb across my bottom lip, and his face tightened as though he was doing something forbidden.

"Don't worry, Kitten," he said. "Whatever he has devised, you'll be the most beautiful pet on display."

It was an unexpected compliment and there was throatiness in his voice that erased my censure of whatever outfit I might be wearing. I let it wash over me the way alcohol flooded your senses. I felt drunk looking at him, listening to his voice.

Something jangled in the back of my mind, warring with the reaction my body had to his. I was supposed to be my own woman. Not succumbing to some whiskey voice and brawny shoulders. I wasn't a girl anymore to be seduced by the threat of danger or the promise of protection.

I intended to push him away but the moment my palms landed on his chest, I felt his heartbeat against my palm and it was such a staccato drumming that I looked up into his face. Big mistake. His eyes were locked on my lips. A quiver dressed the corner.

I realized he was holding his breath.

And I knew those signals. My body drenched my mind with a flood of oily desire.

There was no shouldn't. No never again.

There was only the taste of his lips as I reached for him. I dipped my tongue in the lax center where he made a surprised sound that filled my mouth with the taste of fine whiskey.

My arms went of their own volition around his neck and my hands sought the roots of his hair. So delirious it felt in my fingers, it was soft and lush and smelled of ylang ylang, that I moaned.

I tugged at it. I wanted to feel it curtain my skin, obliterate any visual cues that might make me rethink the rightness of what felt so dreadfully, sinfully, forbidden.

At first he responded. Not expertly, but clumsily, as though he hadn't expected me to take initiative, and then he took control, teaching my tongue what it really meant to be kissed.

However many centuries he'd lived must have schooled him in a woman's every pleasure. There was an almost tentative mastery in his touch. His hands roamed my arms, memorizing the curve of bicep and tracing the line of wrist but they never moved close to my breast, never down past my waist.

It was chaste and steamy all at once. He explored me as though he'd imagined every curve and line in the darkest parts of night and was now testing his practice.

I melted beneath him, every muscle a lubricated gear that sank backward, intent on pulling him with me.

What he was doing to me wasn't enough. I needed to feel his skin on mine. I felt alive and reclaiming myself. I initiated this. I wanted this.

I would drive it.

I pressed both hands atop his hair and eased him, guiding him toward my breasts. He halted at the hollow above my sternum, lighting my skin with feathery kisses that made me arch upward, pressing against him with a need that remembered it hadn't been fulfilled in years.

I squirmed, trying to peel off my clothes without losing touch with him.

"Undress for me," I said. "Let me see you."

The words must have been an icy wash of water over his skin. He recoiled and drew back, the drugged look on his face slowly swallowed up by realization.

"I'm sorry," he said in a husky voice. He shook his head the way a dog does after a swim. "I shouldn't. I can't."

I didn't have time to be hurt. Before I could protest or beg or even feel the shame coat me, he was off me and striding to the door.

"I'll meet you at Errol's," he said without looking at me.

He halted at the door, his posture rigid. I watched him ease his eyes closed as though bracing himself for something and then he yanked on the handle and pulled it open.

When he was half way out the door, he finally threw a glance my way and it was such a look of pain and confusion that I didn't have the heart to feel hurt.

"I'm sorry, Kitten," he said and there was a hint of his normal composure seeping back into his demeanor. "The last thing you need is another bastard."

He shot me a grin and then he was gone.

The cat yowled at me from the kitchen and pawed at her dish.

"Sure," I said to her. "At least one kitten deserves a treat."

CHAPTER 15

Three nights later, we stood in front of Errol's shop. The neon sign above the door was out but the barred door wasn't down. I could see through the glass door all the way to the back of his shop. A basket of what looked like electronics sat just inside on the floor.

Maddox stood beside me.

He was dressed in a crisp dress shirt, open three buttons down. I could see a freckle to the left of his sternum shaped like a star and wanted to trace it with my finger.

The undershirt he wore beneath was one I'd seen Scottie call wife beaters with a knowing laugh. The trousers were tight at the hips, buttoned just below his waist and fell in a straight line to Louis Vuittons.

He didn't mention our kiss and I didn't either. After I went to bed with a laptop of porn, I decided he was still too heavily mired in his relationship with Kerri. I liked her despite not knowing much about her and told myself it was perfectly honorable to pay for a boy toy in the near future if I felt the need to throw myself at a man again.

Yeah. That rejection hurt. I wasn't going to pretend it didn't, but there were things at stake here that helped me at least push it to the back of my mind.

A pro never let personal things get in the way of a heist, and I was already feeling electric with the hum of possibility.

The other thing neither of us mentioned was the outfit Errol had provided me. When I'd pulled it out of the bag I'd retched out of sheer principle. I wore a long trench coat over what reminded me insufferably of a princess Leia slave outfit. Not only did Errol have a revolting idea of fashion, apparently, he was a nerd.

There were only two differences to the costume: one was that the nipples in my bra cups were cut out and replaced with a bit of gauzy fabric. It chafed in awful ways. The other was the small pouch attached to my waist, presumably to hold the substitute stone that Errol promised would be delivered on entry to the soiree.

Maddox held out the chain that was also part of my garb. I sighed heavily and snapped the collar around my neck. The chain was not costume; it had weight and heft and real, honest to goodness locks.

While I'd agreed to wear the thing, I'd been adamant that I would be the keeper of the key. It was tucked into the elven boots I wore, and a duplicate was safely sitting on my bureau at home.

A smart thief always had backup.

I was going to be the smart thief tonight.

"Just remember what Leia did with these chains," I quipped. "So be nice to me."

He gave me a blank stare, punctuated by a breeze that blew his auburn hair across his face. He'd come un-bunned for the soiree as a means to look more roguish and I wasn't sure the look was sexier than the knot he always pulled his hair into.

"Princess Leia," I said. "Jabba the Hut?"

He shook his head with a dumbfounded look on his face.

I sighed. "Plebeian," I said and held out the other end of the chain to him.

He rattled it noisily as I stood there and I noticed he wasn't just doing it to make me nervous. He was fidgeting.

"Are you ready for this?" I said.

"You can't mess this up," he said. "You have no idea what's at stake."

I stared at my feet, enrobed in felt boots. Earlier, he'd made me practice keeping my eyes downcast no matter what he said, and he said some pretty hurtful things. I'd failed the test three times before I managed to keep my gaze downcast.

He then suggested I practice crawling on my hands and knees.

"Just in case," he said, but I had the feeling he was toying with me.

He sported a bruise on the corner of his left eye that told him exactly what I thought of that practice.

Now he was tapping his foot on the sidewalk and fiddling with the chain as though he was the one dressed in a sheer bit of gauze and humiliating chains for the sport of a few deviant guests.

"You need to understand that whatever Absalom wants can't be a paltry thing and that puts us both at risk." He pinned me with his gaze. "You understand?"

"I understand," I said. "I hadn't thought you'd be afraid of anything."

"I'm afraid of no one," he said. "But risk is an entirely different thing. I have others to think about. More lives than a few mortals are at stake."

He looped his end of the chain around his wrist several times, shortening the distance between us. After that awkward kiss, I was surprised he wanted me so close, but I supposed he didn't want to take a chance of me doing something stupid.

"Stay close to me," he said. "Don't wander off. Don't look anyone in the eye. Got it?"

"Got it, I said and noted the way his jaw clenched and unclenched. "Jesus," I said. "You're going to queer the deal."

He gave me a long look. "I just want you to understand what you're up against."

"You told me plenty back at the apartment."

He had. He had gone on for long moments about what I might see inside. Everything from orgies to cannibalism to snuff sex. All of it meant to titillate the Kindred within.

I expected incubus, shifters, and vampires, but I wasn't sure what else could be there and it made me nervous.

"Just don't let anyone eat me, okay?" I said.

He lifted his russet brows as though he wanted to crack off a bad joke and I lifted my chains with an equally suggestive browline.

He chuckled and then squared his shoulders with all seriousness. The muttering beneath his breath was a signal that he was uncomfortable, and I realized just how much when he faced me.

"You're sure he's going to be here?" Maddox said, lifting my chin with his index finger hooked beneath.

I adjusted the gauze over my left nipple where it had begun to chafe enough to make it itch.

"Errol was quite clear that he would be here and that he would be sufficiently pliant."

I'd been sure the incubus was telling the truth when he'd given me a time frame when the target would most likely be near the fire gate. All I had to do was ingratiate myself and lure him close enough to the gate for the item to reveal itself.

I believed Errol because I had the feeling he was getting something out of the deal as well, and while I bristled at the thought that he was using me, I told myself that in the end it didn't matter.

Maddox's eye followed the trail of my fingers from beneath the trench coat to the loin cloth that had begun to creep sideways.

"What?" I said. "A gal doesn't want the whole of her goddessness to peek out at the world."

"You should have worn panties under that thing," he muttered. "It's going to be distracting."

"Isn't that the point?"

Maddox made a sound deep in his throat that could have meant anything. I heard him take a deep breath and mutter something about he hated these things before sending a text on the phone Errol had also supplied along with the outfit.

Immediately, the phone evaporated into nothingness and showed up on the counter inside along with a dozen others.

Moments later, a short girl in a flowing see through dress came through the beaded curtain and headed toward the door. She waved away the locks and bolts from her side and opened the door.

Tiny, elvish ears waggled playfully. Her nipples were purple and I'd have thought it was paint until I noticed that she also had a purple birthmark on her left breast. She was amply endowed for a girl shorter than me, with full hips that curved into a triangle of purple hair.

I tried to lift my gaze to her face but the way she jutted her hip to the sides made looking away tough.

"Like what you see?" Maddox said in my ear. I felt my face burn.

"Just thinking they're all going to be very disappointed to see regular human pink nipples."

"Not half as disappointed as they'll be to see you didn't bother to shave your legs."

He chuckled darkly as the girl opened the door and ushered us in. She said nothing but slipped a heavy object into my bag. The stone, I realized. So. Part one had begun.

I heard the girl locking the door back up behind us and would have turned around except Maddox jerked the chain and I staggered toward him. He wasn't waiting for me at all, just striding toward the beaded curtain with dogged purpose.

"Hey," I complained. "I thought you hated these things."

"Silence, pet," he said over his shoulder. "You know the rules. You speak, you are spanked. You argue, you are bitten. You disobey and--"

"You're enjoying this too much," I complained, and the girl sent a sharp, uncertain look toward me. She was hesitant as she held out her arm toward me, giving me a wary look that said she didn't trust me.

Maddox nudged me with his elbow. "Your coat, pet." He leaned in close and hissed in my ear. "Play the game dammit."

I clutched my jacket tighter. Something about baring my skin, even if I'd agreed to it, seemed wrong. I couldn't go through with it. He was fully clothed, after all. I was the one left exposed.

He gave the chain a hard jerk and I gagged as the collar bit into my throat. I clutched at the edges, glaring at him as I tried to loosen it from my skin. I hissed a curse at him and he lifted an eyebrow in apology.

"It's a privilege you were invited, mortal," he said. "Act grateful."

I sucked in a spiteful comment, reminding myself that I'd agreed to all this. I pulled off the trench and laid it over the girl's arm then heeled like any good pet, coming up along his left side, just in line with his boots.

The girl seemed less flustered now that he had assumed command but when she went ahead of us, I stabbed him in the kidney with a stiffened finger.

"This is a show, remember," I said. "Don't take advantage."

"I don't think anyone can take advantage of you, Kitten," he said.

He pulled me close, wrapping his free arm around my midriff and I felt safe in that moment. I knew he wouldn't just leave me exposed and open to attack or otherwise in unknown territory. He had my back.

At least, that was how I felt until he spoke.

"Get ready," he said. "It's going to get hairy in there."

I'd been in Errol's back room before of course, but I wasn't sure what to expect since he'd admitted that it changed depending on its need and use. I told myself it would no doubt be very much the same as my first visit in the sense that I wouldn't be able to make out any faces or creatures or identify anyone.

With the exception of Kerri, I'd been unable to really make out features or even if the company were human. He'd been careful to either mask my ability to see reality or warp it. No doubt his nefarious activities required some anonymity of most. Maybe his company had their own sorts of glamor. I was still pretty ignorant of the Kindred worlds except for the fact that it existed.

I knew other things, however. More than one of these worlds existed, for example. Nine if I remembered correctly, and no matter what the inhabitants looked like, ate, drank, or breathed, if they were able to come through to the human realm, they had to have some sort of portal.

The inhabitants either had magic or twisted energies and time. Anything seemed possible from what I could tell. But what I didn't know would fill a universe, and I had the feeling that now it was part of my reality, I'd best bone up or risk being caught up in worse than the mire of Scottie.

In short. I needed to suck it up, whatever it was, and get on with why I was here.

One problem at time.

I doubted Errol would let just anyone through, no matter how much energy Maddox told me he'd be trying to siphon off. Incubi fed on sexual energy and that was what this soiree was all about.

In his prime, Errol sold these soirees to other creatures, earning power in return for every lascivious activity. There was at least some sort of safety in that. Errol wouldn't do anything to risk the power he was pulling.

I was already imagining the setting Errol would have cultivated beyond the curtain as I pushed through behind Maddox. At first, all I could see was his broad back and the way it tensed beneath his dress shirt.

He gave off a scent of Old Spice cologne, one he said he'd put on to ground me to reality because he was certain Errol might be after more than just helping me help a powerful alchemist.

I was prepared for a 70s style disco with undulating naked bodies basking on bear skin rugs and sniffing cocaine from silver trays to fuel their lustful adventures. Errol himself looked so much like a 70s porn star when I'd first met him, that I couldn't see him in any other setting despite his more recent glamour to resemble the Irish actor I had a crush on.

And just how he had known that, I'd want to know but for now, I needed to focus on what was important. If I couldn't just have Scottie handle the stone and be gone from my life indefinitely without endangering me and the entire world in the long run, then I'd have to find another way to get rid of him.

And since no plan at present revealed itself other than the original one, I might as well forge ahead.

For now.

That meant I had this one chance to get a replica that might fool Scottie and get it charmed. I wasn't about to muck that up by looking either shocked or angry at what would meet me.

As our hostess guided us toward the beaded curtain, lit behind by an alternating blue and red light, she was careful to wrest the trench coat from my fingers, leaving me standing in the outfit Errol had picked out for me.

I braced myself for that cheesy 70s porn movie, and took a deep breath. I nodded at Maddox and clenched his hand briefly, either giving or taking support, I wasn't sure.

Then the hostess lifted it aside, and I realized this visit would be different. Different because what I heard as I stepped through, was the last thing I expected.

CHAPTER 16

Deep, throaty moans of pleasure swelled across the room, but they sounded tinny, disguised by the dull roar of regular conversation. The muted sounds of jazz tinkled along, filling in the gaps in the lull of voices.

It could have been an upscale meet and greet until you took in the décor and setting.

While the first time I'd been to the back room, most of the patrons had been blurred in a wash of unrecognizable color, this time the room and its inhabitants were all painfully, crystal clear.

I held my breath, certain that when the fog cleared this time, I'd see a chamber filled with large satin throw pillows cast around a gaudily decorated room. Naked bodies would no doubt be writhing over each other, the lights blinking on white backsides and creamy skin.

Chalk one up for Errol. He pulled off the most discreet of sexual escapades. I was even relieved to see that most of the patrons looked very human.

"I thought they were supposed to be escorted," I said.

Maddox tracked my gaze to a sofa where three men and one woman were about to get down to some serious petting.

"You see humans?" he asked and I nodded.

"Glamor meant to keep the true pets from freaking out," he said. "Most of them are incubus, a means of priming the pump, if you get my meaning. But at least all the Kindred I see are humanoid: vampires and shifters and sorcerers. There's a mage in the corner with a human woman on a leash, and a raven shifter staring at you but nothing worse. That's a step in the right direction. It means we can hope that the other spectacles are aimed at and attended by ninth worlders who will no doubt discover tomorrow that they had the most lascivious dreams."

He leaned down. "But that doesn't mean it's a given, you understand. Just my presumption."

I gulped.

"You see why you need to stick close?" he said. "Anything could be beyond those thresholds." He jerked his chin toward three doors that wore signage I didn't understand.

"What do the signs say?" I said. "Is it some strange language?"

The first one was a long, brownish burn mark with a white flower, the second an oblong fire red etching. The third was an orange circle with at least nine crimson rings.

He pulled me close and leaned in to answer. The perfume of wood smoke and whiskey engulfed me.

"You don't recognize a vanilla bean, Kitten?"

"Vanilla," I said, and made a small sound of understanding that made him chuckle under his breath. With the first one decoded, I didn't need further hints to know the rooms got increasingly more risqué.

"Good," he answered. "But you should keep your eyes down. Most of the allure is visually driven. Do you want to hang out here a bit longer," he said, sensing the way I hung back.

I waggled my head up and down, but I had a hard time not looking around me and taking it all in. I doubted a priest could have kept his eyes downcast.

There were sofas, yes, with couples half reclined in semi-upright positions on them, leaning into each other, pressing against each other and kissing. I wasn't sure how many were human and how many were Kindred, but it was all very titillating, to be honest.

Especially the nude statues made of living flesh that entreated passersby to touch them.

I had to admit the sexual tension in the room was enough to make even a nun sweat. I've never been to an orgy before. I'd never had a threesome. Scottie was always so jealous of me, he wasn't about to share. And since he was my only lover, I often wondered what it would be like with another man.

I cast a sidelong look at Maddox. Was he as affected by all this as I was?

Surely we could mix business and pleasure a little bit. We didn't have to go all in, but we didn't have to be frigid either.

"I actually feel over dressed," I said, looking down at myself. I picked at the loin cloth, deciding it might not need to get in the way.

Maddox pulled my hand away and tucked it beneath his arm. "Eyes down."

"But it's so hard," I said, giggling at the pun.

It wasn't so bad, actually. No worse than a few porn films I'd watched. Nothing truly deviant. I certainly didn't see any cannibalism.

And it was making me feel a little flushed.

I began to understand why Maddox had been so insistent on me keeping my eyes downcast. It wasn't just for meekness, it was out of necessity.

Young women ambled around the room, naked from the waist up, with short skirts swinging.

Two of them wore white knee socks and Mary-Jane shoes but nothing else. They had large breasts and neat hips completely void of any follicle of hair. The burnished skin looked as though it was polished and oiled.

They walked together, arm in arm, and stopped every so often to inspect a couple, perhaps touching one or two of them, and then moved on.

It was almost as though to them, the room was the equivalent of a tasting bar where sips of champagne could be taken alongside bolts of whiskey.

"Succubae," Maddox said, following my gaze. "Ancient ones. They're meant to improve the energy."

He eyed the women for a long moment then averted his gaze almost awkwardly. He muttered something to himself that I couldn't hear and then, seeming to know exactly where my own eyes were, he rattled the chain.

"Stop gawking, Isabella," he said.

I sighed.

"You're no fun," I said, but I skated my gaze back to my feet as he led me along.

"You said Errol gave you a mental image of the man we seek," he said under his breath.

"Yes, an older looking guy. Kind of Sean Conneryish."

"Sean Connery?"

I had to swing my gaze to his. "Seriously," I said. "You don't watch any movies?"

"Human drama doesn't excite me," he said and steered me toward the door with the vanilla bean.

"Methinks thou dost protest too much," I said, peering beneath my lashes to see two youngish looking men, completely nude, heading toward us.

In one easy movement, Maddox spun me to face him, his knee slipping between my legs and parting them.

Interestingly enough, they parted easily. My breath caught in my throat. For one moment, I thought he would kiss me and my mind flooded with confusion. I'd misread those earlier signals, and I was resigned not to do it again.

But now, with the feel of his muscled chest beneath by palms, feeling the stuttering of his heartbeat, I wondered if the atmosphere was getting to him too.

I fluttered my eyes way up to meet his. He really was so very tall and in the elven boots without a heel, I only came up midway his chest. He gazed down at me and I had to resist the urge to reach up and brush away the fox-colored hair that framed his jawline. The stubble was still there, all reddish and smoky gray.

I wanted to feel the roughness of it against my palm, pull him down and nuzzle against it until my cheek was sore.

Worse, I wanted to feel that stubble against far more tender areas than my cheeks.

"You're flushed," he said. "You certainly can't be hot in that garb."

"I admit it is a bit overwhelming," I said, and discovered that no matter how hard I tried to look him in the eye, my gaze was locked on his mouth. I swallowed to clear the lump that formed. "I think I'm going to faint or something."

"It's allure," he said. A note of huskiness burnished the usual tones of his voice, and I knew he was trying to get me to meet his gaze.

"That's all, Isabella," he said. "The incubus has woven a good bit of it all over the place. Humans have a hard time resisting. Even a few Kindred have trouble."

I wondered if he was one of those.

"You don't think it has anything to do with all the love-making going on?"

I almost twisted around to see what the noise was to my left but he held me tightly.

He shuffled us both sideways, butting into a table laid out with gargantuan bowls of sex toys. Some I'd seen before, some I had no idea what to do with. My hand reached out to touch something that reminded me of a whip except it had several lashes, each with a hookish barb on the end.

"This isn't love-making," he said with a sudden tightness in his voice that confused me. He pulled me closer still, my chest against his as his gaze darted over my shoulder. "This is cheaply manufactured lust."

"I doubt this was cheap," I said, indicating the bowls of toys.

He cupped his hand over the back of my head and tilted it back so I could meet his gaze.

"As heady as this is," he said. "It's nothing to what will be going on inside the spectacles."

"You say that like you've been to a good number of orgies," I said.

"I'm immortal," he said shortly. "I've seen a lot of things. "

I wasn't sure whether the emotion climbing through my throat was jealousy that he'd been to lots of events like this or relief that he could handle what might be coming.

If this was just the beginning, I wasn't sure what would go on later, and it was almost comforting to know someone more experienced than me was at my side.

"Should we carry on, then?" I said, trying to block out the sight of two very beautiful women peeling off their clothes and heading our way.

"Do you think you're ready?" he said. I noted he took great pains not to look where my eye kept wandering. Good lord, were those breasts even real?

"Isabella," he said. "If this is the fluff room, and you're not immune, we're going to have trouble."

One of the succubae ambling about the room drifted near, pushing aside the naked women already enroute. Both of them devoured Maddox with their eyes but deferred to the succubus.

She ran a long slender finger blood red nails along the skin of my arm. Every inch of my flesh strained to be touched again. I felt myself leaning in to it, aching for a full palm, a stroking touch.

"It's pretty for a human," she said to Maddox. "I might be persuaded to educate her for you."

I watched Maddox's jaw clench. "No," he said.

She scowled at him. "You're not playing by the rules."

"Fuck the rules," he said.

She snapped a nasty look at him but she drifted away all the same.

"You didn't have to be rude," I said.

"Are you forgetting why we're here?"

"Of course not." I squared my shoulders and felt the gauze scratch against my breasts. "I'm not an idiot."

"You're acting like a besotted idiot," he said through clenched teeth.

I noticed a thin sheen of sweat beading on his brow. His posture was tense and rigid. The usual arrogant demeanor was gone. In its place was a man whose face was as tight as a virgin's thighs.

I wasn't sure why, but his awkwardness made me feel a heck of a lot better. I could almost feel the allure receding.

"If you don't unclench that sphincter," I said. "You're going to suck your legs right up your ass."

He looked down at me with a baleful glare. "It's time to find Errol and get the show on the road," he said. "We've wasted enough time."

"You were all teasing and macho outside," I said. "Now you're acting like a monk caught with his cassock open in front of the pearly gates. Buck up, man. We've got shit to do."

I started to spin around, but he jerked on the chain and it rattled against my bare clavicle.

"Stick close to me," he said sharply. "I can't have you wandering off and getting mixed up in this mess."

"How can I wander off?" I said, lifting my arms in the air indicate the state of my shackles.

"I have no idea," he said. "But you have a penchant for getting into trouble."

I might have argued, but I spotted two large men heading our way with determination in their step and commitment written all over their expressions.

They carried dominatrix type whips. Both of them looked like Greek gods with naked torsos biceps hewn from stone.

I felt a flush of lust shiver over my skin. Whatever I'd wanted to do a moment ago slipped from my mind like a drop of oil on a hot pan.

"Oh, Mama," I said before I could stop myself. "Whatever those things are, they're hot as hades."

"It's the allure," he said with a note of pique. "It's got you enthralled."

"Well, I like it."

I felt a pull, almost as though one of them had tugged on my chain and I reacted by stumbling forward. Those pecs. I just wanted to run my palm down along them to find the warmth of one of those hard bellies.

Maddox snagged my elbow.

"Isabella," he grumbled. "Snap out of it."

"What?" I said, turning in a daze back to him and slipping my fingers between the buttons of his shirt.

He sucked in a breath when I grazed his navel.

My mind flooded with images of the two of us together and I felt hot and flushed as they raced through my mind.

"You've seen me naked," I said. "Remember? You gave me a shower."

"Stop it," he said. "Get a hold of yourself."

The men, I noticed, had halted. I waggled my fingers in their direction, inviting them closer. All I could think was how divine it would be surrounded by gorgeous men, crushed in the middle, feeling skin on skin.

"Why are you still dressed?" I asked Maddox. I tugged at the buttons. "It's unnatural."

"What's unnatural," he said, pulling away so that my hand fell away from him. "Is the aura in here. It's making you crazy."

"Not crazy," I whispered. "Wet. What else are we here for except to enjoy it?"

"You know why we're here."

One of the men closed the distance between us and picked up the slack in my chain as though he planned to lead me away.

I thrust my hips to the side, giving him a good view of my thigh. The loin cloth was too long, I decided.

He gave me an appraising glance.

"That's better," he said, addressing Maddox. "Now, let her go. Serena wants her. She's waiting in the Hunn room."

"The Hunn room," I echoed thoughtfully. "That sounds nice."

"It is not nice," Maddox said in a tight voice. "It is the opposite of nice." He nodded in the direction of the Dante's Inferno door. "It's in the seventh circle."

Maddox pushed me behind him. I was stuck between the broad back of an immovable force and a table filled with sex toys and I wasn't sure which was more intimidating.

One of the men addressed Maddox.

"Humans are supposed to be fair play," he said.

"Over my dead body," Maddox said. "I don't share."

"Then you might have rethought your choice to attend," the other man said.

They bustled forward, obviously Errol's muscle. No doubt the slender woman had gone to complain.

Maddox looked over his shoulder at me. "Give me that Trioldo," he said.

"The what, now?" I backed up against the table. Now that all I could feel were Maddox's rigid shoulders, I felt a bit more myself.

He jerked his elbow toward a rather large, triple shafted toy the size of my forearm. I cringed when I saw it, but hefted it with both hands, staring at it with tightness in my jaw that meant I was grimacing. Probably unattractively.

He took it from me and held it like a bat.

"Now," he said to the men. "Where do you want it?"

CHAPTER 17

A quick peek around Maddox's midriff revealed the two handsome men had become four and that they had ceased to be attractive in any way that a human woman would enjoy.

They weren't vampires, but each one of their teeth extended into sharp points and when they opened their mouths, those teeth dripped some sort of fluid that was brackish and stunk like skunk spray as it landed on the floor in front of them.

I clutched Maddox's sleeve. "Sweet Jehosophat," I said, sick to the pit of my stomach that a moment ago, I'd wanted to touch them. "Watch out," I said and hid my face in the folds of the back of his shirt.

His free hand swung around to search for me and I took it. His grasp made me feel safe for the one moment it landed on me. All too soon, he let go to grasp the handle of the trioldo in a partner with his other hand.

He swirled the sex toy in a big arc at his side as the four men turned into six, two of them wavering in from thin air. All of them held cattle prods at their sides that burned with an internal sort of light and were decorated with runes.

"Punishers," Maddox said.

"Which?" I squeaked from behind him. "The men, the weapons, or the toy?"

As if in answer, one of them, a tall bloke with a buzzed haircut and several tattoos of grotesquely painful scenes inked into his bare chest leaned sideways to catch a good look at me.

"Pets are meant to be shared," he said. "Failure to comply means punishment for its host."

"I don't share," Maddox said.

"We've had several requests for your pet already," he said and brandished his weapon. The end of it began to glow.

"I don't care," Maddox said.

"Two goddesses have put their bids in."

"Again," Maddox said. "I don't share."

I tugged his sleeve. "Tell them I only do men; maybe that will help."

I said it into his back and he stiffened. The folds of his shirt stretched out across his shoulders and went taut from hem to collar.

"None of the parties in question are men, Isabella," he said. "It's glamor. That's all."

They swarmed around us and if anyone else in the room noticed, they paid no mind. The razor's edge of one Punisher's weapon touched down lightly on a human looking woman gripping the leash of an old man.

She cried out, and bloody boils freckled her arm in a line from the entry point to her clavicle. They burst with a hissing ooze that burned the old gent's pate.

Apparently the penalty for keeping your human company to yourself was severe.

"Sheesh," I said. "Overkill much?"

But that was all I got out before the swarm became deadly. Maddox shoved me backwards as the men fell upon him and I toppled sideways. I crawled into what I thought was a safe spot to hold out till Maddox could clear up the disagreement.

Because it needed to be a disagreement. Anything else would get us thrown out or worse.

I watched as one by one the men threw themselves at Maddox. He swung the sex toy in an arc that struck one of them in the ear. One heartbeat later and the six men got sucked back up into one.

Next I knew, Errol was striding over with the succubus in tow.

She had a furrowed and angry brow and her breasts swung free, jiggling like massive water balloons. I forgot I was supposed to keep my eyes downcast and openly gaped at her.

"For pity's sake," Maddox complained. "Can't you cover those up?"

Fury did not sit well on her features. She didn't bother to address Errol at all, just lifted her hand and pulled the trioldo straight from Maddox's grip. It landed like a fish on the floor between them and flopped three times before settling.

I snickered. I couldn't help it.

The succubus clawed her gaze my way.

I've never been into women, but I swear, the energy that came from her made my entire body tingle. I lost all interest in what might have been going on. All I wanted was for this woman to run the back of her fingers down my hip.

I stuck my leg out, keen for her to see the skin, to imagine touching it.

Someone grabbed me by the waist and yanked me backwards and only then did I realize I'd been walking liking a drugged mute toward the succubus.

"Get out of here, Kitten," Maddox hissed. He tossed my chain at me, letting go his end. "Run. Somewhere. Anywhere. I'll catch up."

I did run, chains rattling and weighing me down and making my flight an awkward, fumbling thing. I bolted for an opening to the left, not caring where it took me, just careful to keep my gaze down, refusing to meet the eye of anyone who could snare me with allure.

No one lingered at the mouth of it, handing out toys, drugs, or drinks. I paused at the opening, keeping my eyes carefully pinned to my toes and only occasionally checking to be sure I wasn't heading straight into a wall or worse.

I kept my hands close to my chest, with the fetters clutched tightly enough that I didn't trip on them.

It was a short hallway, lit by Grecian looking lamps that hung from iron chains attached to the ceiling every few feet.

Frescoes swathed the walls in color. Mosaic tiles lent a slippery touch to my boots as I shuffled along, trying to work out what the pattern was. It took me several steps before I realized it depicted a nude women peering out from a cluster of tall reeds. A goat kicked up its heels beside her.

The sound of music lured me forward into a grove lush with tree canopies and the sound of tinkling water. A goat bleated from somewhere in the midst of a thicket of roses and came barreling out as though it had been given the bum's rush.

A much larger, much hairier goat emerged from the thicket, strutting through the tall grass with a wooden flute hanging over its chest. It paused as it saw me, front foot held aloft like a dog on point.

I swore I saw the beast smile.

Even as I watched, it stood on its hind legs, its torso lengthening out into a thick human chest. The flute hung from his neck like an afterthought, slung sideways, it swung back and forth as he sauntered toward me.

Giggles came from the thicket and someone called out to him in a foreign language. He smiled at me and held his finger to his lips.

"They think I'm getting them wine." He lifted the flute to his lips and blew out a mournful note, testing the timber. "What do you think?" he said. "Is it to your liking?"

I shrugged. I'd never liked the pan pipe.

"Too airy fairy," I said.

Elegant brows knit together in thought. "I agree," he finally said and lifted the pipe from its string around his neck and breathed into one tube after the other. The instrument trumpeted out a blast of jazz that sounded like the serpent coiling around Eve's ankles.

Sensing this was all a test, I shrugged and he grinned, taking up the challenge. Note after note, rock, country, classical, even something that sounded like punk blasted from the pipe.

Whatever giggles were going on behind the thicket transformed to moans each time the music genre shifted. I wasn't completely certain they were sounds of displeasure.

"You're still dressed," he complained at last, dropping the pipe to his chest again.

"Shouldn't I be?"

He let go a weary sigh and collapsed onto a green velvet lounge that leapt out from the forest as he let go his footing.

"I've never failed to woo the clothes off a neophyte. I must be losing my touch."

He ran his hand absently over his stomach, tickling his belly button and regarding me thoughtfully.

A low, passionate moan trembled out from the thicket and I almost gave in to curiosity.

"They'll keep themselves busy for a while," he said. "You can come closer. I don't bite."

I was already closing the distance between us when he pulled the pipe to his lips again and blew into it. This time it called out names, followed by hollow sounding cries of passion.

"You're trying too hard now," I said with a laugh.

"You're right," he said in disgust and tossed it into the thicket where it wheezed out a bagpipe sounding noise. I put my hands over my ears.

"Seriously?" I said. "Who likes that?"

He shrugged. "Who knows? But it was worth a shot."

One by one, slender, pale looking women with pert breasts and long legs emerged from the woods and clamored toward him, pushing each other out of the way.

He regarded me with something like suspicion. "Like the ladies do you?" he said. "Because, seriously, who would give up a chance to be with a god."

"Maybe someone who is an atheist?" I said and laughed.

At my retort, he merely chuckled deep in his throat.

"And what of women?" he said.

I shook my head. "Men exclusively. Particularly older men. Men that look like Sean Connery. But not the young Sean Connery. The older one. Like in *The Untouchables.*"

"I loved that movie," he said and I instantly liked him.

"Finally," I said. "A Kindred with class."

He canted his head at me. "You should know I can be whatever you like. Classy, nasty, sassy."

He waved away several of the nymphs cavorting around him and they settled into the bed of cushions. They perched there instead of lazing, waiting for a chance to do his bidding. One of them glared at me as though I were an anomaly she didn't understand.

With a wave of his wrist, he held onto two overflowing goblets of wine, pulled from somewhere as though there was an invisible curtain hiding a cornucopia of enchantments. He tilted one toward me.

"Share?" he said.

I knew I should be searching for Absalom's target, and I hesitated. Even in the human realm, I didn't take drinks from someone I didn't know.

Call me cynical, but a gal can't be too careful about belting back a drink that's been in someone else's fist. It couldn't be much different in the Kindred world. A god might be a god, but this was Errol's soiree after all.

He held out the two goblets to his side and stared down at his bare chest.

"It's not drugged, don't worry. I have no need of artificial intoxicants when I look like this."

His chest was hairy and lush like a bear rug but beneath all of the fur, his muscles were taut and thick, even if they did trail down to loins made of goat legs.

"Pan," I murmured and a grin split his face into two cheery half-moons as his cheeks crested over deep dimples.

"My reputation isn't dead, then, even if the rumors of my demise abound."

He scooted over on his lounge, making room. "Sit," he said. "Tell me about yourself."

I accepted the goblet and held it between my knees as I perched on the edge of the lounge. I faced him without fear, liking his affable demeanor. If he was dangerous, it was to goats and nymphs, I decided.

"There's not much to tell except that I'm new to all of this," I admitted.

I must have given him a rare treasure with the statement because he agitated forward, sniffing the air in front of me the way a hound might proffered fingers, testing for character. His eyes rolled back in excitement as he leveled his gaze to the heavens.

"Sweet Zeus and here I am without the powers to divest you of your lovely costume."

He eyed the material over my nipples with sadness.

"Of course, I do have hands. And teeth. And tongue. Do you prefer that mode of undress, perhaps? Newbies are my specialty," he said with a wink. "Mind you, newbies and virgins are different altogether. One must coddle a virgin. They are skittish and in my experience, guarded about their wares. Newbies just need a bit of encouragement."

I was beginning to enjoy his company; looks notwithstanding, he had charisma.

"Can I encourage you, newbie?" he said. "I have every size, shape, and color all ready to tempt you." At that, he brushed his lap with the back of his hand and the nymph closest to him gasped. I averted my gaze when I realized what he was referring to.

He sighed, disappointed with my reluctance.

"You might be a newbie but you act like a virgin. Why are you here if not to cavort?"

He set down the goblet. "Unless you just haven't been wooed the right way." He leaned toward me, sniffing the air again and wrinkling his nose.

"What is that smell, anyway?" he said. "You've got a stink of virgin on you, but you're not virgin. I can tell those a mile away."

I was about to ask what he meant by that but at that, the door flung open and Maddox stormed in.

He was shielding his eyes with one hand and holding that ridiculous looking sex toy with the other.

"Isabella?" he yelled. "Are you in here?"

Pan laughed out loud.

"Oh dear," he said. "Ask and ye shall receive."

Maddox pulled his hand away from his eyes.

"Pan," he said. "I should have known you'd be here somewhere."

"You two know each other?" I said.

Maddox closed the distance, swallowing up the paces of the room in moments. Just the look on his face, all sheepish and shy made Pan guffaw.

"Now I understand the stink, newbie," he said, swinging his gaze to me.

"This place is revolting," Maddox grumbled. "I had to fight my way through six naked nymphs and two succubus demons to get here."

He scanned the room, and seeing me, stormed across it, swallowing up the distance in a heartbeat.

"We have to leave," he said. "I don't think the target is here."

"Leave?" Pan said. "But the best entertainment of the party is yet to come. This is just the prelude, my boy."

He turned to me to explain. "Later, we shall all be joining in one massive cavorting, where gods and mortal pets and sorcerers and all the like combine their lusts. It's really something you shouldn't miss."

Maddox sucked the back of his teeth. "It's disgusting not to mention dangerous."

He reached his free hand out to me, shrugging off one of the nymphs who had begun to wrap around him.

"The danger is part of the fun," Pan said.

"Oh my God," I said, watching as Maddox did his best to extricate himself from the nymphs. "It's true. Kerri was telling the truth when she complained about your reluctance for threesomes."

"Threesomes," Pan laughed. "Maddox here won't even have a one-some."

I squirreled my gaze Pan's way while he sipped his drink, both eyebrows lifted with knowing.

"What does that mean?" I said.

"You don't know?" he said. "Maddox is celibate."

Chapter 18

I stared dumbly at Maddox, who couldn't meet my eye. Instead he was busy batting away feverishly exploring hands as the nymphs began tempting him in earnest at the news. Some of them tangled their fingers through his hair, others decided that their best ploy was visual.

I could almost hear the sensual lilt of belly dance music accompanying their undulating moves. It sounded like it was coming from the thicket where Pan had thrown his flute.

I gaped at Maddox.

"You're celibate?" I said.

Maddox said nothing, but his jaw clenched.

Celibate. This man whose every pore dripped sex. This man whose masculine hands were meant to explore the female form. It couldn't be accurate and yet, the way Pan's acolytes were behaving, and the frigid, awkward response Maddox was giving as he tried to extricate himself said it all.

It all started to add up: the clinical way he'd bathed me, Kerri's complaints those weeks ago that he wouldn't try out any of her sexual fantasies. I'd thought it a show to create a distraction. But maybe Kerri was complaining in earnest and using the information to her advantage.

Maddox's expression had turned markedly sour.

Pan chuckled from behind me. "Ask him how long."

I swung my gaze from one to the other, still trying to process the fact that a man of Maddox looks and raw sexual energy had sworn off sex.

I couldn't imagine what might have initiated such an extreme reaction. Maybe he'd lost someone he loved dearly. Maybe he'd been stung; heck, we'd all been.

But for him to agree to attend a party thrown by an incubus had to mean he was also a bit of a masochist. I mean, who would volunteer for that. No wonder he'd been so anxious. No wonder he hated seeing all the nudity.

"Celibate?" I said again because if Maddox had heard me, he'd decided that the way Pan's acolytes were taking it as a challenge was a bigger priority than answering.

They'd now begun to peel his clothes away and guide him toward a luxurious looking settee that had sprung from the trunk of a broad redwood. He didn't have enough hands to block them all.

He fell backwards onto the lounge and they fell over him. He was all but invisible through the skin, hair, and hands.

"Fuck," I heard him say from within the cluster.

The nymphs tittered as one and drew back. He was shirtless, his nipples hard pebbles and the V line in his lower abdomen trembling above the waistband of his pants. He was breathing hard, trying his damnest not to stare at the breasts swaying in front of him. The hand on the settee was clenched.

Celibate, perhaps, but still very much a slave to primal desires.

"Is it true?" I asked him.

He dragged his gaze to mine and might have answered except a brazen acolyte ran her hand down along that chest, teasing its way down as it tracked his median line.

He tried and failed to pin her hand from plunging into his pants. He caught his breath and his eyes rolled back.

The moan that came from him was anything but a protest.

"Maddox," I said, fighting my way between two fleshy nymphs, and only managing to get a few feet away. "How long?"

It was Pan who answered. "If it helps," he said. "I only found out three centuries ago."

I could feel my jaw gaping open.

"Centuries?" I said in disbelief. "You haven't had sex in centuries and you come with me to an orgy."

At that, Pan let go a peal of laughter.

While the sound might have amused me before, now I was outraged.

I couldn't push through the last three naked nymphs, but I could see the effect they were having on Maddox. His features were painted with bliss. He was enjoying himself even if he didn't want to admit just how good it felt.

Even so, I knew the way he was squeezing his eyes shut, that he was anguished over it. He was loving the feel of hands on his skin, but he didn't want to love it.

And yet, he'd been able to resist me quite adequately.

I wondered which would be the best decision: let him enjoy it and ruin his vows or interrupt his enjoyment.

The way one of the acolytes gasped and caught another's eye with delight made the decision for me.

I shouldered my way through the remaining trio and palmed one of them--the one with her hands down his pants--right in the forehead, pushing her aside more roughly than I'd intended.

She fell back with a glower.

"No means no," I said to her.

Pan called out to her, saying humans could be terribly jealous and not to pay me any mind.

"Shut up," I said, not caring if he was a god or not.

Maddox blinked at me in relief as I peeled another set of hands from his chest.

"Why didn't you just tell me?" I said, my mind reeling back to how I'd thrown myself at him in my apartment. How I'd done it again in the foyer.

I felt foolish. Somehow part of me would have rather that he just didn't find me attractive. But the thought that I had so brazenly offered myself to a man who had sworn off women made me feel ashamed.

Especially since he had such a damn hard time resisting these brazen hussies.

I pinched the bridge of my nose in humiliation.

"I can't believe it," I said. "Don't you think things would have been easier if you had just told me you had sworn off women."

"Oh, that's rich," Pan said and I turned to discover he was standing right behind me.

He was completely nude now, the goat legs transformed to human legs, and his acolytes had returned to him like moths to a candle. The fact that one of them was stroking his member didn't help the blush that was already burning my chest and face.

"What's so funny?" I demanded.

"You." He pointed at me with his hips. "Assuming he has simply sworn off women."

Pan shrugged off his acolytes who sulked away from him. He held out his arms and two of them pulled a purple silk kimono from thin air and slipped it over his shoulders. He tied the belt as he advanced on me.

"What I find so funny is that you're denying yourself me and saving yourself for this."

He jerked his chin in Maddox's direction, indicating he was the 'this' he spoke of. "I'm the God of wantonness," he said. "I know desire when I see it. And it's stamped all over your face."

"What's stamped all over my face is anger and humiliation," I said.

He sighed and sat down next to Maddox, putting his arm over the back of the settee.

"Are you going to tell her, Maddox, or am I?" he said.

I cupped my elbows over my chest. "Tell me what?"

Maddox looked at his knees. "I've never..." he started to say. "I mean, it's not something I –"

Realization washed over me as I took in the look on his face, full of shame and embarrassment.

"Oh my God," I said. "You're a virgin."

The blush that crept up from his neck and colored his face was all the answer I needed.

"You're hundreds of years old and you've never had sex?" I said.

"A thousand," he said.

"A thousand what?"

"Years," he said. "I'm almost a thousand years old. Give or take." He waggled his hand in the air in front of his chest.

Even the nymphs gaped at him.

"Sweet Jesus," I said.

The flute made a comical sound from the bushes.

"But I thought you had been to dozens of these things?" I said, holding out my arms to indicate the surroundings. "You said you've seen plenty of things in your time."

He shrugged. "I have."

Pan laughed. "I've seen him at these things every so often over the centuries, and he's always the same. Grouchy. Prim and proper. I keep telling him that the best thing for him is to just get laid. But no. He won't have it."

Maddox swung on him. "I don't take vows lightly," he ground out.

Pan's lifted eyebrows nearly met his hairline as though he was vaguely insulted that he might consider a vow a light thing.

"As well you shouldn't," he said. "Vows and commitments are binding. No one understands that better than a god."

"Damn right," Maddox said.

"Wait," I said, holding up my hand. "What are you talking about? What vows. What commitment?"

Pan waited until a nymph brought him a large bowl filled with fruit before he spoke. He inspected the contents of the bowl with his finger and finally lifted a string of green grapes to his mouth. He chewed the way a goat did, back and forth as he watched my face.

"You mean you don't know?" he said as he chewed around three at a time. "Maddox here is a monk."

I felt my own eyebrows lift in surprise. "A monk?"

"He's been a monk for as long as I've known him and no doubt longer than that."

"Since I was 18," Maddox said and his eyes fell to his feet.

I sank down onto the nearest velvet mossed log. All thoughts of finding the target gone. This news was even larger.

"A monk," I repeated. I tested it on my tongue. It didn't feel right. It didn't sound right. Not for the man that I'd come to know. But then, he wasn't a man, was he?

"Monks don't act like you do." I said to him.

He shrugged. "Monks like me do. Although, to be honest, my vows haven't been quite as important the last couple of centuries. Not since the stone went missing."

I snapped my gaze up to his. This was getting uncomfortably familiar.

"The stone?" I said. "What stone?"

He pushed himself from the lounge and crouched in front of me. He took both of my hands in his. I thought maybe he was doing it to keep me from hitting him.

"The Lilith stone," he said. "I'm a guardian."

At the admission, Pan clapped his hands loudly and the nymphs scattered. I wasn't sure where they went, perhaps into the wallpaper to cavort among the trees there, but Pan didn't disappear at all. He stood in front of us like a referee, putting both of his hands on each of our chests.

"Wait a minute," he said to Maddox. "Are you saying the Lilith Stone has been found?"

Maddox looked up at him. "In a manner of speaking, yes."

He twisted around so the god could see his ribcage where the tattoo stood out against this skin.

"It's why I'm here," Maddox said.

Pan nodded. "I should have known he wouldn't have come here if it wasn't something important."

He swung his gaze to mine. "The last orgy he attended was to extricate a guardian acolyte." He shook his head. "That was nasty business. Just nasty."

I started to ask about what constituted nasty, curious beyond what I should have been to know some of Maddox's history, but Maddox stooped to pick his shirt up from the floor and cut me off.

"We have business today as well," he said.

Pan paused in shoveling another grape into his mouth. "You don't say?"

Maddox nodded. "It's why we're here. We've got intel that there's a gentleman here who has info on the stone."

It was an outright lie, and I thought Pan knew it too because he held Maddox's gaze for a long time before he spoke. Maddox didn't so much as flinch under the scrutiny.

"A Sean Connery type," he said, flicking his gaze to mine. I did my best to hold it without flinching too, but didn't do as well as Maddox.

Pan sighed. "Well as you well know, Maddox," he said. "People come to me, I don't go to them. And those who come to me and are admitted are only the youngest and most beautiful of form."

He ran his gaze up and down my form, obviously enjoying the look.

He spread his arms. "As you can see we are all beautiful in here, so I would have no way of knowing if the man you're looking for is here in the event at all. But if he's more human than creature, there's only one other room designed for the more delicate of species."

I liked the sound of a room designed for delicacy.

"So where is it?" I said. "How do we get there?"

He laughed at that question as though it was the most delicious joke and snapped his fingers. The nymphs ran in from thin air, crowding around him and pushing him back toward the sofa.

The door I'd come in opened and the room flooded with naked humanness. They all rushed Pan and his entourage with a thrum of lustful excitement.

"Well," I said, the impatience evident even to my ears.

"Oh darling," he said, opening his arms to the throng of worshippers. "It's my concerned opinion that he will not be there." He nodded at Maddox with a sympathetic eye. "And I doubt you want to step over that portal."

"And why is that?" Maddox said his jaw set tightly.

Pan eyed me just before he disappeared beneath a wave of naked flesh that was transforming even as I watched into scaly, serpentine skin. The god gave a wave with a hand that sprouted talons. "Because it's a virgin sacrifice spectacle, dears, and you wouldn't want anyone to mistake you for an offering."

Then he guffawed until he was smothered in flesh.

CHAPTER 19

I wasn't disappointed to leave Pan and his entourage behind. The last thing I wanted to remember was his transformation into a lizard to satisfy the lusts of a few reptilian shape shifters, so it suited me fine to weave down the corridor behind Maddox.

We snaked down a long corridor lit by gas lamps and torches that illuminated frescoes painted with tangles of body and flesh. I guessed that the Vanilla door was a composite of multiple rooms, not just one expanse, and when doorways opened and closed, all but disappearing after guests entered or exited, I realized I was right.

But the hallways themselves were a testament to the thoughtful planning. Errol had outdone himself with the details and I imagine he must have worked his magic for days to create it all.

Either that or we'd stepped into and over dozens of portals, weaving in and out of realms with abandon and ignorance. However he'd done it, the soiree, as he called it, was large and complex.

The hallways beyond the vanilla bean sign were stuffed with tables sporting toys, bars cradling drinks of all colors and the deeper we went, the more incubi emerged from the frescoed walls to tempt me with a scent or a touch. Sometimes they merely watched me, and I suspected that they were transmitting sounds just beneath level of hearing but that my body responded to without me knowing it.

I certainly didn't want to think it was only sight that drugged me with that filmy gauze of desire.

Twice Maddox had to tug at my chain as, blinded by the allure that crept back on me once I'd left Pan, I bumped into servers offering up human pets both naked and costumed.

I couldn't help reaching out to a man dressed as a Highlander Scot. He was brawny and gorgeous and red-haired and I immediately thought of James Fraser from the *Outlander* books. I'd loved that man and devoured each book several times.

I knew the angle of his jaw, the cant of his head.

I wanted to be his Claire.

"Leave him, Isabella," Maddox barked and slapped my hand away just as my fingers lighted on the man's ruddy-haired chest. "Eyes down I told you."

I cringed beneath his tone but my hand lingered behind me as I was tugged further along the corridor, trying to memorize each curve of muscle.

Maddox tugged inelegantly on his end of the chain.

"Dammit, woman. Do I have to blindfold you?"

I stopped short, jostling into his back as he halted abruptly in the middle of the corridor. He was already peeling off his shirt and tearing a strip from the hem. The way his muscles moved like small kittens beneath his skin made me purr teasingly but he just glared at me. The crease between his eyebrows cut into his brow.

I saw his face loom down toward mine as he stretched out the band of material over my eyes, shutting off all but the dim light that fingered through the holes in the material.

"How naughty," I said, feeling coy and in need of teasing the poor bugger. "Are you sure you're a virgin?"

"If I wasn't, you'd be asking me an entirely different question," he replied.

When he tied it off behind my head, his fingers caught in my hair and I thought I felt him tug at a lock. Maybe I heard him inhale; I couldn't be sure.

"Did you just smell my hair?" I said.

I caught the distinctive crack of bone on bone followed by the thud of a heavy weight landing. Something fell on my feet.

"That was a beast with grabby hands," Maddox said. "Now, step large, Kitten. He's a big fellow."

His voice was bright with pleasure that I guessed he enjoyed letting off a bit of steam at some poor sod's expense.

I lifted my leg as high as I could, unsure what sort of gait would land me free of what I presumed was a monstrously sized jerk by the sound of his contact with the floor.

I stumbled, hands out, sensing for something solid to guide me and found the harness of his back. I clung to it and had an image of us cavorting down the corridor in a limbo line.

"I'm not sure what you're laughing at," he said. "But it's drawing too much attention."

He pulled me to his side and the chains sang out as they mated with each other. The allure began to wane so that I could at least concentrate.

"Better," he mumbled as though he felt the lust leave my body. "The sooner we get out of this den of iniquity, the sooner I can breathe again."

His brief respite of pleasure fell off him the way a sheet of rain ran down a gunnel. For every step we took, I heard him beside me grumbling about the debauchery of every species no matter the world it came from as he tugged me along.

"Doesn't the allure affect you at all," I complained, annoyed at my reactions. "I mean, you ARE a man, aren't you? Don't men love this sort of thing. Dream of it? Isn't it in every teenager's fantasies?"

He said nothing to that, and I guessed that was as good an answer as any I could expect.

Someone pushed past me, shoving me sideways. It was infuriating not seeing where I was going. Relying on his sight made me feel ridiculous considering I was a grown woman, and far more experienced than he was.

"Shouldn't you be the one hiding your eyes?" I said.

"I'm immune," he said. "You obviously are not."

"Let me go," I said. "I can take it."

"That's what she said," he drawled and laughed beneath his breath at the campy joke.

"Really?" I said. "That ridiculous joke just proves how naive you are."

"I'm a virgin, Kitten, that doesn't mean I'm inexperienced."

"I thought it was exactly what it meant."

In answer, I felt his fingers brush against the rise of my chest, just above the barely there bra cups. I sucked in my breath, enjoying the way the fine hairs rose to strain against his touch. For one hazy moment, there was no allure filling my nose, intoxicating my mind.

It was a pinwheel of images that shuttered through my mind as though they were animation cards or slides on automatic show. No matter what the woman looked like, he was in each one of them.

"How did you do that?" I said, remembering that something like it had happened before.

The night I'd been at the museum, I'd been blasted with erotic images that included me with him and Kerri. I'd thought it was some deeply hidden rush of lust and not an intentional thing put there by someone else.

Now I thought differently.

"A man has to have some fun if he can't actually succumb to his desires," he said. "And I have skills. Mad skills."

I narrowed my gaze beneath the blindfold. "Pretty skillful if you can inject dirty thoughts into my head when you've got no sense of what you're projecting."

I felt his shrug. "I told you, I've been around." he said. "Virginity just means I haven't taken a woman to my bed or given her my chastity. It doesn't mean I'm not educated."

I heard in the words the rest of the statement. He'd not taken a woman, but he'd touched them plenty. Maybe seen plenty if he'd been at soirees like Errol's before.

I wondered how far he'd allowed himself to stretch the boundary of his vows.

"Cheater," I said.

"I prefer to call myself a smart student."

I was about to argue, but he paused, anchoring me to his side.

"What's wrong?" I said, because I knew by the way his muscles had gone rigid beneath my palms that something was up.

"They're watching us," he said against my temple, so I knew he was leaning down.

A whiff of Old Spice seeped into my nostrils and coated my palate. I squirmed, trying to slip from his grasp because I found it ridiculously alluring all things considered.

"Maybe they all know you're celibate and don't trust you," I said.

"I am a man of my word," he said.

"A monk in a whorehouse is about as trustworthy as a whore in church," I said.

I tried to peer beneath the fabric where a crack of gloomy light shone through. He merely grunted his displeasure at my joke and went silent for long moments as he guided me along. It was getting downright uncomfortable dealing with his seething silence.

"So?" I said. "Why didn't you tell me what you were when you asked for my help? Why use a fake client?"

He sighed as he steered me to the left. "I did not use a fake client. I really do have to reclaim the stone and they really are a client."

"Except it's not because they're paying you; it's because you have to."

I was beginning to believe I'd been duped. "Were you ever going to pay me?"

I felt his hand smooth down my hair to cup the back of my neck.

"I have refrained from sex for millennia, Isabella, despite many, many temptations," he said. "What do you think?"

I could barely hear him over the sounds of partying all around me, and I could tell by the shift in energy that we were nearing a new spectacle. I got shoved and brushed against more often, but Maddox was careful to keep me from being man-handled again.

I matched his pace as well as I could with my feet taking three steps to his one, but I could always feel him there, guiding me. I began to trust his guidance and stumbled less.

With each step, the sounds and smells shifted.

"That mark," I said. "It marks you as a member of this stone order?"

"The Guardians of the Stone order; yes."

"Does it do more than that?" I said, thinking of his ability to give back to someone the pain they'd inflicted.

It took him a while to answer and I thought at first that we were nearing a space where he didn't want anyone to hear but the noise was so loud around us, I doubted it could be that. When he did answer, I heard in it a note of wariness.

"The mark has its own powers," he said carefully. "But they belong to the stone. Some things are my own, earned after centuries of work, and some are bestowed. Dormant, lost, or found, those things cannot be stripped from me even if the stone ceases to exist."

I heard the hidden meaning in those words. Celibacy, Immortality. All those things were irreversible.

"How are you going to get me to finger the guy if my eyes are covered," I said, then laughed out loud at the pun, admittedly as ridiculous as his earlier joke.

"I'm sure you'll find a way to shove that finger where it doesn't belong," he drawled. "It seems to be your specialty. Now, hush. We're almost there," he said.

I snickered beneath my breath at the sound of my surname mixed with such an obviously ribald euphemism.

"You do know you left yourself open there."

"Juvenile," he said, but there was humor in his tone, an indulgence that wasn't there before.

The sounds of our footfalls and the clamor of the corridor got swallowed up suddenly in something soft and lush enough to reach up over my elven boots to tremble against my ankles. My skirt swished against my legs as he spun me forward. The chains bit into my skin and I swore at the sudden discomfort.

"Hush," he said. "I think I can see the light from the gate."

"I think you like saying my name," I said and began humming a Beyoncé song until he clamped his palm over my mouth and whispered that I should listen.

I cocked my head to the side, trying to make out what had his attention. The low thrum of chanting broke through the veil of moans and whispered obscenities that filled the corridor. I thought I heard a feminine scream, a high pitched warbling sound that died out the way it does in horror movies: slow and stark.

"Sweet Jesus," I said. "That can't be good."

I had images of bloody knives and altar stones and virgins in white cascading dresses.

"Take this damn thing off," I said, scraping the blindfold from my eyes but getting it no further than my eyelid.

His hand touched down on mine, the warmth of his palm radiating to my face as he eased it to below my nose.

"Just for a second," he said. "I can't risk you getting all hot for me."

It was a joke, and I knew it, but something in his expression spread a flush across my chest, made it bloom up my neck to my cheeks. I wasn't sure why my body wanted to react to a man who was the supernatural equivalent to a priest.

I guessed forbidden fruit had its own allure.

"I feel ridiculous blindfolded," I complained. "I'll stand out, and not in good way." I didn't want to admit that I really wanted to see what I might be facing. Foreseen meant forewarned.

He ran his palm down along my arm, stopping at my wrist. I thought he could feel my pulse speed up.

"Whoever the princess is that you mentioned earlier, she couldn't have rocked that bra like you do."

It was a compliment that flustered me, and I reacted with exactly the same amount of dignity that the costume imbued to me.

"She's not real." I yanked the material down. "She was a character in a sci-fi movie."

"Ah, that explains it," he said.

"Explains what?"

"What kind of man would think that getup was sexy."

I rocked against him as someone jostled by. He grabbed for me as though he thought someone was going to make off with his pet.

"Are you afraid?" I said. "You're acting afraid."

"I've never been afraid," he said.

"Tell that to the nymphs that just made you run like the devil was on your heels."

"Maybe he was," he said.

He halted mid-step and held me against him as someone fell against us, jostling me enough that I stumbled. I thought I smelled caramel and candy floss and then the pungent aroma of sulfur and smoke seeped along beneath it, lifting to my nostrils and smothering me.

"What is that?" I said.

"The sacrifice spectacle."

Clipped and tension filled if ever a statement could be.

"Prepare yourself," he said. "Because the hairy part just got dirty."

Chapter 20

He sucked in a breath and I felt his palms on my shoulders. Whatever he planned to say, it mattered to him. I looked up into his face.

"Before we commit to this," he said, "I want you to know I've not been called to service in a hundred years. I didn't think it important to mention."

Not important, meaning I was nobody. A human. A pet. He wanted to be perfectly clear what I meant to him. What he thought of me throwing myself at him. I recalled his disgust with the flat out lust of the place, and imagined he felt the same about me except he was too polite to say anything while we were working together.

I stiffened beside him. "I understand," I said.

"Do you?" he said. "Because you look like you don't."

I waved my hand, getting caught up in the length of chain and I wrenched it back against my leg.

"I'm fine," I said. "Let's just get this over with."

There was a bit of pressure as his fingers loosened the knot from the back of my neck. My forehead butted into his chest and for one moment, I let it lay there, soaking in the feel of hard muscle and the sense of comfort and safety he gave off.

It was totally inappropriate to be annoyed that the kiss we'd shared in my apartment meant nothing but hundreds of years of sexual frustration and I knew I shouldn't have spared more than a passing interest in it.

And yet it bothered me and the thought that it did was a wound I didn't expect to suffer. I watched his face as the fabric unwound from my neck but my mind started its necessary machinery, shutting down the last remnants of my feelings where they couldn't bother me anymore.

He held me an inch away and I knew he was looking down into my face. I couldn't look at him. I could barely speak for heaven's sake. My throat ached and my eyes were burning.

"Isabella?" he said. "Are you alright? Did I hurt you?"

I shook my head, not trusting my voice.

He knew I was lying. He had to. He thumbed a stream of liquid from my cheek, smearing it into my hairline and I twisted away from his touch.

"What did I do?" he whispered. "I've done something."

It was laughable and it showed exactly how experienced he was with women. A virgin indeed.

"It wasn't anything you did," I said.

No. Because it was all on me. I'd imagined something more in his touch, and I only just realized how much when he'd admitted what I meant to him.

I was a means to an end.

"Let's just do this thing," I said.

Work was as good a balm as anything. Maybe in time, I'd be able to touch on the memory and laugh over my own sexual frustration.

"So," I said as I surveyed the area that stretched out before us. "This is where virgins come to die."

There was no hint of room at all. We could have been standing on the top of a mountain for all the surroundings held no hint of Errol's back room. Misshapen stone and beds of red hot coals surrounded an open pit.

Sulfurous smoke rose from various pits, leaving bits of ash everywhere. I held out my hand, palm up, to catch a few flakes.

The dull thrum of chanting rose from somewhere behind my ears, and through the smoke, shapes took form, shadowy and black at first, but becoming clearer with every waft of breeze that moved the smoke.

Nude forms danced around the open pit as sparks rose from its depths. I blinked, the smoke burning my eyes. I could swear an altar stone stretched out on the other side of the pit and that one by one, creatures of all sorts clambered atop a woman tied to the stone.

Maddox tried to steer me to the side so that I wasn't facing the show anymore but I held back, studying the way the women were one by one settled onto the altar stone, and almost reverently handled.

If it was the allure that was letting them endure the act, that was one thing, but if they were inviting this as some sort of ritual or out of consent, that was another entirely.

I shuddered as I realized what was happening.

They didn't struggle. Not even when they were led to the mouth of the pit once the deflowering was done.

"This is the Virgin sacrifice," I said, hearing the dread in my own voice.

Maddox wrapped my chain three times around his wrist.

"Virgins no more," he ground out. "Come on, we have a man to find."

Six of them stood lined up along the mouth of it by the time we had edged along the periphery of crowds that were chanting and swaying back and forth. A gentle hum came from one group, like a chorale, and echoed by the others in a wave.

"What in the heck is going on?" I said.

He peered down at me and raked his hand through his hair. It was greasy with sweat, and I realized I, too, was perspiring. It was hot in the chamber. No breath of air relieved the suffocating press of sulfur.

"The second act," he said shortly.

Oh. The sacrifice bit.

The belly of the pit burped and sparks shot into the air, lighting the shadows and it occurred to me what I might be looking at.

"Is that the fire gate?" I said.

He followed my gaze to the open pit belching out sparks and smoke. A ring of fire shot up around it, outlining the mouth in a blaze of light.

He sighed tiredly. "The bastard has no imagination. He could at least have avoided the cliché." He sounded put out, like he'd been insulted.

"How can you not recognize your own portal?"

"The gates look different and act differently," he said. "Based on whether they are on ley lines or created by magic. On my side, where they initiate, most are created by magic. The fire gate was born in fire magic, so..." He let that trail off and finished with a wry smile as the pit belched again and a curvy looking creature, presumably a virgin, leapt into its center.

Applause went up around the room.

"Oh my gods, he's such a drama queen."

I gathered he said it because once the girl leapt, a purple burst of light spewed from the portal and rose to the air.

Drums tattooed out a sensual rhythm and the remaining virgins swayed in time to the beat.

"What now?" I said, curious to know what happened to the girl.

"Now, she's no doubt on the other side, having her every sexual whim catered to."

I glanced at him when his tone soured.

"You have a problem with that?" I said. "Gals have fantasies too, you know."

"That's not why I'm pissed," he said through gritted teeth. "The damn incubus is no doubt sending them to my bazaar somewhere."

I couldn't help a chuckle. He was taking this a little too personally..

I studied the portal again, getting a better glimpse of the patrons around it since the light hadn't receded.

About three feet away from the altar stone, I spied an older gentleman whose body was suspiciously trim and taut for the age he must be. His biceps were sheened in sweat as he held his hands out over the mouth of the pit the way one did when they're cold and have a campfire to hand.

He didn't have a stitch of clothing on.

"Well, if it is the gate," I said with a happy sigh. "Then things just got a hell of a lot easier."

"Why is that?"

I pointed to the gentleman who had sidled just behind a cassocked giant at the mouth of the pit.

"Because there's our target right there," I said.

Maddox went rigid as he followed the direction of my finger. He dropped my chain.

It fell in a heap with a nasty clunking sound.

A patron noticed and made a grab for it.

"Oh hell no," I said and stepped on his hand. I felt bones spread beneath my foot.

He cursed and I had two seconds to grab for it before another patron shoved him onto his ass and scrambled to take the end closest to him.

"Seriously?" I said and kneed my way forward. I had to fall on it to keep three more guests from taking possession.

I gathered it up as best I could from my prostrate spot on the smoldering ground. It was as hot against my skin as Lucifer's tiled floor had been. I suffered a moment of panic. I couldn't see. There were too many feet and hands, some of them touching me, grabbing for me.

I yelled out for Maddox and scraped my gaze over the area, looking for him.

I caught sight of his shoulders pressing through a throng of naked dancers, already a dozen feet away.

"Hey," I yelled.

He looked back at me over his shoulder and gave me an irritated look. He'd forgotten me, that was clear. When he headed back in my direction, I scrambled to my feet. He threw off the creature still clinging to me, but not before the glamor stuttered over its skin, revealing the authentic creature beneath.

A vampire. I was sure of it. He hissed at Maddox but withdrew into the shadows that played about the walls.

"What in the hell?" I said and punched him on the foot with the butt of my hand because being sprawled on the floor, it was the fastest way I had to hurt him. "You just left me here?"

"Dammit, Isabella," he said. "Take my hand."

I looked up to see him reaching for me, and chagrined, I took it, but his attention was back toward the portal and not on me at all.

He was off again without so much as a grunt or grumble. In fact, he was strangely silent as we threaded our way toward the target.

"OK," I said. "So maybe a virgin like you shouldn't be so quick to run to a sacrificial altar."

I tried to pull my chain back, to slow him down because I was having a hard time keeping up.

At one point, I wasn't walking fast enough to keep up with him and he hoisted me against his hip for several paces to speed me up. I complained. He was being an ass and entirely too rough.

He dropped me back onto my feet but he didn't halt or slow down.

"You're gonna queer the deal," I said. "How am I going to lure the object out of him if you're charging at him like a bull."

I stumbled along with him, trying to keep up. We were within five feet of the older gent, by the time I knew for sure we had the right guy.

"Do you see that?" I said.

"What?" Maddox said in a distracted way. "What do you see?"

He sounded befuddled and I imagined he was just preoccupied. But I couldn't imagine that he couldn't see the same thing I did, even if he was distracted.

Errol had said there would be a glow to indicate where the item was being hidden. It would be my clue both to know I had the right guy and to figure out where I could slip my fingers to divest him of the object.

I hadn't done petty thievery for years and years, and I worried at first that my skills with sleight of hand would have waned.

Now I was a bit more than worried because the whole damn man was glowing. It was subtle, a bluish wash of light that must have been residual glow from where the spelled object was.

He had the relic, all right. And he was within a foot of the portal. Easy toss.

Sweet. Things were finally starting to go my way. Maybe we'd be out of here before sunrise and I could call it all a day.

I scanned the target from head to heel, trying to see if there was a stronger glow in any one place that would give away where he'd be hiding it and it was in that instant that I realized I was in trouble.

It seemed I'd have to charm the damn thing out of him. Literally.

"The thing Absalom wants," I said. "He's got it."

"Eh?" Maddox said and dragged his gaze from the portal to my face.

"The reason we're here," I said, snapping my fingers up at his face and fell short by a good foot.

I pointed with my elbow at the old gent.

"I don't know where he's keeping Absalom's item," I said. "But if you're thinking the same place as I am, you can have the job of searching him."

This time when Maddox swung his gaze to mine, I saw something in his face that made me stop dead in my tracks. The chain went taut and then he returned to gather me up.

"Maddox," I said. "What's wrong?"

"You've got it all wrong, Kitten," he said. "There's no object to steal."

"What?" I said. "Of course there is."

He shook his head. "No. No object. It's him. He's the thing you're supposed to steal."

"Impossible," I said. "You can't steal a man."

"Not a man," he said beneath his breath. "Not anymore."

At that, he started to run and I got pulled headlong along with him, stumbling, tripping over the chain when I did manage to catch up. One moment, my feet were scuffling along the rough stone of the floor or ground or whatever it was beneath my feet. The next, the tinkling sound of links of chain cried out, screeching to the air with a gritty, gut-wrenching sound.

My feet left the safety of terra firma as he gave a hard yank.

The heavy collar bit into my neck.

Hard.

I lost my balance one last time and pitched forward, just barely catching myself from hitting my knees by grabbing onto the closest thing to hand. I felt my nails scratch into something soft. A feminine shriek drilled into my ear.

I tried to buck backwards but the pull was too strong.

Forms and shapes spun as I lurched forward, unable to control the movement of the chain that held me by the throat and throttled me sideways as I fought its pull.

The fire gate gassed out one long and blazing stream of light and I could see that I was heading straight for its maw. Maddox weaved ahead of me, ignoring my pleas or not hearing me in the cacophony of chanting. He elbowed through a clutch of drugged-looking men, drunk on the incubus's allure.

Before I knew it, we'd skidded to a stop next to the old gent. He looked up at us with a look of alarm.

"Maddox," he said with a bemused tone.

"Dad," Maddox said through tight lips.

I might have found a chance to register my shock at the exchange but right then, Maddox lunged forward and shoved him into the mouth of the fire gate.

Chapter 21

Right then, I knew Maddox was going to jump in after him and no amount of digging my heels in or of grappling for purchase would keep me from going along with him. The firelight climbed his legs and illuminated his face in a reddish glow.

He looked huge, standing there, angry looking, a god of sorts preparing his vengeance. My heart called out to him, proud and scared at the same moment.

I thought I might be reprieved. Everything in my body went still with hope.

I staggered sideways as an allure-drugged guest fell against me. I shoved him back into his partner.

Heads turned toward me. Slow, movie-like panoramic motion told me my peripherals had seen something dangerous.

Several Incubi, dressed in robes, launched themselves at Maddox from all directions. The crowds parted to give them room.

The movie-like quality vision freeze-framed.

Maddox on the ridge. Several of the sexual demons, maybe half a dozen, flashed their true visages at me; teeth and gleaming red eyes, and naked scaly skin shuddered under a wave of change and then they were men again.

Or were they men and the demons were the glamor? I couldn't know.

Maddox sent me one final look over his shoulder.

My hope at reprieve died, a sacrifice to Maddox's mania.

He leapt.

The chain rattled along the edge, snaking away from me.

I was going with him.

All in the space of three heartbeats.

I hurtled down into the depths of the gate and all I could think was that I wasn't a virgin. I'd never survive the journey.

When I'd charged through the blood gate, back before I'd even know there worlds other than my own, I'd had Kassie's blood as the bond that gave me permission to move through it safely. It was painful, and frightening and existential all at once but I'd landed on the other side unscathed.

This time I had nothing, no key, no bond. I knew it was just me and a length of chain falling like Alice down the rabbit hole.

The insides were lined with hissing coals and seeping lava. Smoke and steam in equal parts coiled around me, making me cough, making my lungs burn.

I think I might have cried out. At the very least, I swore. Repeatedly.

Then the pain came. It sliced into me from every angle. While there was no flame, my skin bubbled into sticky boils as the heat assaulted it. My throat cracked like sun-aged and un-oiled leather.

I smelled burning hair.

The gate was meant for Kindred. I thought of the virgins who had leapt and wondered if they were screaming their ways to the bottom the way I was.

No one had prepared me. No one had given blood for the permissions I needed to see my way through the portal.

I was going to die in there.

Gusts of hot air clawed down my throat and sucked out scream after scream and when they'd finally dried up my tissues, nothing but an exhale wormed its way from my lungs.

I was hurtling downward at a speed I didn't think possible. How could I ever find one body, let alone control my direction? I fought the descent, scrabbling for purchase. I kicked at empty air and bucked against the wind. But the gate refused to release a safety net.

Something brushed against my hair. A voice sounded in my ear.

"Come to me, Isabella," it said.

Maddox. Dear God. Maddox.

I twisted about, emitting timid shrieks to echo-locate to the sound of that voice.

"Isabella," he said again. "Listen to me."

Listen. I was trying, oh how I was trying. But where was it coming from? Below me? Above me?

"Here," he said.

Right in front of me. I sobbed in relief. All I had to do was reach out for him.

I flung my arms out as wide as I could to grab onto whatever met my fingers. I prayed for his shirt, his hair, his foot for Pete's sake. I needed something tangible to grapple for, but nothing met my reach.

I was lost in there, falling end over end. I was coming apart at the seams.

Then, the chain caught between my legs and knotted around my ankle. The thrust of it bit into my neck as the links strained against each other in one wrenching movement. My ankle received a vicious jolt and I bit my tongue.

Tears leaked from my eyes and dried before they tracked a line down to my cheeks.

As if the gate knew I couldn't take one more assault, I was enfolded in a massive embrace. I felt Maddox's hard chest beneath my palms and my fingers crawled of their own accord toward his back. I hugged him, tight.

"Oh thank God," I said into his chest.

I was terrified to let go. I mashed my cheek against his chest and sobbed against him, clinging like a dying woman.

"Thank the gods, Pan, Jesus, whoever the fuck I need to, to make this be ok."

"You can thank me," came his caustic reply, but it wasn't unkind, more like an attempt to reclaim some level of norm.

He didn't so much pull away from me as ease my arms out from around his back. I wasn't ready. I grabbed for his collar instead. Then missing that, fell to the buttons. His shirt tore beneath my hold. Skin, sweaty and hot, met my palm.

"It's alright, Kitten," he murmured. He cupped his palm behind the back of my head and he let me lean against him, sagging into every hollow his body made, fitting in like I belonged there. "It's all ok."

It evaporated: all the pain, fear, blistering heat.

I peered along his chest to the world around us. It was entirely too fortunate for all that to have disappeared. I didn't want to believe I was fine.

What met my eye was neither fine nor awful. It was as neutral as my imagination could find: a dull, greyish place. Mists and smoke billowed around me, the first smelling of brine and the other of sulfur.

I felt like I was everywhere and nowhere at the same time. It was warm, but nowhere near as hot as it was within the portal. A comfortable temperature, as though it was my own body heat.

All I could see of Maddox was his shirt and a brief bit of skin that tensed and let go, visible through the tear I'd made. I could see the buttons had come off in two places.

I hiccupped out the last of the adrenaline.

"You're safe," he said. "For now."

Maddox plucked my fingers from his collar and eased me away from him. When he looked down at me, it was with slitted eyes that showed nothing but wariness and something else...some fear of my discovery, perhaps.

I let go reluctantly, cupping my elbows then rubbing my hands down along my bare arms.

"For now?" I said.

He nodded. His expression was inscrutable, but his body language was tight with emotion. I wasn't sure what he was feeling: rage, fear, anxiety. I just knew whatever was firing his synapses and muscles was a deep-seated, primal thing.

"We're in the Abyss," he said. "It's safe here. But we can't stay."

"Where is he?" I said, swinging my gaze left and right. "The target. Where is he?"

The man Maddox had shoved into the portal. His father, apparently. I was still processing that one.

"On the other side," he said. "I had to wait for you."

He didn't say he was worried I wouldn't make it through, but I heard it in his voice.

I swallowed down, trying to whet my throat. He'd pulled me in with him, thinking I was too fragile for the intensity of the portal, and yet he'd done it anyway. I wasn't sure why he'd do that, but I imagined there must be something going on that I didn't understand. I couldn't find words, and I wasn't sure if I could whether they'd be angry or grateful.

I pulled in a hitching breath, hugged myself tighter.

I kicked at the links of chain that hung from his wrist. They had no weight here. Even my collar felt nonexistent. I touched it with a finger to be sure it was still there.

His palm laid over mine as it wrapped over the collar and he squeezed the fingers gently before putting my hand in both of his, holding them between us.

"We're nearly there," he said. "The abyss holds time in an elastic band of energy, but it won't last long. We need to continue on."

Fear rose in my throat. I shook my head.

"Not yet."

"You have to be, Isabella. We can't leave him there. I can't help him if I'm here."

"Help him?" I said. "We're supposed to rob him." I inched away when he reached for my hand. "How in the hell am I going to do that now?" I could see it all veering off course and straight out into the rhubarb where the tangles of weeds and leaves would swallow up opportunity forever.

"You're wrong," he said. "Errol was wrong." He raked his hand through his hair and I noted it trembled. Not a comforting thing to witness under the circumstance.

"Wrong about what?" I said. "That man has something Absalom wants--something we need so we can get that stone back--and now he won't let either of us close enough to lift it."

I clenched my fists at my side. I was weary. The chains were heavy and beginning to cut into my skin. I dug at the collar as I stared at him.

"I'm taking this damn thing off," I said. "It's over." I bent over retrieve the key from my elven boot and I had it clutched in my fist when he grasped my wrists.

He snagged my gaze with his. "You don't understand, Isabella," he said. "Either Errol set us up or he was wrong because my father doesn't have what we need. He *is* what we need."

I thought about the way Maddox's father had glowed, not just in one spot as he got close to the fire gate, but the way he glowed all over.

"You mean--"

"Yes. He's the target."

"Your father," I said, prodding.

His jaw clenched. "Yes."

"You looked surprised to see him," I said.

He spun on his heel and peered into the mists. Shoulders that were tense went rigid, as though he felt anxious.

"He's supposed to be dead."

Dead. An immortal man who looked to be in his seventies. I eyed Maddox carefully. If his father could age and he was immortal, just how old was this council of the stone, anyway?

"Why?" I said. "What makes him so important to Absalom?"

"He's the stone master," Maddox said, avoiding my eye. He peeled off his shirt, since it was flapping open anyway and mopped his face with it. I only noticed then, that he was sweating heavily while I felt perfectly comfortable.

"The stone master who is bonded to the stone?"

"Yes," he said. "I'm not sure what he has in mind, but if he wants Doyle, it no doubt has something to do with the stone."

He tossed the shirt into a nearby fog bank. It disappeared into the mists. My eye caught on the angry looking weal that made up his mark. He looked like he was exerting, lifting a heavy weight and yet he was simply standing there.

"We're all bonded to the stone in some way," he said. "All of the acolytes and monks. We are initiated into the order by taking the same trip you did. But the Stone Master has a unique power. One that becomes all the more threatening now that the stone is back in the ninth world--your world."

He laid his palm on my shoulder and it felt moist and hot. It shook, just a little, as it rested there.

"Now we need to go. I can feel the time elastic tightening. It's getting unbearable and I have no idea who is waiting for him on the other side of the portal. We're wasting time here."

I had a host of questions, but he was right. If Absalom had arranged for the artifact to be thrown through the portal, he would have someone there to retrieve it when it came through.

"But why push him through, then?" I said, edging away from the way the mists were coiling into a funnel in front of me. "Why not just grab for him and run like the devil out of the spectacle?"

"Because it's my portal. I created it. If it goes to the bazaar, I have some control. Now please, Isabella. We have to go."

I sucked in a bracing breath. In for a penny in for a pound. I'd made my decision long ago. And I needed to follow through, no matter how terrifying it was.

I let him take my hand and his felt smooth and warm and mine.

His fingers tightened around mine and his other arm moved to snuggle at the waist at the small of my back.

I'd forgotten to take off the collar and I felt it grow heavier as I clutched at it.

"Take a deep breath," he said.

I did.

The next thing I knew he was pushing me through the funnel. But this time there was no pain. He was wrapped around me like a cloak, protecting me or taking whatever pain the portal was delivering.

We stepped through with the ease of stepping across a threshold. My first impression of the area was that we were in a shop of some kind. The room was in semi-darkness except for the flickering glow of a streetlamp streaming in through the window.

I could just make out yellowing skulls lining the wall ahead of me, leering at me with open jaws. Jars of black powders and bottles of viscous fluid companioned them. It looked like an old-fashioned apothecary shop. Nothing special. Nothing terribly frightening. Maybe the portal had sent us somewhere else. Maybe the whole thing wasn't a set up at all.

I swung my gaze about the room, scanning for Maddox's father, and only meeting shadows and, where the light touched, bookshelves and herb counters.

And yet in one of those shadowy corners, I could swear I saw movement. Not a lot, just a bit of writhing greyness where the dark wasn't so deep. My eye caught on something that looked like the edge of a sheet and a bare toe flirting with the light.

In the next instant, dozens of jolts of electricity sizzled down into my skin. They burrowed into my tissues like worms. My hair felt like it was rising, standing against my scalp. The hair on my arms and legs strained outward, prickling my flesh. A gentle hum reverberated deep into the core of my chest.

I spasmed. My back arched painfully.

Just like I had been throttled by Scottie's thug's Taser, I was being juiced again. The collar heated up like a griddle and made me cry out. I dug at the thing, trying to pull it away from my skin, but the heat burned my fingers.

I fell against something--a counter, maybe. Something crashed to the floor on the other side. I squirmed there like a bug against a pin, writhing around my pain.

"The incubus was right," said a familiar voice, but it wasn't Maddox's.

Absalom's I realized. I'd barely heard him speak in Errol's shop, but I knew the timbre of that arrogant voice nonetheless.

"She's been sanctified," he said with certainty. "She'll be perfect. Take her."

The pulse of energy evaporated and the heat left the metal, leaving me panting and hanging over my knees.

I thought I'd be sick.

I peered up through my hair to scan the room as a cluster of men advanced on me from the shadows.

Apparently the moment of respite was for their benefit, not mine.

My gaze clawed over the room, seeking escape, seeking Maddox, Absalom, some sort of hint that I'd stepped through to the right end of the portal and wasn't lost in a realm without them.

I couldn't see Maddox at all.

I couldn't see the portal I'd just stepped through.

But I did see the target I'd been hired to steal. Doyle: Maddox's father. He stood in what looked like a kiddie pool except the water wasn't any liquid I'd ever seen. It was molten and moving and it swirled with steam that reminded me of Errol's green neon sign.

The old gent looked stuck in that mire and was trying to lift his feet over the lip of the container to free himself. Each time he lifted his foot, the steam rose and circled him, twirling about his body like the wand of magic from Cinderella's godmother as she transformed a shabby tunic into a gorgeous gown.

Instead of doing a beautiful thing, this magic seemed to strip him of his reason. He looked befuddled and blinked down as though he'd lost the ability to process simple thoughts.

I tried to move and found I was caught up in a sticky substance too, one that contained my movements the way a spider might a fly.

Whatever held us was the same thing. We weren't meant to move freely.

By all rights, I should have panicked, but I watched the men approach with clinical detachment, noting how they moved quickly but cautiously, their eyes scanning me with trepidation.

Something was wrong with me that they were afraid of. Something they didn't want to touch.

Chapter 22

My eyes flitted to my fingers and I splayed them out in front of my face. Some sort of webbing coated them, and it sizzled with a blue-grey light. I barely felt it.

Absalom stood a short distance off, his hands were still lingering in the air as though he had thrown two balls at me with a basketball kind of free throw.

It took several seconds to realize that he wore that same strange sort of sleeveless glove that wrapped around the base of his fingers. Small round pads nestled into the base of each, forming a sort of flower on his palm.

I might not know the Kindred world well, but I knew a weapon when I saw it. And that weapon had been aimed at me.

I traced the blueish glow from those pads to the air around me, and realized that what he had thrown had been energy, and that it was wrapped around me like a spider web. A similar bit of magic had pooled into the container that held Absalom.

Whatever magic he held, I knew it wasn't his own but was manufactured and its source was there in those finger pads.

I could feel a faint sort of sizzling in its pulse of energy. I could hear it buzzing in my ears.

Absalom had planned this alright. Right down to the last detail. He'd taken the time to create or buy a weapon that could hold the Stone Master because he'd known he needed him. Maddox was right. This had everything to do with the Lilith Stone. That much was clear.

But what it had to do with me beyond getting the Stone Master through the portal, I didn't understand.

I might have admired his planning but for the way he stepped toward me with a predatory gait. And that was the moment I realized that somehow, all of this had everything to do with me as well.

"She's the perfect conduit," he said, rubbing his chin. "Errol was right."

Targeted by that piece of shit. If I lived through this, I'd make the incubus pay.

"Errol is a dead man," I said through gritted teeth.

Absalom canted his head to the side. "Errol is not a *man*," he said.

"No shit, Sherlock," I said.

Another jolt went through me as Absalom flicked his finger in my direction. This time I did cry out. The shock went all the way down to my toes.

I was vaguely aware that the men who had tried to swarm me cringed away from me, afraid of the webbing the way an animal is of being cornered.

It was in that moment that Maddox stepped through the portal. He took one look in Absalom's direction and followed it to me. Once Absalom realized Maddox had stepped through, he pulled the webbing of electricity that surrounded me and threw it toward Maddox.

I watched it fly like a net about to wrap around a feral beast.

I was free of the magic, but not safe from the goons. I dodged left, seeking a harbour as I wrestled with possibilities. Could I do something to help? Was there a weapon nearby?

Absalom's thrust landed on empty air as Maddox leapt from his spot and bulled his way across the room.

I had no idea a man of his size could be so quick on his feet. I'd seen him fight before, but not charge and feint as Absalom retracted his energy and flicked it out again over and over like a whip being cracked and withdrawn.

The men who had swarmed me shifted the way geese do in the air toward Maddox. He in turn, upended several shelves and ripped a freestanding beam from the wall. When he swung it toward Absalom, the alchemist countered with a blast of light that splintered the wooden beam.

It missed Maddox by mere inches.

Freed from Absalom's attack, I was able to duck for cover beneath the table. The chains scraped along the floor and I had to gather them up. My breath was coming in gasps. My hands shook. Whatever was going on, it was a game that was in deadly earnest.

I wasn't just a hired thief, I was part of the heist the way Maddox's father was. My eyes skirted the area, searching for him, scoping out the distance between us, thinking maybe I could find a way to reach him.

I couldn't see him from my vantage point.

He could be dead for all I knew.

I scoured the floor around me for a weapon that I could wield while in chains because Errol had made sure to supply real ones, not large and hefty, but true steel links with a lock on the collar.

Now I finally understood exactly why. The bastard. He was doubly dead if I got my hands on him. As I was thinking of all the ways I'd like to see him die, my eye locked on the snaking curve of the links. Seeing them curled on the floor, made me realize something.

I had a key.

If it was still in my boot, then I could be as good as out of there. But could I just leave Maddox there alone to duke it out with a host of nasties in a bid to save his dad. Besides: just where in the name of Jesus did I think I would I run to?

I had no idea if I was in the ninth world, Errol's spectacle, or the Shadow Bazaar. Running blind was not a good idea when you had no idea what waited for you a few steps away.

But I could at least get the Hell out of these chains. I stuck my finger in the left boot, fishing around for the key. I'd not felt it embedding into my sole for a while now. I hoped it was still in there.

A clatter of bowls and jars cut through the air just then. A sucking sound tugged on the air currents in a way that made me think of taffy stretched out from a spoon.

I dared lean out from behind the table. It was almost too far for my comfort, but I was terrified someone was coming for me. And if they were, I wanted to see them.

Doyle had somehow managed to step over the container and free himself from whatever had held him. He was coated in energy, but it shed from him in sheets that didn't seem to slow him down as he entered the fray.

It crackled and evaporated into steamy puffs that fogged him in special effect fashion.

Pretty damned impressive, I had to admit.

He ducked adroitly and with as much agility as a man half his age as one of the goons charged him. The attacker sailed over his back. In a swift motion, the old gent spun on his heel and grappled for the man's hand, twisting it in a painful motion that made bones snap noisily.

"Wicked," I said despite myself.

I fished around my boot in earnest, then, because I was sure we'd be getting the upper hand any time now and I wanted to be ready.

I needed to be ready.

I caught sight of Maddox as he snapped his foot out at his opponent and knocked him to his knees. One more powerful blow against the man's shoulders, and the creature slumped to the floor. Maddox stepped over him, aiming for Absalom.

Absalom tried and failed to lob another ball of web at Maddox. The webbing went limp in his hand and he called out for cover.

Three of his goons shielded him.

I thought we might be winning.

So did Absalom, apparently.

While Maddox and his father cut their way through the men standing in direct line, shielding the shields with an almost deadened and dogged gaze, Absalom fiddled with the weapon that encircled his hand.

Whatever he did to it showed in the bolt of crackling energy that he sent sailing off into the shadowed corner of the room. It sizzled past Maddox to strike into the darkness.

A scream shredded the air.

I realized that in the shadows of the shop, cowering in one of the corners, were the half dozen virgins who had leapt through the portal before us, expecting a frenzy of pleasure.

Absalom sent through another jolt of electricity in their direction. One of them fell. Her body spilled into the light, enrobed in a white tunic that had scorched directly in center mass.

She spasmed for at least thirty seconds before she went perfectly still.

I would have thought the act would freeze time, but it didn't. Maddox fought on, bringing down one more goon as he advanced on Absalom.

I had to give Maddox credit; he looked terrifying, and Absalom's hand trembled as he took aim again at the shadows. I knew Maddox wouldn't care about those women. They were human after all, and I knew Absalom would kill them all before Maddox got to him.

I also knew he was doing it for a reason.

He wanted me to see it.

He knew I couldn't let another human being die. I was sure he was banking on it.

His arm lifted again, resting against one of his goons' shoulders. The whimpering in the corner grew. A mass of greyish clothes moved as one, out of clear shot and behind cover of several of the men

"Greys," Absalom said. "Move aside."

Maddox leered at him.

"Greys or not, humans or not, I'm coming for you."

Absalom released another jolt from the weapon. The shadows shrieked.

"Stop it," I heard myself yell. "Stop. Maddox, he's going to just kill them all."

Wherever Maddox was, it wasn't in his right mind. Every feature in his face was curled into red blotches of rage. I wasn't sure he could even hear. Bodies of what Absalom called greys littered the space around him, and there was no way he was going to stop. Only two greys remained guarding the alchemist.

Absalom leaned sideways, aiming past his greys shoulders to get a clear shot at the shadows.

That was when Maddox charged.

His father snagged him by the arm. In the moment Doyle's grip tightened on Maddox, something passed between them. It was subtle and as quick as the time it took for a heart to pulse, but it was distinct.

I thought maybe Maddox would relent, but he swung his gaze to me where I was by then feeling into my other boot for the key. I found it, clenching it tight in my fist.

His expression hardened and I suspected that humans or not, he was not leaving this place while Absalom breathed. He sent another withering glare at the alchemist, trapped behind his greys but leering as though he was the one who was winning.

They were all too busy to notice me slipping the key into the lock on my collar, twisting it till the click snapped free. I pulled the chain slowly back toward me, link by link.

Absalom was right there, not five feet away.

I pushed myself to my feet, the chain spilling down my front. I inched forward on crouched legs, crabbing toward the alchemist.

Absalom's eyes were for Maddox only.

"There's two prizes," he said, and it was such a shock to hear him cut through the air with his voice that one of the virgins shrieked. He ignored her and continued. "There is the master, and there is the conduit. Which one of those would you choose to save. Not the useless humans, surely, and yet the conduit seems to think they have value."

He raked his gaze over Maddox's form with a smirking eye.

"Isabella," Maddox said without taking his gaze from me. "You need to run. Now."

It was obvious he thought Absalom's threat to harm his father was an empty one, and maybe he didn't care about the women, but I did.

And Absalom knew it. I shook my head. I wasn't running. I would never run again.

I couldn't look at Maddox or his father as Absalom edged closer. The chains were heavy in my arms, cutting into the skin of my breast. I could barely hold them aloft anymore.

Absalom scanned me head to heel as he drew closer to me. He was working out his plans even as he closed the distance between us. I could see the inner workings of his mind written clearly on his face. He obviously assumed he could take control of at least one of the prizes so within his grasp.

He was counting on Maddox rounding on his father, saving the master of the order he so revered and leaving the human women to their fates. But would Maddox also make an attempt on me? He wasn't sure, and so he ordered his greys with one motion of his hand to surround his father while he advanced on me.

He didn't plan to lose any of his leverage. The way he looked at me, I had the feeling he wanted to open my mouth, inspect my teeth. He rounded me, circling ever closer and murmuring to himself.

"Yes, perfect. She should be pleased."

I swallowed convulsively as he stopped in front of me. His black eyes pinned to mine.

"You've been to hell, yes?" he said.

"Isabella," Maddox warned and my eye tracked the sound of his voice. He was as still as a mouse under a hawk's gaze.

Absalom smiled broadly as he regarded me. He knew the truth of his question without me answering.

"I thought so," he said.

Over his shoulder I could see Maddox tensing. It truly did look like he couldn't decide who to save: his father or me. The thugs were less interested in the virgins in the corner now. They were rigid with expectation, standing to the ready for Absalom's orders.

We were at an impasse. One that everyone in the room was aware of.

"How long did you have the stone, woman?" he said and smirked. "Not long enough judging by the scent of you."

"You've got a nerve talking about how I smell," I said, waving a hand in front of my face.

The length of chain clinked against itself.

He smiled but it wasn't one of good humor.

"What you sense as stink is the fragrance of ritual." He held up his hands to show me that they were changing in front of me from human hands to something else. Something claw-like and feral.

"One taste of your blood, that's all," he said.

From over his shoulder, I could see Maddox tensing to strike the grey that crowded him. His father behind him was edging for the gaggle of women.

I needed to stall, I realized. Neither of them was going to just accept the impasse. I almost sighed out the relief that those women would be spared.

Maddox lunged at Absalom at the same time his father aimed for his greys. A flock of women broke through the ring of greys blocking them and scrambled to escape in every direction. Maddox hoisted the grey he'd grabbed over his head, crushing its skull in as though it were an aluminum can.

The grey's legs twitched and blood spilled black and viscous, raining over Maddox and the floor.

His father slipped in the fluid. A grey grasped him by the throat.

One moment Doyle was standing looking fierce and deadly, and the next, I heard a sharp crackling sound as the grey dropped him backwards over his knee.

Doyle collapsed onto the floor. It took a long moment of me holding my breath before he rolled to his knees. He hitched himself upward and fell again, pain lancing his expression. Bone shone through the blood and flesh.

My stomach lurched at the sight of him cradling a fractured leg.

He cried out as the grey advanced on him, murderous intent on his face.

Absalom spun around at the sound. His movement knocked over a chair and it left him wide open to me. It was the perfect moment, given like a gift by the heavens and I used the distraction as though it had all been planned.

I launched myself at Absalom and slid my hands around his throat. I fully intended to choke him until I felt no give anymore in the tissues. But my hands were still wrapped around the collar. And I'd have to drop it to choke the life out of the bastard.

And then I realized. I was still holding the collar, and it locked in place on closing. I almost laughed at the irony of it. Two steps more and I was able to snap it closed around Absalom's neck. He swung on me, eyes wide from surprise, mouth in a grim, angry line as he realized what I'd done.

I had time for one quick smirk as I lifted the other end of the chain to his view before I tossed it toward the fire gate.

I'd always wondered what it looked like to see someone enter a portal. I got to see it then, as he began to disintegrate in front of my eyes. Small pieces broke off and while he struggled against it. He was gone. We should be home-free.

But Maddox obviously didn't think so. I heard him grunt as he hefted his father onto his back.

"Run," he shouted at me.

CHAPTER 23

Next I knew, we were running headlong toward the door because something snarled from beyond the portal. And it wasn't going to stay there.

I was out of breath already by the time we rounded the doorframe and headed down a tight alleyway filled with cardboard boxes and red dumpsters. Rats skittered ahead of us in the darkness and the rotten stench of old fish assailed my nostrils.

The adrenaline and fear was robbing me of energy.

I clutched at my chest and willed my legs to carry me just one more step.

I hung over my knees, dragging in frantic breaths.

"Don't you have somewhere we can go?" I gasped out in the general direction of Maddox's retreating back.

He reached behind for me, his fingers waggling past his father's waist.

"This isn't my bazaar," he said. "The bastard incubus switched out the portals somehow. We're back in the ninth world."

The ninth world. Home. That was comforting, if you didn't count the sound of a half dozen sets of dogged feet pounding the asphalt behind us.

"I thought you weren't afraid of anything," I panted out as I clutched at the wall, and seeing it laced with excrement, grimaced and scraped my palm against a clean section of brick.

"I'm not," he said giving me a queer look. "But you should be."

"What is it?" I said, using the question to sag against the wall instead of leaning on Maddox's arm.

Maddox eased his father against the wall, holding him there pinned between brick and back as he caught his breath.

It was his father who took up the gauntlet of informing me what we were truly running from.

"I recognized that claw," he said. "Absalom is more than just a soul-eater. He's a shape-shifter."

I cupped my elbows, not daring to ask the question that was utmost in my mind, averted my gaze from Doyle's naked haunches as he clung to Maddox's back.

"Chupacabra," Maddox said, not paying attention to the wild way my eyes were traveling the space around me, trying to take everything in at once. "Do you agree, Doyle?"

His father nodded. "He'll have our scent. There won't be a good enough place to hide. And if there is, we got a tribe of greys to face before we even think about finding a haven."

He dragged his gaze over my clothes, ratty and askew from the run, but fetterless at least.

"You ever face greys before?" he said but didn't want for an answer.

Maddox snorted. "She's human, Doyle. Newly aware of Kindred."

Doyle looked displeased but not at my ignorance. He leaned his head against Maddox's shoulder with a wince, pain etched in the skin around his mouth.

"They're creatures from the first world with impressionable bodies. Kind of like blanks. A soul-eater can siphon out their essence and fill the body with their own intent, keeping the souls of the creatures as hostage."

My knees regained a bit of strength and I made the effort to stagger along the alley to swallow up the uncomfortable distance between us. I much preferred to have Maddox at my back where I didn't have to see Doyle's bone shimmering against the blood and tissue of the wound.

"I'm guessing Absalom is a soul-eater?"

I'd never heard the term before but it sounded positively awful. I felt a new empathy for the creatures that'd attacked us.

Maddox hoisted his father a bit higher on his back and Doyle sucked in a breath.

"It's dark magic that he filled them with, that's for sure," he said. "I could barely withstand them. You can bet those greys will do his bidding until the body dies or he returns their souls."

"So," I said. "In other words, they're the Terminator. Nice."

Maddox sighed. "And I don't like killing them since they are at heart a peaceable Kindred. But they do have a doggedness about them that might make that impossible."

I thought I saw in his face regret about the ones he'd taken out in defense of his father and me.

Doyle let go a resigned chuckle. "Nice is for kittens and rainbows. A soul-eater can suck out human energy too. And it can swap it. I'm guessing that's what he's after."

I perked up. "You guess?"

He nodded and caught my eye in a viselike stare. "You're a conduit for Lilith. I don't think he's a goddess acolyte, but it's obvious why he wants you. He wants to perform the re-animation ritual."

My head snapped up at that. "A conduit for what now?" I said. "Ritual to do what exactly?"

Maddox had already begun pacing back up the alley, seeking the open street.

I had to run to keep up.

"Maddox," I said. "What is going on?"

In that moment the sound of trash cans being skittered across asphalt sounded behind us. Several of the greys entered the back end of the alley, and spying us, came at us with all the speed of lightening.

Maddox was already sagging beneath his father's weight.

I gripped him by the arm.

It was clear we couldn't out run the greys.

His dad was slowing him down that was obvious. I could tell he didn't want to let him go, but that he knew I was right. He couldn't carry the man on his back forever.

He dropped him and sent me an entreating look. "Take him," he said. "I'll hold them back. Fayed's. As soon as you're able."

Then he backed up, making sure I had crouched down next to Doyle. I sent him an encouraging look, as best I could create it, and then he spun on his heel to face the two the greys who rushed him.

"Come on," I said, urging the old man. "We need to get out of here."

He was as heavy as a fifty pound sack of flour and I couldn't imagine how Maddox had been able to just heave him up over his shoulder and run as though the man was nothing but a bit of fluff and feathers.

The old man shook his head. "I'm not sure I can," he said.

I caught his eye, and I was surprised to find that instead of being blue or green or brown like regular irises, his were blood red. They were so reminiscent of the stone that it made me shiver.

"You can," I said, lowering my gaze to his whiskered chin. It didn't matter how prepared I might have been for that look, I couldn't keep it. It was too penetrating and altogether too creepy.

"Thanks," he said. "But no thanks. You go. I'll hold off any that get by Maddox."

"Don't say that."

"Sweetness," he said. "Immortality is fine if you're young when you're made – but being 70 as an immortal really sucks. Do as I say. He needs us both and you can run. Now go."

I couldn't lift him and he looked like he was in so much pain. I knew he couldn't travel. Maddox was working his way through grey after grey and I was beginning to think the inching progress we made was futile.

I wasn't sure what to do. I couldn't just leave them both. I couldn't leave Maddox.

Then the greys simply stopped.

They retreated, backwards through the alley.

They were gone into the shadows the way darkness filled dark crevices.

I watched as Maddox's hand ran down along his ribcage. He swung around to face us; his face was cloaked in bewilderment and wonder.

No sense running anymore," he said. "The stone has gone dark.

Gone dark. I knew what it meant as soon as he said it. The stone was off this plane and into another. Meaning, it had traveled to Hell.

Maddox ate up the distance between us, and stared down at his father who was holding his leg in stiff and awkward grip.

"Find a drugstore, Kitten," he said. "And a men's store. This one needs shirt." He ran his palm down his sweaty chest. "Badly."

He gave me a list of items to procure, and while I haggled in the first clothing store I came across still open, he got his father to a safer bench a few streets away that bordered a fenced off playground.

We made it to my apartment without further incident and it was a bit surreal to sit on my chair watching the way my cat lay spread-eagle on Doyle's lap.

He sat there next to me on the sofa, absently stroking my cat's tummy, the letters spelling out God is Love but lust is better peeking out from the souvenir shirt I'd managed to find. Maddox's shirt simply said: I shaved my balls for this.

Maddox had done some sort of magic that he insisted was just plain ancient healing arts but I doubted a few cups of herbs from my cupboard and a few supplies from the pharmacy could have helped Doyle already. He was able to limp to the bathroom twice already and pee with the door open.

When Maddox peeled up his T-shirt for the third time with disgust to look at his mark, it really hit me. Really hit me. Scottie was in hell. He had touched that stone and been transported through its magics to a place no person should ever have to go. Lucifer would greet the appearance of a living mortal in his realm with sadistic glee, but that wasn't even the half of it.

I'd been there. I saw what he did with what he called his menagerie--how he tortured them. He was the original sadist, the sociopath with psychopathic tendencies.

I wanted free of Scottie, but I wouldn't wish that awfulness on him. What kind of person would that make me?

Not that kind of person, that was for sure.

"We have to get him out of there," I said.

"Are you kidding me, Kitten?" Maddox said. "That man has ordered you throttled twice already."

"A dozen," I said.

"What?"

I took a breath as I inhaled the courage to tell him the truth. "A dozen times. He ordered me beaten one dozen times already."

Maddox just gaped at me, and I wasn't sure what the look on his face meant. I just knew I was happy to be on his good side. I thought he was going to say something but Doyle interrupted.

"By the gods," he said. "And you survived it all?" He shook his head. "You are one crunchy piece of saltzat, girlie."

My brow furrowed in confusion. "A saltzat?" I said. "I hope that's not something catching."

"A treat in my world made of salt and caramel," Maddox said. "Chewy on the inside, but crystallized chunks of tooth-breaking treat on the outside. We eat it with herring."

I gave him a look of revulsion. "And you are revolted by my housekeeping?"

He shrugged.

Doyle leaned forward, not willing to let the topic go.

"He beat you a dozen times? Really?"

"By a proxy hand," I said. "I tracked every one of those because they felt more like a betrayal. But the amount of times he beat me himself? Too many to count unless I wanted to drive myself insane with the guilt that I let it happen."

I found I couldn't look either of them in the eye. All of those years I'd stayed with Scottie despite the times he'd taken a hand to me. I'd not been a woman who thought I could change him. I just always thought he was better with me in his life. I thought I softened him in some way. I still wasn't convinced I hadn't.

But what he'd have been like without me, I wouldn't want to imagine.

"I'll kill him," Maddox said.

It was a nice sentiment, if not overkill.

"There's no need to now," I said." "He's in hell, remember?"

"Too good for him," he said. Maddox took to pacing.

Doyle, however, slid closer, careful to do so gingerly so as to not dislodge the cat or his wounded leg. He pulled me close. His arm slid around the small of my back and he tugged me in, enfolding me in a fatherly embrace.

I was stiff at first, awkwardly trying to figure out what I should do. He cupped the back of my head, ran his fingers down my hair.

"Shh," he said, as though I was crying. "Shh. He can't hurt you. You're not to blame, child."

I choked up. I couldn't remember my own father. I'd never known him. If I had ever met him, it had been in the small times when I'd been between infancy and toddler. I'd been in foster homes for as long as I could remember, not just bouncing from one to the other, but being tossed from one to the next. Halfway houses held me when a foster home wasn't available, and that was all too often. I was too difficult. No one wanted me.

"Abuse is the fault of the abuser," he whispered against my hair. "No matter how much they deflect their own blame onto their victims. Stop blaming yourself. I know the type. We have them in the fifth world too."

I wiped my nose on his shirt and realized it was full of snot.

I lifted my eyes to his. I expected those eyes to be soft and sympathetic, but he was looking down at me with mock revulsion. A playful grimace twisted his features.

"Now that atrocity," he said directing his gaze to a slimy patch on his shirt. "You are to blame for."

He shoved me away and with delicate fingers, he pulled the buttons loose. He peeled it back and turned to Maddox who was busily washing down my cupboards with soapy water because according to him, my house was a petri dish.

"Got another?" Doyle said to Maddox, holding the material between pinched fingers.

"Afraid not," Maddox said. "You're just going to have to suck it up."

He frowned as he regarded the thing still hanging from his fingers. "Please tell me you at least have a place where I could wash the goo off," he said.

Maddox jerked his chin to the left and his father followed the direction. He held the shirt at arm's length and marched away to disappear behind a door.

I looked at Maddox. Now that we were alone, I felt awkward and needy. I cupped my elbows.

"Is it over, do you think?"

Maddox sighed. "I honestly don't know. The greys retreated. The mark is gone dark."

I ran my hands along my arms, wishing I hadn't changed into my pajamas. I felt like I needed to be able to flee at a second's notice and ducky flannel pants might make me a bit conspicuous.

I tossed the replica stone up in the air and caught it, studying the precision of it. He'd made it like he'd known it intimately.

"I guess we don't need this damn replica anymore..."

"Don't bet on it," he said. "Absalom isn't about to give up altogether. You don't think that was all about helping you, do you?"

He poured the water from the bucket down the sink.

"But the stone is in hell," I said. "So ipso facto – no issue." I felt pretty good about things actually. Despite the fact that we been chased through the streets, surely things had changed even for Absalom upon discovering that the stone had taken another mortal to hell.

"Theoretically, yes," Maddox said. "But now he knows my father's alive and there's that issue of a conduit –"

"You said that before," I said, looking at him through narrowed eyes. "What do you mean by that?"

He chose to wipe his wet hands on his pants instead of the towel hanging from the oven door.

"The stone master, my father, can release Lilith," he said. "It's his blood and bond that helped entrap her in the first place. But there was always a need for a third-party. Someone needed to have gone to hell and back in order for Lilith to find release from the stone."

I watched him eyeing the cat when she headed in his direction and he took a wary step to the side.

"But why would you build an escape hatch in the first place?" I said. "If she was so damned frightening that you needed to entrap her within a stone, then why would you build a way for her to get out?"

"We didn't build it. Magic just works that way. The energies aren't unidirectional. They stretch out everywhere. They have a mind of their own sometimes. And magic creates its own breathing spaces."

"And the risk was too great," came a voice from behind Maddox. I looked up to see his father pulling on the shirt again. There was a large white spot in the front where he'd obviously rinsed it. He was buttoning it up over a heavily muscled chest with the smoke of grey hair.

"So that's why you hid the stone," I said, thinking that this must have all started with him.

He nodded. "I took the stone with me to the world of the gods, and I entreated them for sanctuary. They allowed me to stay, but I had to give up the stone to fate who said she needed it."

"Kassie," I murmured. The girl who I thought was just a runaway teenager, but who was really the disembodied goddess trio known as the Morrigan. "And now here we are."

"Yes," Maddox said.

"But surely the threat is over," I said. "Your mark has retreated back into nothing more than a silver scar. Your father is safe." I leaned back into the chair. "What could possibly go wrong?"

"The threat is over," his father said. "But the council must now resume. We need to be ready."

"Resume?" I looked from him to Maddox. Maddox looked very unhappy.

"What does that mean?" I said.

"It means now that the stone is no longer in fate's hands, it must return to ours.

Maddox did not look pleased. His other hand dug into his pocket and I could see it was clenched into a fist in there.

I tried to catch his eye, but he stared out over the window, refusing to acknowledge me or his father behind us.

"I can't do it again," he said and at first I thought he was talking to me and angled closer. He looked over his shoulder, raking his glance at his father.

"You were dead," he said. "Gone. The order disbanded. I can't go back to that life."

"You're ordained, Maddox," Doyle said. "You have no choice the way I have no choice."

Maddox shot a look my way, one that made his Adam's apple bob in his throat.

"Things aren't the same anymore," he said.

"No," Doyle said. "They're not. The stone is under siege. The little mortal is in danger."

Maddox swallowed convulsively. He gave a short nod and stared at the cat.

"I know what needs to be done," he said and heaved a sigh. "I'll prepare."

Doyle placed a quiet hand on Maddox's shoulder.

"You won't," he said. "I can't live through another loss," he said. "I'll go."

Maddox flung his hand off, spinning on his heel to put distance between them.

"No, Dad," he said. "You said yourself that we have a duty. Yours is not to do the soldiering. It's what I was made for. What we sacrificed for. I'll collect it."

I had no idea what remained unspoken between the two of them, but I realized one thing. It was a knowledge that gripped my heart with dread because no matter what Kindred he was, no matter his creed, his powers, the things he would face now would be on my head. And I knew exactly what he planned to do.

Maddox was going to hell to retrieve the stone.

Chapter 24

There wasn't much I could do to help Scottie and I knew it. Maybe a different Isabella, the one borne of a decade of abuse and petty thievery might have opted to leave him to his own devices and his own fate.

Then there was Maddox

He might be an immortal, one that had possessed abilities I still didn't understand, but I'd seen Kassie--a goddess--ensnared in Lucifer's realm. I'd made my way out only because of fate and fortune.

It would be easy to let Maddox cross the threshold and bear all the burden of a mistake I'd made. It was an ignorant mistake, yes, but it still needed to be rectified. It was my fault he was going to have to do so. I couldn't wear that guilt.

The younger Isabella, the one filled with hope, chasing after a man she thought might be able to save her from herself, that one wanted to find some sort of innocence again. Some way to burrow back into a world that dreamed of compassion and hope.

That was the Isabella who tapped me on the shoulder and begged me to remember that taking control of her own life also meant walking forward into it with a clear conscience.

It was my fault Scottie had that stone in the first place. It was my fault Maddox planned to cross the threshold to retrieve the stone.

I didn't care what Maddox or Doyle might think, whether or not they would try to stop me. I had to fix what I'd messed up.

But how? I certainly couldn't just step over a threshold into hell, nor did I want to. The thought of it terrified me. The only way that I knew of for a mortal to enter that realm was either through the magic of the stone or death.

But were there are other ways? Other beings – Kindred, as Fayed called him – that could step across that threshold?

The Morrigan could. She'd come to claim me from Lucifer, citing that she had a blood bond with me and offered up a replacement in my stead that would please him just as much, if not more, than having a breathing mortal in his realm to play with.

I chewed my lip, thinking. I hadn't seen the Morrigan since. Or even Kassie for that matter. The goddess had renounced her powers and separated into three aspects as penance for her role in ChuCulain's death and transport to hell. Wherever she was, or whether or not she was reintegrated or in her separate aspects, she was the only chance Scottie and Maddox had.

I hadn't seen her, hadn't heard from her, and if she'd gone into hiding, then she no doubt didn't want to be found. But I wasn't the only one looking for her, and I realized it as I sat there. Fayed also wanted to know where she was.

He wanted his progeny back and as far as he knew, the Morrigan had her. When he'd tossed Kelliope the fae assassin out of his bar, had he hired her to help him find the goddess who stole his progeny from him?

Fayed would know as well as I did, maybe even better, exactly how good Kelliope's tracking skills were. She'd managed to find Kassie and had dragged her into the shadow bazaar. Used her for bait to get me to turn over a priceless artifact.

There was no question about it: I needed to go back to Fayed's bar and feel him out. Find out if he had managed to hire the assassin.

The plan wasn't perfect by any stretch. It was entirely possible that Kelly had found the Morrigan and told Fayed that his progeny was Lucifer's new plaything. In that instance, asking Fayed for any information would be about as useful as a spigot on Niagara Falls.

There was no way he was going to tell me anything when I was the reason the Morrigan took his progeny in the first place.

He might already be disposed to hate me, to want vengeance, and I'd seen the feral look in his eye when he thought about revenge on Ismé's behalf.

Walking into a vampire bar was risky enough, but before I had Fayed watching my back. Exactly how inclined to protect me he would be if he knew Ismé was in hell on my ticket was anyone's guess.

I knew backtracking my way to Fayed's bar this close to dawn was a risky endeavour. He hadn't said so, but I suspected the basement of his bar to be a hostel of sorts to rogue vampires all over the city. That made the danger doubly risky.

I started rummaging through my cupboards, and complaining I was dying for Chinese food. Maddox had taken to pacing, running through a list of things he would need to do to prepare to pull out onto his highway to Hell.

Maddox didn't seem impressed at my declaration, but Doyle licked his lips.

"Sweet Jesus," he said. "I haven't eaten in days."

"Order in," Maddox said.

"You don't understand," I said. "I'm a regular, and if I schmooze up the son, he always gives me a big container of wonton soup."

"I love wonton soup," Doyle said. "Go, child. Go quickly."

Maddox crossed his arms over his chest. "Trust a thief to find ways to steal from the poor."

"They're not poor," I said. "They're the best place in the city."

I opened my smart phone and tapped my destination into the Uber app. Three minutes later, they were stopped in front of my step. I grabbed my bag and slung it over my shoulder amid protests from Maddox that I shouldn't be going out alone.

"How dangerous can it be?" I said. "I'm getting in a car and going directly to point A. I'll be getting in a car at Point A and coming directly back here. By the sounds of it your preparations are going to take hours. Should we starve while we wait?"

His palm sealed over the seam in the door as he scowled down at me.

"We're not in the bazaar," he said. "I have no way of tracking you or keeping you safe."

I put on a big show of impatience, heaving a heavy sigh and rolling my eyes.

"Then come with me," I said, hoping he wouldn't take the bait. "The line ups aren't that long. And there's usually only two or three families with screaming kids."

Doyle threw an empty can at him. "Maybe your body can live off all of your fat," he said. "But a body with this much muscle chews up energy pretty quick. If I don't eat soon, my metabolism is going to start chowing down on my liver. And I hate liver."

Maddox rolled his eyes heavenward and I had the feeling they had argued like this too many times in the past for him to appreciate it.

Maddox's lips pressed together in a thin line and he pushed himself off from the door.

"Direct," he said.

I nodded. "Direct to my destination and back. Not a single side-trip." It wasn't really a lie.

I grabbed my satchel from beside the door, and yanked on the handle, knowing full well I'd slipped my replica stone in the bag when neither was looking.

I fled down the stairs before they could change their mind and I waved to Maddox who was peering from behind the curtain at me. Then I slipped into the back of the Uber.

"Rot Gut Alley," I said.

I caught the driver's eye in the rear-view mirror.

"I don't go that far," he said. "Get another driver."

"Just take me as far as you do go," I said.

In the end, he dropped me off three blocks away. I checked my watch. 4:30 AM. I checked the skyline for signs of sunrise.

Nothing pink in it anywhere. Hopefully, that meant Fayed was still awake and prowling or whatever vampires like him did.

The short walk to the Rot Gut Tavern was brisk. I didn't want to tarry any longer than was necessary, and the rats were already scurrying along the graffitied walls and carrying off bits of trash bigger than they were. For some reason, this part of the metro grew them big.

When I opened the door to the bar, Fayed was over his counter in a heartbeat, placing both of his hands on either side of me, pinning me to the wall.

I could feel my heart hammering in my chest. I stared up at him, doing my best to look casual and unafraid. His nostrils flared, no doubt scenting my fear. I could feel every muscle tense up as I waited to see a flash of fang.

"You're all right," he said.

I was pleased that I managed not to sag out my relief all at once.

"Of course I'm alright, I said, ducking beneath his arms and heading toward a stool. I jumped on it as though there was nothing more to my visit than a casual visit.

I could hear him spinning around behind me. "The last I saw of you, you were supposed to meet me."

I looked over my shoulder at him. He was supposed to help me wrest the stone from Scottie's possession. He was going to be my muscle. In all the hubbub, I'd forgotten that.

"Sorry about that," I said. "It was foolish of me to ask. I wasn't thinking that you couldn't possibly help me in the daylight." I hung my bag on a peg jutting out from the bar. "You know, you being a vampire and all."

He nodded slowly. "I would've thought you'd consider that before you asked me."

"I guess I'm not used to all this nightly supernatural stuff."

"So you're telling me that thieves do all their dirty work in the day?"

I laughed, a forced chuckle that I didn't feel, but that was for his benefit.

"The bar looks undamaged," I said, twirling around on the stool and scanning the premises. "I would've thought Kelly had torn the place into splinters," I said. There. It was out there. I prayed he'd pick it up.

He raked a hand through his hair.

"She very nearly did. She only gave up after I helped her subdue the crossbreed."

He came around to my right and settled himself on the stool next to me. He laid his arm against the counter.

"That was smart of you," I said, careful not to meet his eyes. The last time he'd explained about his compulsion, and now I felt as though the smart thing to do was avoid direct eye contact.

"Nothing smart about it," he said. "It was pure self-preservation." He grinned. "But it did at least net me some information."

This was what I was hoping for. My heart jumped.

"You mean about Kassie?" I said.

His fingers walked toward my hand. He tapped each fingernail thoughtfully.

"I had no idea she could be so amenable."

"Don't tell me what you did with the poor crossbreed," I said.

He smiled.

"So did she find the Morrigan for you?"

I held my breath as I waited for the answer.

"She did. Sort of."

"And that means –"

"It means the Morrigan has divested herself of her aspects again. Renounced her powers. She's useless again as a goddess."

I groaned inwardly. I'd expected as much. Guilt like that didn't just evaporate like steam. It took hellfire and the threat of having my soul eaten to do that.

"So she's more no more than a body again," I guessed.

"Body, mind, and shade."

He turned my hand over so that the palm faced up. He poked his finger into the middle. "She has no idea where the body is, but the shade moves around wherever it wants."

"So you did find her," I said.

His jaw clenched. "Yes. Apparently she sold my progeny to the devil."

My heart skipped. "How do you know that?"

"She admitted it to Kelly," he said. "I paid the assassin to track her using her power. She had a taste of it from before you see." He gave me a beady eye. "I think you might know something about that."

His intense gaze was too much for me to hold and I dropped my eyes to his mouth instead. I was sure if I didn't he'd read the entire history of my trip to Hell in them. Heck, he might even compel me to detail it all, and the last thing I wanted was to revisit that nasty bit of business.

Especially since I was guilty as charged. Kassie had used his progeny to rescue me and I'd not felt one bit of guilt at the time. I just knew I wanted rescued any way I could get it, and Ismé had cheated her way out anyway.

As far as I was concerned, Hell was her home. She'd earned it. Not that I would tell that to Fayed.

I decided the best truth was the closest truth.

"I know more than I'd like to be honest." I withdrew my hand. "Did she say why she sold your progeny?"

While I certainly knew the answer, I needed to know if he did. If he was going to still be my friend after all this. Because if he wasn't, I needed to rethink the entire plan.

"Not sold." He tapped the middle of my palm again. "Bartered. One useless vampire for a mortal about to change the worlds she said."

Those eyes landed on mine, and I met them without thinking, unable to help myself. He had the most gorgeous eyes. Moss green irises turned black and then silver and then black again.

"What are you planning Isabella?"

I spoke without meaning to. There was no hesitation, no thinking that I shouldn't confess. It just came out like breath.

"I want to rob Lucifer of another soul he shouldn't have. One that I sent there and I need to fix it."

Fayed's expression hardened, transforming the handsome features into something dark and ugly. His lips pressed together.

"My guess is if you want to fix it – you have to barter with something of equal or greater value."

No word of warning, no begging me not to do something foolish.

I had a feeling I knew what it was. Lucifer did not like to give up anything. But I had to ask. I had to be sure.

"And what would that be?" I said.

"Your soul."

CHAPTER 25

I had no intention of trading my soul for Scottie's – heck, I'd already given him a good deal of it already, along with almost a decade of my life. But if a soul was necessary to fix all this mess and clear my conscience, I'd find a way to get it without putting anyone else in danger, without subjecting Maddox to it.

And the only person I knew that might be able to help was not quite human.

Absalom had wanted me for a conduit when the stone was available. Surely Scottie would be a suitable replacement now that it was in Hell.

I just had to convince Absalom that since the stone was no doubt in Scottie's grasp somewhere in that straddle of line between chaos and fire, that he could kill two birds with one blood-drenched stone.

And, of course, leave me out of the whole affair of ritual and soul-eating.

Fayed was giving me a strange look. "What's going on in there?" he said.

I tried to smile at him. I couldn't tell him what I planned. He'd never understand, even if he did want his evil progeny back. She was his evil progeny. Scottie was a mortal who didn't deserve to live in Fayed's opinion. Maybe he didn't. But that wasn't my call.

"Don't worry," I said. "I'm not planning to hop the Lucifer trolley into chaos town. But if I can find a way to screw him over without putting myself in harm's way...Well, what would you do to get your progeny out of his hands?"

He flashed his fangs. "I'd kill for the chance."

I shuddered at the fierceness of his expression. Sometimes it was easy to forget he was a vampire. He was amenable to me, even friendly. But like he'd said the last time I was here, I amused him. It made me wonder what would happen if I ceased to do so.

I cupped my hands over my elbows, squeezing my arms against my chest. A gleam lit in his eyes, a predatory one, and I realized my protective posture might have ignited something primal in him.

I very slowly and carefully laid my palms down on the bar and leaned away from him.

"I might be able to help with that," I said. "Do you have a portal to the shadow bazaar?"

He shook his head. "I stay away from that shit. It's hard enough keeping my head above water here in my own world let alone jumping into a portal that will take me to another one."

I cocked my head at him. "Your world?" I said. "You're from here?"

He smiled. "Most humanoid kindred are," he said. "We started as mortals here in this world, and so we are of this world. Other kindred: the Fae, sidhe, gods. All of them originate from a different world. And then there those other ones that no one knows. I learned about the world after I became a vampire. Decades later. Not everyone knows they exist."

He shook his head the way a dog might rid itself of water. "My initiation into that knowledge wasn't exactly pleasurable. But I eventually learned that we've mapped out at least nine worlds. Two of them are inactive."

"Inactive?" I said.

"Yes. Either there is no portal or there is nowhere to go to."

"But the Shadow Bazaar," I said. "Surely it has portals to multiple worlds."

He picked up a cloth and began to mop up the counter.

"You'd have to ask Maddox how many portals into how many different worlds he created. It's his. I'm not even sure it exists on a separate plane or straddles all of the worlds. Portals are difficult magic and they're unreliable."

"So you've never gone?"

It interested me that he'd not visited Maddox's bazaar. I wondered at the reason, considering every manner of supernatural goods was up for grabs there.

"I've been," he said shortly. "Let's leave it at that."

His hand paused on the counter and he looked up at me, trying to lock eyes with mine. I quickly averted them, remembering his admission of using compulsion to get what he wanted.

I chewed the inside of my cheek. This was getting me nowhere. I had a feeling Absalom was still there in the apothecary shop, hiding out or waiting. He didn't strike me as the sort of man who would just give up.

It was in the memory of the shop that I had my answer. We'd not escaped Absalom from another world, but from right here in the ninth one. Absalom had a shop in the city.

I ran down the route in my mind, passing by the pizza shop I frequented and a pawn shop that I rarely used because it was too close to the docks for my safety.

I retraced that flight, back to the dirty walls of the back alley we'd fled to.

I knew the place.

"I have to go," I blurted out and pushed off from my stool.

I had the feeling he'd found his way back from his trip in the fire gate and was planning out his next mode of attack.

I decided I'd reroute those plans.

His shop wasn't hard to find. The skull and crossbones on the sign that formed a mortar and pestle were the dead giveaway. I pushed open the door just as the streetlights went out and heralded the end of the dark hours when most bogeymen like Fayed would be climbing into their crypts or coffins.

Absalom was reclining in a leather chair when I found him, thumbing through an old text as big as a desk top.

I pulled out the stone from the satchel I carried with me, presumably to carry the Chinese takeout back to my apartment.

He looked mildly surprised to see me, and I guessed he didn't think I'd have the nerve to show up on his doorstep after he'd tried to kill me. His mistake. I knew my body was useless to him without the real stone.

"Did you ever intend to pay this to me?" I said, holding up the replica he'd made. "Why did you even bother to make it if you planned to use me?"

He shrugged. "I didn't make it for you," he said. "I've had that kicking around for a century or more."

"Meaning you planned to swap it for the real one, but Doyle gave you the slip and took the Lilith Stone with him when he disappeared." I would have chuckled at the old gent's moxy, but I didn't want to insult Absalom. I needed him.

He shrugged. "He's a crafty old fart, but yes, I originally hoped to make all this a clandestine affair."

"You can still succeed," I said. "We can make a deal."

He narrowed his eyes at me. "Says a woman who has nothing to barter."

"Who says I don't?" I said. "I have what you're looking for, and I'm willing to trade on your other skills. The ones with your unique magic."

"You couldn't possibly," he said. "The stone is gone."

"But I know who has it," I said. "And I know how to get it."

He leaned forward in his chair, resting his elbows against his knees. His gaze was intent and terrifying. "And where is it?"

"In Hell."

He lost interest then, waved his hand at me. "I can't just go gallivanting into Lucifer's realm. It would take too much...e nergy," he said.

"Not even if I provide the conduit too?"

I had him then. I could tell by the gleam in his eye. He waved over one of his greys from the shadows.

He spread his hands. "What do you know of the conduit, little girl?" he said, but he didn't take his eyes off me.

"A conduit is someone who has entered hell via the stone. A vessel that's been sanctified by its energy." I stared him down. "The stone is in Hell. Your conduit is in Hell. The math is easy. If you could call it Math."

"You make it sound as easy as going to the store."

I felt my jaw tightening.

"It's not easy," I admitted. "But some have done it. Maddox has done it. It's how he gained his immortality. Doyle has done it. I have."

"But you're not immortal," he said.

"No, I'm not. But I know who has the stone. Someone who has a blood bond with me."

I thought of all the times I'd bled under Scottie's hand. The amount of my blood he had on his. I prayed it would be enough to call out to him when he returned. It would have to be. Maddox's life might depend on it.

"If you can access the gate to open the door, I know he'll find me."

He eyed me suspiciously. "If I could access the gates to hell, I would've done so long ago."

I eyed him speculatively. "Except you had no reason. The stone wasn't in hell before," I said. "But then you knew that, didn't you? It's why you sent me to tackle Maddox's father. He's had the stone forever."

"Not forever," he said.

"No. He lost it to Fate. Fate gave it to another human man. And then I ended up with it when he gave it to me. Access the gate and you'll see. The man who loves me, who is blooded to me will find me. He'll have the stone."

"And why would I risk one of my greys for that?" he said, nodding at the man who held me.

I knew then what I suspected. He could access the gates. But he'd never been able to trace the stone. He had no bond with it. No way to extract it.

"Because you can't get the stone otherwise," I said.

I'd already thought it through.

"You wanted me to be a conduit for Lilith," I said. "You want to release her from her prison."

"It does take a certain set of prerequisites."

"And one of those prerequisites is that I must have had possession of the stone at some point and used it to enter hell."

"That's true," he said.

"But you also need the stone." I walked along the wall, letting my finger trace a path through the dust on the shelves. "You also needed Doyle," I said.

I gave him a long look. "You don't have the ability to extract Lilith, but you do have the ability to empty the soul from a living vessel in order for her to inhabit it. Doyle will do the rest."

"Why would you care?" he said. "Why would you help me release the goddess?"

"Because my ex--the bastard, may he suffer for all eternity--will be a conduit when he returns, and you can use him to release Lilith."

"And so trap him forever in unyielding, inescapable stone?" he said. "You are a heartless little thing."

"He is a bastard," I said. "And I want you to leave me alone. If I substitute him as a conduit for me, then I'm safe. I don't care what happens to him."

"So," he said. "It's not philanthropy at all. It's self-preservation."

"Exactly. The way I figure it, you have time on your side. As long as that stone has the capabilities it has, and as long as I live, you could come traipsing after me at any time."

He nodded. "I do have long life."

"Exactly," I said. "And I don't. What does it matter to me if some demon is released?"

I spread my arms wide. "I have maybe 50 years left on this earth? I'd like to live them not looking over my shoulder."

He ran his thumb across his chin, leaving smudge marks from the textbook.

"All that remains is to extract the man," he said. "If I could do that, don't you think I would have done so already?"

"Maybe," I said. "If you knew how to contact him. But you don't. You have no way of grasping onto him because you don't know who he is. You have no bond. It's why you need me. It's why you'll do as I ask."

I remembered how so many of the portals, and so many of Lucifer's tortures were bound in blood.

"If it was that easy to go to hell, I'd create my own conduit."

"Really?" I said. "Because it sounds like the round-trip is the problem. Am I right?"

I stared him down. I had the feeling I was on the right track. If he could bleed souls, surely he could tap into them somehow. Regardless of where they were. So long as he had the right key.

I faced him. "Getting in is easy, isn't it?" I said. "When was the last successful round-trip? Before me, I mean? Chu-culain. And he never made it back to the ninth world at all. Lucifer sent him to the sidhe world––out of your reach."

He wore an odd expression as he looked at me but he didn't deny it.

"You're very clever," he said. "You think you've got it all figured out, don't you?"

He pushed himself up from the chair and closed the distance between us.

"You might be right in some ways. My power does stretch and tap into things beyond. I'll make you a bargain. I'll send in a minion to get your friend, but you must wait here as insurance."

I gave it a lot of thought. Was there a catch?

"So you don't want to send me to hell?"

"Why would I want to send a perfectly good conduit in case things don't work out. I have generations to wait for the stone to return."

"But I can get it back for you now."

He chuckled. "Then maybe we can make a bargain. You do know that the only way to travel to the first world is to die right?"

"Not the only way," I said. "The stone."

"A stone we don't have, but there is a way in. One gate available to all the worlds."

I nodded. I'd been expecting that.

"The death gate," he said.

At that he took a step toward me, and I knew in that moment exactly who he wanted to send through the death gate. Not a grey. Not himself.

Me.

CHAPTER 26

I sat in a dank and stinking basement, lit only by braziers whose light flickered along the cement walls like water tunneling down the side of a sunlit boat. It was like I was living in a cliché horror movie.

A rusted iron cot clung to the left wall, out of my reach. Not that I would have lain on it. The mattress was stained with mould and sunk down in the middle so far that I knew the old-fashioned springs had let go years earlier.

The only thing missing was the scuttling sound of mice. But that was replaced by the hum of a clothes dryer busily spinning its contents around the bin.

I suppose even dark alchemists needed to do laundry.

I hugged my knees to my chest, laid my chin on top of them. I wasn't sure what time it was. I wasn't even sure how long I had been chained here.

All I knew was that I was hungry. Thirsty.

Dog-tired.

I was shackled at the ankles by a length of rusty chain embedded in the mortar that held the stones together. It was laughable, really. I'd picked the lock within half an hour, then carefully arranged the chain to hide the fact that I was free.

I could hear Absalom and his greys preparing upstairs for the ritual in anticipation of Scottie's arrival with the Lilith stone.

He'd taken great pleasure in explaining to me as he shoved me down the stairs that it wasn't just any old conduit Lilith would need. She would require a feminine one. So Scottie was out, but I'd do just fine, and since I'd been helpful enough to provide the blood he needed to bond to Scottie, his ritual could take place within the hour.

I wasn't sure what the heck they were doing up there, but it was noisy business. Every so often I heard heavy objects being dragged across the floor. Terrible smells were coming from up there, too. Leaking through the lintel of the ill-fitting door that itself from the basement where I was being held.

There was one small window to my right, small enough that I could scurry myself through it if I could reach it, but I was short and it was well above my head. The only other thing besides me in the basement was that ratty old bed. Trying to drag that across the entire basement wouldn't do much more than make unwanted noise.

Besides, it would be ridiculous to try and escape while there was still a chance that Scottie and the stone could be retrieved. And while I was pretty sure I could sneak my way up the stairs without alerting Absalom or his greys, I wasn't exactly sure what they were doing up there.

For all I knew, I might be running straight into a trap on my way out the door.

So I waited. Eventually they would come down the stairs. I doubted they wouldn't lock the door behind them because they would expect me to be chained.

I looked around the cell holding me, telling myself patience was a virtue. What I was doing was the right thing. But all the while in the back of my mind, a little voice kept telling me it was foolish to wait.

A trip to hell and back wasn't something that could be made every day. What in the name of heaven made me think pulling Scottie out of there was even possible? There was no way he was getting out. All Absalom had done was send the grey to his eternal torment.

But the sounds coming from upstairs and the smells of sulfur and something else I couldn't name bolstered my hope, sending threads of it out like cobwebs.

I was rocking back and forth with my knees to my chest when lightning crackled through the chamber, like the sound of thick material being torn apart. I had to stopper up my ears with my hands to protect them from screams that cut through the air.

Every hair on my body strained to attention, the muscles tensed. I felt as though I was hurtling through another portal.

The next instant, a man dropped through open space onto the cement floor in front of me.

He lay cowering in a ball with his knees pulled up tight to his chest, arms wrapped around his shins as he protected his core. His head was tucked so tightly with his chin in that all I could see was a blondish shock of hair. Clots of blood clung to the locks, with one of them hanging down by a thread of viscous fluid that looked like spit and tissue.

Convulsions wracked his body and whatever part of him that wasn't shivering was spasming. His clothes were torn into ragged strips that reminded me of the tatters of mummy rags. Where his skin showed through, it was burned and boiled and bloody.

It was a horrific sight, one that made the bile rise to my throat, but even as it did, I realized with some satisfaction that his fists were clenched tightly together. Because I knew who it was by those fists.

It took Scottie a moment to realize something was different about where he was. I wasn't sure if he felt the coolness of the room instead of the burning blaze of hell he'd been in, or if whatever torture device Lucifer used on him had ceased its assault on his skin.

He lifted his gaze cautiously as he registered that his surroundings were different. He peered out from between his knees with obvious trepidation, lifting his gaze to look around him.

He spied me and I saw the recognition in his gaze.

"What in the hell?" he said.

"Not anymore," I said and was surprised to hear it come out as no more than a hoarse croak.

To say the man had been brutal to me was an understatement. But still, this was a man, after all. A mortal human being with pain sensors, a psyche, and a soul. I knew what that trip to Hell had done to me, what it cost me, and I wasn't sure he would ever be the same.

My heart hurt for the things he'd endured, knowing I had put the stone within his reach as a means to distance myself from guilt. I'd told myself it was his choice, his fate, to make, and that whatever happened would be on him.

I couldn't shake the fact that I had been the catalyst and the guilt ate at me.

But there was something else, too. I felt hope that maybe he would be different after the experience. Now that his body was out of physical danger, he could be grateful.

Maybe he'd change.

His eyes landed on me and I reached out for him, the chains rattling. Footsteps sounded above me. They had heard his arrival.

"It's okay," I murmured to him. He was like a wild animal, eyes darting about, muscles tensed and ready to leap into flight or fight. I could see his throat convulse as he tried to swallow down the adrenaline.

"Sis?" he whispered.

"Yes, it's me." I waggled my fingers at him, encouraging him the way I might a wild rabbit.

"It's all right, Scottie," I said. "Come here. Come to me."

I squirmed forward slowly on my bottom to meet him, wanting to help close the distance between us but not wanting to scare him.

He began to crawl forward on his hands and knees. My heart lurched when I saw how swollen his face was. I couldn't imagine how he could see through the slits that were his eyes.

The door opened at the top of the stairs; I could hear the sound of it being wrenched open. I waved my fingers at him.

"Please, Scottie," I said. "Come closer. I won't hurt you. You're safe with me."

Absalom's voice sounded from the top of the stairs. Feet, shod in strange looking Persian type slippers, scuffed on the treads.

"What's this?" He demanded. "You're not one of mine. Where is my grey?"

He was rigid with suppressed anger.

"Come to me, Scottie," I said, dragging my eyes from Absalom's face and pinning them to Scottie's eyes. I needed to reach him. His body was here, but his spirit was still running afraid.

I tried not to sound afraid or rushed, but I knew why his fist was clenched. I knew why he was here, why he looked so afraid.

"Come to me," I said.

If Scottie would have trusted anyone in that state, it would be me. He scurried forward no matter how much doing so must have hurt, and I reached for him and pulled him close, cradling him the way I might a child.

I ran my hands down along his torn shirt, pulling at the tatters, drawing them closed over his skin. It must've been what he was wearing when he'd been taken.

A piece of his shirt tore off in my hand.

Absalom rushed down the stairs, two greys following.

"You're safe now," I said to Scottie. "I've got you."

I put my hand over his, Tapping his fingers the way I would a child who had picked up something dangerous. It opened obediently and the stone dropped into my palm, nestling nicely in the scrap of shirt that protected my skin from its touch.

"He's been assaulting me," I whispered in a ragged voice. "He thinks I'm *his* bitch, not yours."

If the feral animal in Scottie was roused by anything, it was jealousy. Now with fear and rage added to the mix, it roared to the surface.

I knew what he'd just been through. I imagined it was all the horrors that I could imagine and more. But I also knew Scottie would need to strike out in response. The man in him could only survive if the animal could fight for him.

Scottie would have made a great shifter. He gave over to that part of himself frequently – and not just to save himself. It was part of his nature. He lived and thrived to control.

He wanted his vengeance. He didn't need an excuse to exact it, but he would want it all the same.

I watched him struggle to his feet, and I thought I saw the ghost of a smile play across his lips as the two greys charged at him. The animal in him knew better than I did how important it was for him to reclaim his ferocity.

He wasn't a victim. He would never be a victim. And he wasn't about to let the things Lucifer had done to him turn him into one.

The moment Scottie launched himself at Absalom and his greys, was the same moment I hurled myself toward the stairs.

I heard Absalom cry out to one of his greys to grab me, and I ran like fire was licking at my heels, thudding my way up the stairs, stumbling twice before I managed to get to the top.

I couldn't catch myself as I stumbled against the door, trying to open it with closed fists. I had the real stone in one hand, and the fake in the other. I couldn't let either of them go.

I had to use my wrists and the friction of skin to open the door. Too much sweat made my grip a slick, ineffectual thing.

Scottie roared, an aching, animalistic sound that reverberated in my chest and buckled my knees.

I had to get the door open. The thing wouldn't budge.

The wet and harsh sounds of struggle preceded that of a meaty sounding thwack. Someone or something hit the floor.

Hard.

I prayed it wasn't Scottie.

I worked at the knob and cast a harried glance down the stairs. The bed was on its side, mattress separated from its partner. The springs of the iron frame clawed at the air. One of the legs was missing.

A quick scan of the rest of the room showed me the leg was planted in the grey's stomach. What should have been blood pooling from the wound looked more like tar.

Absalom, face suffused with rage, stood over the puddle that formed. A thread of light stretched from his fingertips to the fluid.

I was transfixed, unable to make a move.

Scottie pounded up the steps behind me.

"It's a fucken lever, Sis," he bellowed. "Yank on it."

He reached past me and pulled the knob upward and pushed me through the maw as the door shrieked open. We both fell through the door into the apothecary shop.

I twisted my leg when he landed on top of me but I didn't have time to inspect the damage or cradle the pain. He pushed me to my feet, shoving me forward so powerfully, I gobbled up three steps in one from the sheer force of it.

"Run, Sis," he said, breathless with adrenaline. "I don't know what the fuck is going on or even if I'm dreaming the shit out of all this but there's no fucken way I'm living through hell to let a pussy in slippers take me out."

I had to give it to Scottie. He'd always been a take charge sort of guy. Nothing short of death would keep him from winning. Competition fueled his heart beat and danger was the pool he dipped his toes into for refreshment.

I hadn't exactly banked on his fierce brawler spirit, but I was grateful for it.

One look over my shoulder showed him barring the door with both arms, giving me time to propel myself deeper into the shop.

"Holy fuck," he said to the opening of the doorway.

That was it. Two words to describe the mangy looking, greyish coyote that leapt from the basement stairs at him. It was three times the size it should be, and it had Absalom's long mane of silver hair. I gaped as its mouth unhinged and dripped brackish looking saliva onto the floor. Where it landed, the floor sizzled and hissed.

I thought the beast was going to swallow Scottie's head.

It snapped his forward, aiming for Scottie. But Scottie was a fighter. He knew how to dodge a blow. He fell backward just in time.

A brawler Scottie might be, but he was used to having back-up. It had been years since he had engaged in hand-to-hand combat of any sort. And that combat had been fists, feet, and the occasional weapon.

I wasn't sure how effective he would be against soulless zombies more dogged than a Pitbull and more deadly than a wiry accountant refusing to cook the books.

All I knew was I had to run.

My elbow yelped as I smashed into a shelf, and realized I was still running, so intent on what was going on behind me, that I wasn't watching where I was going.

I clambered over the mess of skulls and mortars, pestles, vials of powder and liquid. My feet squished into fluids that drained onto the floor. I sneezed as the powders rose to dust into my nose.

I fled the shop, pulling things from the shelves with my fists and kicking things ahead of me as I went. Crystal orbs shattered as they struck the door. I could see the street, people milling past. Taxi cabs blared horns and people, regular everyday human people cursed and laughed.

A sob fled my lungs.

I was almost there. I prayed it would be enough. I prayed Scottie wasn't already dead.

But I didn't stop to turn around. I didn't stop to look over my shoulder. I didn't have time to wonder if Maddox felt the re-entry of the stone to the mortal plane and would know he was saved from a Hellish journey.

I just flung myself headlong toward the door.

CHAPTER 27

At first, the only thing I heard behind me was the door slamming shut.

As I skidded to a stop in front of the apothecary shop, scanning this way and that for best escape route, I felt worry for Scottie raising a rash of thoughts in my mind. I would never have taken him for a knight in shining armour, but he had just saved me. Given me a chance to save my life in an act of selfless chivalry.

I owed him. What had begun as a way to give Maddox an out, had ended with an unexpected realization that my ex could be compassionate.

The thought gobbled up all my mental gears and I wasn't sure how to react.

The sun was sinking down over the buildings, casting a fiery glow across the brooding sky line. The streets were emptying out of people who had been working for the day and were going home for supper.

It was filling up with nightwalkers, but not enough that I could disappear into the crowds. Certainly not with a chupacabra hot on my heels if Absalom stayed in that form at all. I wasn't sure how the shapeshifting thing worked. Would he have control? Could he change at will?

I dimly wondered if someone would spot the beast and call animal control.

I skirted to the side, pressing my back flat against the brick wall of the building in case Absalom came rushing out at me. I didn't expect the mangy animal to hang sideways before it burst forth. A man, maybe. He might be more careful, inspecting the area the hopes of finding direction I'd gone. It gave me maybe, what?, Three minutes?

At best.

I edged along the bricks, feeling my way with my fingers as I kept my eye on the door. Fear thudded against my chest. My breath was coming in rasps.

When the door creaked open, reflex almost let escape a shriek of surprise and fear, but I bit down on it, sucking in a breath and holding it.

Someone did burst out of the door, but it wasn't Absalom or the chupacabra. It was Scottie. And he panned his gaze left, not right, knowing exactly which way I would go because he knew my habits, my nature.

He swung his gaze along the brick wall to find me, my eyes straining wide at his exit, unable to shutter down because of the fear.

"I thought I told you to run," he said. "Get moving, Sis."

And then he was coming at me, full-tilt.

"I don't know what the fuck that was or what's going on," he said, "but there's two more of them."

He shoved at me so that I staggered ahead of him, surprised by the sudden force. When I almost fell, he grabbed me by the elbow and yanked me along with him as he sprinted down the alleyway.

"We have to hide out somewhere," he said. "Lay low."

His breathing was ragged and he was limping, and even if his gait was somewhat slower than normal, the power in his arms was unmistakable.

He yanked me along without concern for my welfare or whether I was stumbling or stopping. The grip he had on my elbow was so ferocious it hurt as it dug in.

We rounded another corner, one that led into the bowels of the seedier part of town. A streetlight sizzled to life around us and he swore at it, muttering something about being too bright. They'd see us.

"Get over there," he said and pushed me into the shadows where the glow couldn't reach. He stood beneath it, bathed in light, almost taunting whatever decided to burst into the mouth of the alley like an old-fashioned bait and switch.

He planned to distract whatever came around the corner.

And come it did. It wasn't the chupacabra, though, and for that I was grateful. Instead, what rounded into the opening from the street were three greys, this time brawnier than the last.

I wasn't sure where Absalom had kept them, or how many he had at his whim, but they took one look at Scottie standing beneath the wash of streetlamp and they tore for him.

Scottie held his position. I stuffed my hand in my mouth, biting down on my fingers to keep from shouting.

Absalom strolled along behind, his long silver hair swinging behind him in the breeze. It was like watching a horror movie in a disco setting. One moment he was lit by light, the next he was swallowed up in shadow.

Scottie waited until the greys were several feet from him before he came to life.

He was exhausted, and I knew he was. And yet he marshaled the strength he needed to fight them off. One by one they went down, not with the grace of battle that Maddox had, but in brutal and cruel fakes and jabs that spoke of his street savvy and the decades of bringing men to heel.

When the last of them fell at his feet, I could see that the adrenaline had long drained from his body and he was acting purely on instinct and determination. His movements were slow and he had a drugged look to his face as he swung about, tracking my movements, searching for one more opponent to attack.

Absalom halted, his head canted to the side, and I realized whatever he was doing, it would inevitably end in more greys rounding that corner.

"We need to get out of here, Scottie," I said to him. "You need to rest. We need to run."

Scottie hated running. It was my thing. He made fun of me over the years for hightailing it with my tail between my legs. This time, I ran for Scottie and wrapped my arm around his shoulders.

I hauled him with me. This time it was him stumbling over the cobblestones being dragged along. I hailed a cab and made it zigzag through the streets until it came upon the first hotel I could find.

The lobby was filthy. Several kindred hung about. I was getting good at recognizing them now. I didn't care. It was only moments away from the alley, but it would have to do. Both of us were fading.

"I need a room," I barked at the clerk.

"Cash only," he said without lifting a brow.

"The regular rate in advance or scads of it later?" I said.

He looked us over. "Scads of it later," he said.

I'd lost my cell phone, but there was no doubt a phone in the room. I'd call Maddox or, failing that, my landlord. Bar the damn door. Recuperate for a few hours. Maybe get some sleep.

Scottie wasn't ready for sleep. Exhausted as he was, he was amped up on endorphins and his body wasn't about to give in to what it so desperately needed that his blinks resembled a cartoon.

"Isabella," Scottie whispered. "What was all that?"

I laid him backwards on the bed and peeled off his bloody socks. "Never mind," I said. "I'll explain later. Right now you need rest."

His shoulders were hunched and he sagged over his lap. Spent of adrenaline, he didn't have the energy to lift his face to mine. He just numbly let me peel his ragged and bleeding clothes off him.

He lifted one arm so I could drag the sleeve off before pulling it across his back and down the other arm. His hands fell limply to the bed. He reminded me of a boxer who had taken too many blows to the head. Punch drunk.

I wondered at the willpower that kept him upright.

"Just lie back," I said and lifted his feet sideways onto the mattress. He collapsed backwards onto the pillow.

"What's going on?" he said. "Did I really just see all that?" His words were slurred and mumbled.

"You touched the weapon, didn't you," I said, giving him the best explanation I could. "I told you it was dangerous."

"The bag," he said. "I put it in the safe. But it kept calling to me."

I ran my fingers across his forehead, sweeping his hair back and blotting aside clots of blood from his cheek. His eyes were still a remarkable shade of blue. My breath caught in my throat. Whatever I thought of him, whatever brutish things he'd done over his years, he had risked it all to save me.

"Thank you," I whispered and leaned over to plant a moth of a kiss on the least bruised place on his cheek.

He was already comatose when I lifted my head.

I let go a heavy sigh. I needed a shower. But more than that I needed rest. And there was the phone. I really should call Maddox. If not just to make sure he hadn't taken that railroad trip to Hell in a handbasket.

All intentions aside, I woke up--I wasn't sure how many hours later--lying across the bed with my arm over Scottie's waist.

He was turned in to face me. Those piercing blue eyes, not so many hours earlier drugged and bloodshot, were now bright and inquisitive.

"That rock was able to do all of that?" he said.

I nodded, my face scraping against the satin pillowcase.

"And what exactly was it all about?" he said, his brow creased with the intrigue. He was already measuring out how it could benefit him.

Looking at him so close, I knew I couldn't lie to him. I explained as much as I could without giving him too many details. The gist of it was the stone was able to send the handler to hell, that there was a supernatural world parallel to our own. That goblins and vampires and banshees were real.

I did not tell him he had come a hair's breadth from immortality.

He listened without interrupting until I finished and he stared at me for a long while, digesting it all.

"My throat is a ragged mess," he said, coughing through the words.

I fingered the candy bowl and found a cherry flavored cough drop.

I held it in my grasp as I regarded him. We'd just lain together for hours and I was no worse the wear. He seemed different somehow. Maybe I wanted it to be so or maybe Hell had mellowed him.

I climbed onto the bed and kneed my way toward him. He watched me with half slitted eyes until I unwrapped the candy and pinched it between my fingers. Then he popped open his mouth like a baby bird and I laid the lozenge on his tongue.

He sucked the candy, his cheeks hollowing in. A small sound of pleasure rumbled through his chest.

"Better?" I said.

He eased his eyes closed and nodded.

He looked so damn broken. There was nothing vicious about the man that lay there.

He'd been ravaged by a fight that must have cracked open his very soul and left it to bleed like an egg from its shell. He wore the struggle of it in the set of his shoulders, the way his leg lay crookedly against the bedspread. Exhaustion and the effort of breathing made his skin sallow.

The Scottie of my youth peeked out from the shadows of the pain that crested and let go on his face. He winced with each movement and held his left arm tightly against his stomach like a broken wing.

And yet he'd survived.

And then he'd risked his life once more.

For me.

Something in me cracked. I found myself lying down next to him, snuggling in tight the way I'd done for years in the early morning. My memory jogged back to a sunny kitchen, the smell of fragrant coffee fingering its way down the hall, the happy sound of him snoring next to me while I waited for him to wake up.

The times after that didn't matter. I wanted him to change, to soften, and maybe if I wanted that, I had to offer him the same thing.

Forgiveness.

I think I sniffled.

"Poor Sis," he murmured. "All alone through all that."

I raised my eyes to see him looking at me.

"You believe me?"

"Fuck," he said. "I lived it."

He ran the back of his knuckles over the crest of my cheek. "You shouldered that all alone?" he said. "My brave Sis. Such a warrior."

The pad of his thumb whispered along the line of my bottom lip, tracing the ridge until his palm found my cheek. He heeled his hand until it burrowed in my hair, and he cupped the nape of my neck with his palm.

"Alone," he whispered.

His voice touched something deep inside. A place I'd forgotten existed, one where I was safe in his arms, safe in his world. My eyes welled, looking at him. Bruised, still bloody, his face showed concern and grief for what I'd gone through.

He pulled me close and laid his forehead against mine.

"I'm so sorry," he said. "Fuck, I'm so, so sorry."

His breath swept my cheek and perfumed the air around us with cherry.

My whole body was clenched in a fist of confused anxiety.

I didn't know this man, and yet I did. I knew the curve of his cheek. My heart had once touched the most intimate parts of his. I knew he checked his toes for fungus when he showered. I knew he was worried about cancer.

And now I knew he'd come face to face with his own mortality. I knew he'd seen the devil.

Had he come out of it stronger and resigned or had he realized how weak we all are in the face of death? Did he find empathy in Lucifer's fists?

I dug into my pocket and pulled out the fake stone. I held it in the air over the both of us. Absalom had done a fine job of creating an exact duplicate. The ruby colored blood drop in the center winked when it hit the light.

Take it," I said. "It's safer with you than with me."

I thought it might be a good memento of the struggle he'd endured, of the man who could face all that and come out better for it.

He nodded and let me lay it on his chest.

"I'm going to shower," I said. "You stay here and rest."

He eyed me but said nothing. Instead, his gaze kept lighting on the stone as his brow creased a heavy line over and over again into his forehead.

CHAPTER 28

When I came out of the shower, wrapped in a large, if not ratty bath sheet, he was putting the phone back on the cradle.

"What's up?" I asked him, rubbing the hand towel through my hair. It felt glorious to be clean and even though the cheap hotel soap had a strong perfume that burned my nose, it was far better than sweat and grime.

The buoyancy of my mood was a miracle all in itself.

"Lance is coming to pick us up," he said.

My feet refused to move any further. I caught the name and didn't need to know who he was or what he was to Scottie. He'd replaced Alvin. He was the one who stun gunned me as a proxy threat by Scottie.

"What do you mean, us?" I said.

He rolled over on the bed to face me, his feet falling to the scruffy carpet. His hands rand down the length of his thighs, smoothing out the holes in his jeans.

"I didn't exactly arrive in a limo," he said and squinted at me. "And I don't have a single dollar in my pockets to pay for a cab."

I wasn't aware I'd dropped the towel to the floor until he leaned over to retrieve it and wrapped it back around me. The other part of his statement, the far worse one than the fact that a sociopath was coming to pick me up, was the fact that Scottie still assumed there was a 'we'.

"I thought we agreed on a sabbatical," I said.

He took to his feet the way a fighter did, with a determination that challenged exhaustion.

"All that is changed," he said. "I can't leave you alone now," he said. "What kind of man do you think I am?"

"A man of your word?" I said, biting the sentence through my teeth.

My stomach knotted up.

"I'm not going anywhere with you, Scottie," I said. "I've made a life here –"

There was no sound from him of protest or insult. Just the noise the carpet made as he stormed the distance to me. He gripped my wet hair in his fist and pulled me sideways, making me cringe and hunker down as the pain shredded through the nerves in my scalp.

He dragged me the few feet to the bed and threw me hard enough that I bounced twice before landing in the centre. The well-worn and threadbare towel wrapped around my midriff came open and he gripped the corner of it, pulling it out from beneath me in one motion that burned the skin of my backside.

"I just risked my life for you," he said. "I faced off against God knows what, and you have the nerve to disobey me. You're an ungrateful bitch, Isabella."

"It's not disobedience, Scottie," I said, crawling backwards up to the headboard and trying to swing my legs over the other side of the bed while at the same time trying ineffectually to cover myself up.

He gripped the edge of the towel and snapped it at me, landing a painful bite into my inner thigh. I sucked in a hissing breath and bit down on the cry that lodged in my throat. I rubbed at the sting ferociously.

It surprised me, that flare of temper, a mercurial thing as predictable as the toss of a coin. But it shouldn't have.

His tongue darted out to the corner of his mouth as though he was tasting the temperature of my fear. For a second, I glimpsed the old Scottie, and I inched away like a worm, covering my hips with one hand and my breasts with the other.

That seemed to inflame him all the more.

A low grumble rolled in his throat.

"What in the hell is your problem, Sis?"

He shot over the bed and grappled for my wrist, yanking my hand away from my breasts and holding it out sideways. "I've seen those little apples before. I know every inch of them."

He grabbed for my other hand, yanking it away from my hips as he parted my legs with his powerful knees.

"I know that slipper too. I've worn it a good many times." He rocked his hips against mine. "Since when do you hide from me. I OWN that shit."

I swallowed down my protest, knowing exactly what it would gain me. He lowered himself over me, boxing me in and pinning me down. I lost my breath. Terror climbed the ladder of my spine.

"Please," I said. "Please don't."

"I'm not going to rape you, for fuck's sake," he ground out. "You make it sound like I'm a monster."

It was on the tip of my tongue to say he was a monster, but I bit down on the words and went as docile as I could. I hid somewhere inside, behind that new veneer of empathy, scolding myself for falling for it again. Falling for it the way I always had.

And even that didn't help.

He tightened his fingers into a vise against my wrist. Tight though it was, it wasn't as strong as I remembered, but I knew it wasn't because he was being gentle with me. He was weakened by effort and exhaustion.

That knowledge, that certainty, was the only thing that enabled me to break free and claw my way out from beneath him.

I made it to the edge of the mattress before his fists came down between my shoulder blades.

The sudden pressure knocked the air from my lungs in a painful exhalation.

"Is this what I get for my trouble?" he complained. "I let you live well. Have a few years to yourself to grow into a woman not a child – and this is what I get back? A mouthy and ungrateful bitch."

Of all the hateful things he said, the only thing I cared about was one word.

"You didn't *let* me," I spat out. "I ran from you, you bastard. You beat me nearly to death. You cracked my tooth. I ran out in the rain in my bare feet for Jesus' sake."

His eyes lit up as though I'd ignited some deep and dormant flame.

"Beat you near to death?" he said. "That was just a lover's spat. It's nowhere near what I'm going to do to you now."

I didn't need to hear anymore. I'd been down this road enough to know every curve and pothole. I'd sped down it at breakneck speed and slammed into the back end of another car. I knew exactly where it went. And I knew exactly how long it would take to get there.

I scrabbled toward the edge of the bed. There were only two things running through my mind.

Get up.

Get out.

Everything else was extraneous.

Shoes, clothes, bits of hair that he tore from my scalp. All of that could be left behind.

I ran for the door. Tired as he was, I underestimated his sense of commitment. He ducked around me and laid his arms over the wall, barring my escape. I landed into him full throttle and his bear-hug lifted me from my feet.

The next I knew, I was sailing across the air toward the bed. I hoped for a cushioned landing, but I struck pay dirt only halfway there. My ribs caught on the edge of the box spring and I fell into a crumpled heap on the floor.

All of the oxygen fled my lungs like rats from a sinking ship. Traitorous, merciless body. I couldn't even catch enough wind to put out the fire in my chest.

Dust rose from the carpet and tickled my nose as though all that happening was a bit of rough sport when my ribs lanced me with pain at every gasp for air.

He loomed over me, watching me intently. I think he knew he hurt me badly. There was even a brief look of concern on his face. I watched his jaw seesaw back and forth.

I blinked at him as though I'd had seven drinks too many, trying to force my body to connect to my mind and do something, anything, to move.

If I could just shimmy the three parts of him that my vision showed me back into one man, I might be able to decide whether he was going to raise his hand again or not.

He flinched when I wiped the corner of my mouth and felt sticky fluid there.

"Drew blood that time," I said with a crooked smile. I coughed wetly. "Nice job."

His jaw clenched when he heard me speak but something in his face shifted.

"Get dressed before I lose my temper."

I laughed at that. I mean what else could I do? It was obvious he'd already lost his temper, and not that he regretted it, but he wanted me to know that it could be worse. So much worse.

I stared him down for a long moment, trying to decide exactly what I should do.

In the end, I crawled my way on hands and knees to the bathroom where I'd left my clothes on the damp tiles.

I plucked my filthy clothes from the floor of the bathroom and pulled them with trembling hands over my legs. I hitched the jeans over my hips and buttoned them. The lump in my pocket gave me pause as I tried to remember why there was something in there.

Then I remembered I'd had two stones: one, the real one, and the other, the fake.

I could have kicked myself for giving him the fake one.

He came into the bathroom before I buttoned the shirt.

"I'm dog tired," he said, raking his fingers through his hair. He bent over to turn on the faucet and I watched the way he winced as he turned on the taps and adjusted the temperature.

"Don't even consider walking out the door while I'm in the shower," he said with all the conviction of a man who believed he'd be obeyed. Maybe he had right to expect it. I had stayed, after all. I'd saved him from Hell.

"You can't hide from me anymore, Isabella. You're coming home. That's it."

I clutched the sink to keep from weaving off my feet. Everything was spinning. My lungs cried out every time I moved.

He peeled off his jeans and shirt, revealing every last cut, abrasion, burn, and bruise Lucifer had inflicted on him. He wanted me to see them, I realized. He wanted me to feel guilty.

"Stuff that stone in your pocket, before we go," he said. "You were right. It has a hell of a kick. We'll get it back home, and we'll figure out how we can use that thing."

I noted his hand trembled as he stuck it beneath the stream of water. Beaten and assaulted, he still wondered how he could use such a weapon to his benefit. He still planned to use it to strike out at someone else.

I blinked at him, wondering if proximity was the same thing as possession. And if so, exactly how long before he became immortal. How long had we been lying there? Hours? A day?

Was it too long already?

"You want me to wash your back?" I said as he climbed over the rim of the tub.

Steam billowed out, misting my face.

He grunted in satisfaction. "Mind the sore spots," he said.

"All right," I said. "Just let me get the stone before I forget."

He chuckled to himself. "Always so absent-minded for someone so smart."

I chuckled with him. "Yeah. I'm not sure what you saw in me."

"A weak little kitten, that's what," he said. "And who doesn't like a kitten?"

I bit back a sob at the word. Maddox leapt to my mind, all six feet four of him. I lifted my chin, pulling in a breath as I felt my way from the bathroom.

I didn't feel like myself as I walked stiff legged straight over to the bed. I didn't look like myself when I caught a glimpse in the dresser's mirror.

My black hair was tangled at the side where he'd gripped it. Blood pooled in the corner of my mouth.

My eyes had a wild, frenzied look.

The fake stone was still nestled into the pillow. If it had been the real one, I wouldn't have been able to touch it. He'd not noticed my bare skin against it as I showed it to him.

He didn't know how the thing worked. He hadn't realized that merely touching the stone had triggered the portal.

I lifted it in front of my face and inspected it.

I weighed it in my hand.

Hefty for such a small thing.

I hadn't realized how heavy, but now that every part of my body ached, it seemed like I was hefting a thousand pounds.

Scottie called out to me from the bathroom. He wanted his back washed.

He hadn't even bothered to close the curtain, just turned back to beneath the spray of water while he hunched over as though every droplet was a needle in his skin.

"I've never been so sore," he complained. "Hurry up. I can't take much more."

The first strike of the stone hit him behind the ear, and while he slumped forward, he didn't collapse completely.

And it was too late to turn back.

I hit him again.

This time over the eye socket. His hands went up to defend against the blow, reaching for my wrists.

I fell into the tub with him, the spray of soap making me slippery.

I didn't stop fighting until the soapy water turned the bottom of the tub red and then pink.

I stared into the tub, my eyes traveling his unmoving form but I didn't see him. Not really. He was just a bit of naked flesh.

"I'm not weak anymore," I said. "And I won't ever be your victim or anyone else's ever again."

CHAPTER 29

There was something wrong with me. I felt like a wooden puppet being strung along a cardboard stage, marionette strings lifting one foot after the other.

It was as though someone else decided to check my pockets for the Lilith stone, and finding it still wrapped snugly in its rag, grunted with an almost primal sense of relief.

Someone else's hand, bloody and trembling, reached for the door knob and twisted it.

Someone else waited for the clicking sensation of release as the lever withdrew like a clam inside the belly of its shell.

If the door swung open noiselessly, I couldn't have been sure if it did because its hinges were well greased or if I simply couldn't hear any more.

The floral wallpaper of the hallway and its gaudy broad-leaved border seemed to be growing in, creating a lush forest of the stinking hallway.

I thought of Pan and his nymphs and I laughed, a sound that cut out in my throat like a motor gagging on bad fuel.

I stood in the middle of the doorway, half in and half out of the hotel room for a long time, watching those flowers waltz with an invisible breeze. A small light blinked and changed color somewhere to my right.

I turned, deadpan and stunned, toward it.

My puppeteer lifted one foot after the other in the direction of the light, but the strings offered only awkward movement and I ended up shuffling along the hallway carpet. Each step dug free the smell of a thousand dirty feet and lifted it to my nose, rasped accusations in my ear.

I'd gone into shock once before. Scottie had lost his cool unexpectedly when a delivery boy, one of the University students he employed as the fourth in a networking chain to drop off a booklet of numbers that included everything from payments to gambling bids.

Three of us had been sitting in a crushed leather booth at one of his more upscale bars. One moment we were laughing, the next Scottie's phone rang and he answered it.

There was silence on the other end for several moments, I could hear the tension of that vacuum, and at first I wondered why Scottie didn't just hang up. But then I caught the sound of someone sniffling from the sender's end, and I realized it hadn't been silence after all, but quiet and barely controlled weeping.

Scottie said nothing. His knuckles went white and his lips paled, but he didn't say a word into his end of the phone. He just flipped it closed and laid it on the table in front of him.

The delivery boy dropped his booklet down onto the table next to Scottie's phone with a smack that was too loud in the dead quiet of the room.

It was the thing that ignited Scottie's fuse, and in the next instant, he exploded from the booth, charging in his direction. The boy took a step backward. Just one. Then Scottie was on him, and in a flurry of hands and feet, began to pummel the poor boy.

I think I saw blood fly. I know I heard bones break with the sickening sound of a dog chewing on a knuckle of pig's feet.

I'll never remember what happened immediately after that. Someone told me the boy lived, and learned to walk again after a year of rehabilitation. At the time, I just think my mind went on a lovely vacation, letting me sail down a sunlit highway with the ocean on both sides, throwing up diamonds to shine in the sun.

But I do remember with the clarity of a crystal clear lake wavering over shining stones, the moment reality returned. And it was a small thing, really. A very tiny, probably insignificant detail that put the brakes on that little vacation of hurtling down the summer highway with the wind in my hair.

A droplet of water on the outside of my glass as it condensed and slipped down the surface. The trail beaded down to the table where my hand lay, palm down. The coolness of the wet touched my finger and I realized my fingernails were digging into the tabletop.

Now, another small detail thrummed the strings of memory, but it was the bright chime of a bell and the sound of elevator doors whooshing open.

Everything snapped into focus the way a camera's diopter shifts over the crosshairs.

I caught sight of Lance exiting the silver doors.

I held my breath. There was no coming back from what I'd done. Would Scottie's man exact revenge, or did he even care? He wouldn't involve the police, I knew that, but what exactly does a crime organization do when its leader is murdered?

Murdered.

Oh God. I couldn't just stand there waiting for him to see me.

I had to run.

Thankfully, he panned right, away from me.

I took that moment to slip away, down the stairwell and when I eased the door closed behind me, I ran like the devil was on my tail all the way down to the lobby.

If I expected normalcy down there, then I was a fool.

The lobby was deathly quiet. I skimmed the area with a nervous gaze. The clerk who checked us in stood like a statue, his fingers steepled on the check-in desk while he stared ahead at nothing. The bellhop, the concierge, the doorman, all stood at attention but facing into the lobby as though they didn't care if anyone came in through the front doors.

The front doors.

Four men stood in front of each of them, their backs creating an impenetrable barrier between the lobby in the street.

Something was wrong, but whatever it was, it had to have happened between the time Lance strode through it and the time I ran down the stairwell.

I could hear myself swallowing repeatedly.

The door clicked closed behind me and all eyes gathered to where I stood, frozen like a deer being jacked in a 4 x 4's headlights.

"Don't move, Isabella," I heard someone say. Doyle's voice. I was sure of it. But what was he doing here? How had he found me?

I didn't dare move, but I didn't like the idea of the door behind me so close. If Lance came through it he'd find me standing just inches away.

I gathered my courage--at least, the tatters that I could manage--and swung my gaze in the direction of Doyle's voice.

There. In the lounge part of the lobby where the builders had erected a small coffee bar with plush leather seats and sofas. The shirt Maddox had given him had been washed but not ironed. The cuffs were rolled up nearly to his elbows, showing off thick forearms with a dusting of salt and pepper hair. He stood surrounded by a cluster of greys.

Opposite him, Absalom spread his arms across the back of a buttoned down leather sofa. His legs were crossed one knee over the other. He waggled one foot in the air. A steaming mug of coffee sat on the table beside him.

"Come," Absalom said. "Join us."

"I think I'd rather get my coffee from Starbucks," I said.

He chuckled without a trace of humor. "It will be a pity to lose such razor sharp wit."

He flicked a finger in my direction and both the concierge and the bellhop advanced on me.

I decided I'd rather go on my own steam then be wrestled between those revolting clutches. I might have simply run if it was just me, but there was Doyle.

"Can I at least sit down," I said to Absalom when I drew close enough to smell the tea tree oil he put in his hair and the coffee beans that sat in large glass canisters. "I've had a rather rough day."

I met Doyle's eyes and I was perplexed to see that he didn't look the least bit sheepish or afraid.

Rather, there was a proud set to his shoulders.

It should have offered me comfort, but it didn't. I felt resigned, instead. Maybe he did too. Going down with dignity, I guessed.

Absalom shifted on the couch, nestling in for comfort, I supposed, or just to show me he was so casually confident about his control of the situation that he didn't need to get up.

I considered telling him I'd just killed a man.

"You've been difficult to find," he said. "But luckily, where the stone is, the master follows." He rounded his neck to skim a look over to Doyle.

Doyle's blue eyes pinned to mine. Something flickered in their depths as he lifted his shoulders in half a shrug. A coy sigh eased out from his lips.

"It's like a phantom limb," he said. "I knew it was in the ninth world again. Damn thing is worse than a rash."

He nodded down to his forearm, where a similar mark to Maddox's had raised into a painful looking weal. I could almost see it pulsing with his heartbeat, and it looked like a worm undulating over his skin, seeking blindly something to sustain its life.

I nodded silently. So he'd tracked the stone, probably knowing Absalom would too. Had he known he'd find me and end up giving Absalom everything he needed to complete the ritual, or was he just led by the stone, the way a salmon is to its spawning grounds?

I knew the end was inevitable. I'd drained the last of my adrenaline running from Lance. I could feel a pinch in my flanks where my kidneys twitched and a burning had begun to radiate down to my hips.

I supposed it was always going to come down to something like this. Escaping Scottie, escaping Lucifer. Who did I think I was anyway? People like me didn't just walk away from brutes like that. They didn't make new lives. And if they did, their deeds caught up with them eventually.

But was I going to just give up after all that, through? I'd worked hard to live.

I felt my fingers twitch against my leg, and they struck the stone within my pocket. I had one last gambit.

"I'll break the damn thing," I said. "Shatter it into a thousand pieces."

Absalom leaned forward, propping his elbows against his knees. "Doesn't matter," he said. Stone or sand, all you will do is make a hell of a mess."

"Sure," I said. "But Lilith will be in as many pieces."

Doyle made a snorting sound, drawing my attention. He shrugged as he caught my eye. "Can you see your soul?" he said. "Can you pinpoint where it is?"

Absalom rose from the sofa, leaning over to pick up his coffee cup. He drained it and then flung it aside, where it struck the coffee bar and split in half.

"Time is up," he said. "We already completed the prelude to the ritual. All I need now is you."

Before I could protest, he drew in a long and shuddering breath. I felt my lungs burn. They bellowed out so far that the straining of the tissues made my throat hurt.

I blinked at Doyle, willing him with my eyes to do something.

I was suspended there, unable to exhale, feeling as though I'd become buoyant on the currents of air.

With a shock, I realized my feet had left the floor. I was slowly arching backwards, my solar plexus straining toward Absalom.

I lost my contact with Doyle, and that terrified me.

A low frequency hum began to move through the greys, like a series of tuning forks finding a perfect and synchronized a note. I was arched so far backwards that my spine had begun to crack. I couldn't hold my head aloft and it hung there, tying my neck muscles into a dozen knots as I fought gravity.

From beside me I heard Doyle choking and then as though he were struggling to keep his vocal chords from vibrating, sounds came from his throat that might have been language but that was foreign and filled with enough consonants that it would be impossible for a linguist to pronounce. The words sounded more like pained utterances of expressed agony.

The stone grew hot in my pocket. It rose in temperature until I felt as though the rag surrounding it had burned away to nothing and that it had set fire to my jeans.

The skin on my thigh felt numb, as though it had been dunked into ice water.

And then the incredible pain of freezing erupted around my leg.

I wanted to scream. Hung there, with my face pointed toward the doors, and my throat closed off, I couldn't make more than gurgling sounds.

Tears dripped from my eyes onto the floor.

My shoulders ached from the suspension.

And then something changed in the greys' tone. Something seemed missing, it was less of a swell.

Doyle had stopped chanting.

From upside down, I could make out a pair of legs rush across the room toward us. A second pair sprinted along not two feet behind. For one second, I glimpsed a studded iron mace swinging on its chain. The stomach-churning sound of bone against iron clawed through the air.

Something cut through my core.

I dropped in one second of terrifying freefall.

Pain bit into my shoulder as I thudded to the floor. I let go a howl of pain.

I couldn't move. I'd broken my neck. Broken my back. Maybe I was already dead.

And yet I was pulling in hitching breaths, trying to re-condition my lungs to breathe again and pull in the oxygen my muscles needed. Prickles of oxygen scattered through my tissues like puzzle pieces thrown in anger.

My vision cleared, but I felt foggy. Like I was searching for an image of myself through a haze of fog. Where was the mirror? I needed a reflecting pool, a steel pan, a spoon for heaven's sake, I just needed beyond everything to *see* myself.

A grey fell in front of me. I jumped in reaction and pain lanced down my shoulder and into my back. I bit down on the outcry, terrified he would reach out for me while I couldn't defend myself.

But his face stared just into mine, the blackness of his eyes wavering into a beautiful green.

His mouth was agape and worms wriggled from beneath his tongue. I gagged and struggled to push myself onto my hands and knees. My palms slipped on something fluid. Blood. His blood. It was only then that I realized his skull had been crushed from behind.

I felt myself swaying from the threat of passing out. I thought I heard my name. It grounded me. Telling me to get up.

Dumbfounded, I skimmed my gaze around me.

Fayed, covered in blood head to toe, was tearing into the throat of a grey. There was no scream, no proof that the man he'd been resided any longer in the zombie body. Maddox was surrounded by four of them. I watched him swing his mace with one hand while simultaneously reaching out with the other.

Maddox's fingers closed down over the grey's face, his fingers jamming into the eye sockets. With seemingly little effort, he lifted the grey high over his head where it writhed in agony and then dropped like a wet teabag onto the floor.

Two more launched themselves at him, and Maddox spun, thrusting a leg out in a roundhouse kick that took the legs out from beneath them. The mace came down mercilessly. Chests heaved; blood splattered upward, coating Maddox.

A scuttling sound beside me, far too near for my comfort, drew my attention. I cringed in reflex and sucked in a breath as the pain in my shoulder reminded me who was boss.

Absalom had engaged Doyle in the fight. And at first I was incensed at the unfairness of a man so much younger attacking an old man. Then I realized it was Absalom who was at the disadvantage.

Doyle obviously had centuries of fighting skill and training.

Without his greys, Absalom was pitiful at hand to hand combat. Doyle was playing with him the way a cat does a mouse.

I wondered if he had been playing Absalom all this time, pretending to be powerless, waiting for Maddox.

Doyle's shirt had torn from his shoulders to his waist, and for the first time, I really took note of how muscled his back was. Bands of sinew moved and writhed as he fought.

Absalom reached out his hands sideways instead of thrusting magic toward Doyle, and threads of silver light leaked out his fingertips the way a spider sends out gossamer. The tendrils of light locked on the pools of tar that surrounded each fallen grey.

Everything in the weapon discharged into the viscous fluid, and left Absalom bereft of manufactured energy.

All he had left was the magic of his nature.

It made no sense why he would discharge his weapon's energy until he tore the thing from his hand and grit his teeth, sucking in a breath that expanded his chest.

"He's going to change," I shrieked, but it only came out as the sound of a rusted hinge protesting sudden use.

Too late, Maddox, Fayed, Doyle realized the shift of energy.

Hair, teeth, and claws erupted from Absalom's body.

The chupacabra had taken over.

Chapter 30

Fayed was the first to react. He threw himself at the chupacabra's neck with a guttural roar. It raised its head, bracing itself for attack and I almost saw it smile.

Its mouth snapped open. Foul looking spittle dripped from its fangs.

Fayed met it just as it closed its mouth down over his midsection. A roar of pain lit through the room. The chupacabra thrashed its head back and forth. Fayed sagged, a doll in the clutches of that great maw.

I cried out, but I doubt anyone heard. Doyle and Maddox had already taken the chance the distraction offered and launched themselves toward the beast.

I felt powerless as I lay there. But I had to do something. Had to intervene somehow.

The stone. I still had it. I could make all this stop.

With no stone, none of this would matter.

I rolled onto my uninjured shoulder, biting down on the shock as pain lanced through me. My fingers crawled toward my pocket, making a sure, but slug-like trail toward the stone.

Inches. All I needed was a few inches. Skin to stone instead of fabric to stone and this, all of this, would be done. I just needed to aim my throw accurately, make sure it shed its wrappings as I hurled it toward Absalom.

The chupacabra chuckled beneath its breath, deep in its chest. Or maybe it was a growl. I couldn't tell. All I knew was the thing rose up on hind legs and dropped Fayed to the floor as it whirled on Maddox.

Doyle advanced on it from the other side. I could clearly see the muscles in his back tensing as he flexed his fists.

Maddox was drawing its attention so Doyle could attack.

Fayed twitched on the floor. He wasn't dead. Thank God, he wasn't dead.

And then a sharp, hot shot of electricity sizzled into my thigh.

Doyle rounded on me, his jaw dropped open, his eyes wide as moons.

"She's connecting," he said.

I spasmed, crying out as the needlepoint of pain grew into a dime. I started digging in earnest then, trying to grab for the stone to extract it from my pocket before it could hurt me anymore. To fling it away and at anything so long as it was gone.

"Isabella," Maddox shouted and I lifted my gaze to his. He wore a strange expression: one of joy and fear co-mingled.

My leg felt like ice. I was growing numb.

And I knew what that meant. I was bonding to the stone.

I didn't think about immortality. I didn't think about Lilith or the chupacabra. I didn't even think about Lucifer and the consequences of touching the stone.

I did not want to be bound to anything real or magical.

"No," I said. "Hell no."

As though the stone understood, it tore through my jeans, burning the material on exit. The smell of scorched cloth struck my nose. I fell back in relief, and watched it sail past my head to lodge into Doyle's outstretched palm.

It smacked into the skin with a wet thwack.

I expected to see him evaporate into thin air, hopping his freight car to Lucifer's domain, but he made a sound somewhere between a sigh and a moan.

Then he glowed.

It was enough to capture both Maddox and the chupacabra's attention. For one instant, both sets of eyes lingered on the ethereal looking light that wrapped Doyle in a red glow. He could have been standing in front of the fire, the light from the flames, licking around him.

That moment was all it took for the energy to shift in the room.

Doyle almost looked younger in those seconds before the glow burrowed into his tissues.

Maddox cried out, letting go the chupacabra and gripping his rib cage as though he were being branded from within by a hot iron.

Both men lifted their heads, almost involuntarily to the ceiling, their bodies rigid.

It was a second, and no more, certainly not enough for the chupacabra to launch at either of them, but when it was over, I realized it didn't matter anyway.

Absalom was already shifting back into human shape and running for the door.

I expected Maddox to run after him, but instead when the stone's energy freed him from whatever it was it had anchored into his core, he dropped his mace and ran at me.

I heard his knees popping as he crouched in front of me. His face was full of concern, and while he moved with great deliberation, as though he were hurt, he reached out to lay the back of his fingers against my forehead.

"Are you hurt?" he said.

I nodded, not trusting my voice.

He leaned in toward me, cupping my face with both hands, splaying his fingers over the back of my neck. His thumbs stroked my cheekbones.

"Did he hurt you?"

He. Meaning Absalom.

"No," I said.

"Then I can't heal that pain," he said and there was a note of sadness in his voice. "But I know where to –"

I shook my head. "No. No more magic. I think I need a break. I'll heal on my own, thank you."

He gave me a look like he wanted to argue, but instead, he laid his forehead against mine. I felt his breath against my cheek. His eyes closed in relief.

I looked up to see Doyle looming over the two of us.

"Is she well?" He looked concerned.

Maddox barely looked up at him, instead choosing to search my face.

"Nothing that won't heal, I don't think?" he said.

I shifted my body so that I was able to roll over onto my back.

"Just fell the wrong way, is all," I said. "I might have cracked a rib."

"You could have had immortality," Doyle stated. There was admiration in his voice.

I groaned through a spasm of pain as I adjusted myself on the floor.

"At what cost?" I said. "I finally just managed to get rid of one demon from my life. I certainly don't need another."

Doyle and Maddox exchanged looks.

"What?" I said.

Maddox slipped his arms beneath me, scooping me up and holding me against his chest. He stood as though I were no heavier than a basket of clothes.

"It's nothing," he said. "Don't worry about it."

He carried me over to the sofa and sat me down gently on it. Just that moment made me realize things weren't so bad after all. I winced, but I would live.

I surveyed the room, taking in the aftermath of the fight. I'd not expected the two of them to be able to hold up against the dozen or so bodies that littered the room. It was testament to the strength and cunning, but it was also a reminder of how dangerous things could be in this new world I'd come to know.

"So many people dead," I said. "Fayed. Is he--"

"He's a vampire," Maddox said. "He'll be fine after a swallow of living blood." He eyed the space where Fayed was even then beginning to move.

I felt the sofa give next to me and turned to see Doyle perched there. He caught my eye and immediately wrapped his arm around me, pulling me close. I buried my face in his chest and he rubbed my back.

I didn't realize how badly I needed to cry until then. I let go without shame, and his other arm came around me, hugging me tightly.

"It's all right, child," he said. "Just let it go."

I did. I wasn't sure how long I held onto him and sobbed into his chest, but with each passing moment, I felt lighter.

Finally, I withdrew. My face felt puffy and my nose was running.

"Hold it right there," Doyle said.

I froze and caught his eye.

"Don't even think about wiping that snot on me again," he said a smile touched the corners of his mouth. "I don't have another change of shirt."

The blue of his eyes was spectacular. It winked at me like sunlight on the ocean's surface.

"You're a piss poor excuse for a father," I said, teasing, but he wasn't and he had to know exactly how I felt.

When his smile broke, it was like the sun had come out. "Who said I was a good father?"

I let go his shirt finally, and leaned back against the sofa, running the cuff of my sleeve back and forth across my nose. I snuffed the rest of the fluid up into the back of my throat.

I thought I heard Maddox gag.

"Oh please," I said to him. "You just pretty much bathed in blood. A little bit of snot won't hurt."

"I hate to break this up," Doyle said. He stood up and took Maddox's hand. Maddox cupped his elbow. His expression looked tight.

"What?" I said. "What's going on?"

Both Maddox and Doyle embraced. I thought I caught Maddox's whispered words: "I know, Dad," he said.

"Know what?" I demanded. "Someone tell me what's going on."

Doyle looked askance at me. "It's not safe in this world for both the stone and I," he said.

"Not safe," I said. "I just watched the two of you mop up a platoon of nasty business plus a shape shifter."

Doyle touched my chin with his thumb. "Not a platoon, young one, just a few soulless minions. Now that the stone is viable again, we'll need to reconvene the order. And that's my duty." He ran his hand down along his core, patting down his torso as though checking for his keys.

"Some order," Maddox chuckled, but it was a tight, nervous laugh. "An order of one is no order."

Doyle lifted a finger as though to correct him. "Two," he said. There are two of us. You're not alone. Not anymore."

I thought I detected a look of sadness in Maddox's expression.

"It's best you don't know where I'm going for now," Doyle said. "But I'll call you to service when it's time."

Doyle leaned over to kiss me on the forehead. One small moth like touch with lips that were searingly hot.

He withdrew and cuffed Maddox on the shoulder.

"Now take this young mortal home. She looks exhausted."

He turned on his heel and strode away without looking back, and as he went, he leaned over to touch each grey's body, crossing the forehead with a motion of benediction. Each time, he would touch his thumb to his lips, and the grey at his feet would crumble to ash without a single eruption of flame.

When he met the door, the piles swept up into a vortex and followed him out in a tunnel of swirling dust.

"Show-off," Maddox mumbled, but his voice was filled with pride.

###

I was exhausted.

I might have even fallen asleep. When I woke, it was to the sound of a low rumble reverberating through my chest.

I peeled open my eyelids to discover I was in my own bed, tucked neatly into fresh sheets. My cat was sitting on top of me, her paws folded beneath her chest, eyelids half closed as she faced me.

She wasn't much of a purring type of cat, nor did she usually sleep on top of me.

"You must've missed me," I said.

I reached out to scratch her behind the ears. Of course, her eyes flew open at the movement, and she jumped off the bed, streaking toward the half open bedroom door.

"Should've known better," I mumbled to myself and lifted the blankets to peer beneath.

I was in fresh pajamas. I smelled of soap and sleep.

There was no way I stumbled home, took a shower, and climbed into bed without knowing or remembering.

This was Maddox's doing.

"Sonofabitch," I said. I had a discomforting image of him propping me up in the tub, all comatose and drooling.

"You met my father," said a voice from the doorway. "He wouldn't be happy with that assessment."

Maddox stood there, hands on his hips, feet crossed at the ankle as he leaned on the jamb.

"He's not the sort to bed down with a bitch," he said then shrugged as though he'd just thought of something he hadn't before. "Or maybe he was."

I tested the idea of movement by shrugging my shoulders. I was sore, but the pain in my ribs had decreased quite a bit.

He must have noticed because he came toward me.

"Nothing's broken," he said. "I did a quick rundown. You'll be up and terrorizing the city in a few days."

I eased myself up, wavering a bit as I found my balance with my palms behind me. He was right; my shoulder hurt far less than it did before, and I could breathe without wincing.

"A rundown," I said, testing the word. I raked my bottom lip in with my teeth as a picture of him running his hands down my body replaced the one of me drooling in the tub.

"Like, while I was naked or before?"

He held his hands up in protest.

"Please," he said. "I'm a monk. It's as good as going to the doctor."

His tone was earnest but the way he kept staring at my chest indicated he was remembering every savory detail. The thought of it made something heat up in my belly.

"Indeed," I said, not wanting to give him any reason to press the point.

I threw my legs out from beneath the blankets. There was a nice chill in the room that whispered over my skin and made me wiggle my toes in reflex.

"And exactly how did you get me in and out of the tub without me waking up?" I asked him.

He snorted. "The way you were snoring?" he said. "I don't think Lucifer himself could've woke you."

"Not funny," I said.

"It wasn't meant to be."

He strode into the room, closing the distance between us. I noticed he was wiping his hands on a towel.

"I gave you the military sponge bath," he said. "In some circles, otherwise known as a whore's bath."

I groaned in embarrassment. While the thought of having him rub soap over my body might be something steamy in a fantasy as I lay in bed at night, what he was suggesting came nowhere near an ideal fantasy.

"Please tell me you just washed my arms and legs."

Chapter 31

He lifted his eyebrows suggestively. "I could tell you that, if you really want me to."

I waved my hand at him, eager to be done with the discussion and change the subject.

"Never mind," I said. "I don't think I want to know."

My feet touched down on the familiar floor and I sighed with all the pleasure of being home. I took a step, aiming for my dresser and felt immediately dizzy.

He was across the floor in seconds and holding me against his chest, with one arm slung over my shoulders.

I shrugged him off.

"Trying to cop a feel?" I said. "God. You can just never trust a frustrated male virgin," I said. "Especially one who's been kicking around for a century."

"Centuries," he corrected. "And if you thought a few centuries would make me as desperate as a three year old goat, you're wrong. I passed my puberty the way most teen aged boys do, and I'm none the worse for wear. In fact, all that time practicing being celibate hardens the resolve."

"Sure. Practicing," I said with a snort. "That's what they call it in your world?"

He scowled at me but sent another lingering glance at my chest. I put my hand over my shirt and realized I wasn't wearing a bra. I felt my face flame all the way down to my collarbone as I realized the full truth of what he'd been saying.

"You completely undressed me."

He shrugged. "You were filthy all over. I threw the clothes in the trash."

"I could have washed those," I said.

One russet eyebrow lifted. "I think not. There were cooties on them."

"They were my favorite jeans."

"Torn and scorched."

I lifted my eyebrows inelegantly.

"And my panties?" I said, realizing as I stood that I chafed in my pajama pants.

"Those were particularly awful," he said. "An abomination meant to ward off men of all races. And a relief for a frustrated male virgin." He lifted a russet eyebrow playfully.

I squared my shoulders as I imagined the big cotton bloomers I'd pulled on that morning.

"Well," I said, thinking about the granny style underwear I'd had on. "I wasn't planning on seducing anyone."

"You went to a sex party."

I blinked. "Your point?"

He shook his head, mumbling something about being grateful he was a monk and put his fingers to his chest as though I'd offended him.

"I was the very picture of gentlemanly restraint," he said. "You might thank me."

He grabbed my robe from the side of the door and threw it at me.

"I'm not sure I like the idea of you looking at me nude when I can't defend myself."

"No worries, Kitten," he drawled. "I closed my eyes at the dirtiest parts. The trouble was, there were a lot of dirty parts. I might have had to peek now and then to make sure I got you all clean."

He waved me toward him as he retreated to the kitchen.

"Come on," he said. "The only thing worse than your snoring is the sound of your stomach growling."

I followed him meekly, enjoying the solid feel of bare feet on familiar ground. I entered the kitchen to the fragrance of curry and ginger.

"Butter chicken?" I guessed, inhaling the aromatic perfume. It swaddled me in ways that made me feel warm from head to toe. My stomach roared its impatience.

"How long have I been asleep?"

He eyed me.

"Two days. Well," he said, counting on his fingers. "About forty seven hours, actually."

I sniffed at the air to inhale the fragrance onto my palate.

"So you cooked?" I said. Apparently, the non-man was full of surprises.

He crossed his arms over his chest and scowled at me.

"Not an easy task in a house full of snacking crackers and squeeze cheese."

Then he twisted to reach behind his shoulder. He pulled open the cupboard with a flourish and I gasped. It was full of food. Real food. There was pasta and canned goods and bread.

I caught sight of a bag of nacho chips, nestled toward the back--a holdover from a week earlier.

"Gimme," I said as I took an involuntary step toward him.

He slapped my hands away from the shelf.

"Not until you've eaten properly. I noticed you're far too skinny." He poked me in the belly, almost as though to prove he was lying.

"Scottie said I was fat," I said.

And then the wash of what I'd done to Scottie flooded over me. I lost the strength in my legs and had to find the nearest chair. I sank onto the armrest.

"He's gone," Maddox said.

"I know."

"Not the way you mean," he said carefully. "I removed his body."

My head snapped up at the words.

"I couldn't leave him lying there," he explained. "So I took care of it. Fayed helped."

"So that's why you were there."

"We were there because Doyle told us where you were. He sent me to your hotel room after...well, after I tucked you in."

"If that's the case, then why didn't he just trace it to Scottie and retrieve it while it was in his safe? Why didn't you know Doyle was here? Why did we have to hunt him down?"

"His mark is a bit different, you see. You saw how it reacts to my skin, but it does other things too. Doyle says his mark is more attuned to all his senses, because they are bonded. What it sees, he sees. What it smells, he smells. Mine is more like scent. You touched it, remember? I could smell its magic on you. Kind of like a bloodhound.

"I couldn't tell if you still had it or if it was just somewhere in the city. I just knew it was in the realm somewhere and that it had been in your apartment."

"Sounds creepy if you ask me," I said. "You're telling me that thing can see? Wouldn't it have been easier if you had magicked it so it could talk too?"

He had the grace to laugh.

"Our marks aren't exactly like science, you know. But I imagine its sentience comes from the demon goddess trapped inside."

I plucked my fork from the table and tapped it against a slice of coated chicken.

"I know," I said. ""Magic doesn't work that way, but it would be hell of a lot more convenient if it did."

"Did you just make a pun there?" he said, scooping up a saucy bit of chicken with a hunk of Naan bread.

I grinned, feeling the smear of greasy curry coating my teeth.

"Well I'm glad it's over."

"You did well," he said, passing me a slice of warm Naan. "I'm impressed, actually. You handled it all like a pro."

"I am a pro," I said. "At least, I used to be." I frowned at the implication of the words. "I'm not sure what I am now. Just a regular gal, I guess."

While Scottie was gone and I was free of his threat, I wasn't exactly ready to take up my old habits. If anything, the loss of the kingpin would send the organization into a tailspin and I wasn't sure if the new boss would be indulgent of a freelance thief in its territory.

I was sure that Scottie had moved most of his operation to the metro and had been in the midst of starting up a faction here. I imagined the new boss would expand and continue.

I wasn't even sure if they would want retribution.

I couldn't just take that chance.

Maddox must have noticed the way I was moving the chicken around the plate and barely tasting it. He took my fork and placed it neatly beside my glass of lemon water.

"If you're worried about him finding you, don't be. I doubt he'll attack again so quickly. He'll want to regroup. Build up his army again."

I raised my eyes to his across the table.

"Army?" I said. "They're pretty well organized, but I wouldn't call them an army."

He leaned back, obviously just realizing I wasn't thinking about the same concern as him.

"I was talking about Absalom."

"Absalom?" I said, confused. "He's gone. The stone is gone. Doyle is gone. What do I have to worry about him for?"

He laid his hand on mine across the table and I couldn't help looking at the way they fit together. His palm was warm and dry, calloused in places. I got lost in thoughts of how they'd feel on my arm, my back. Count on me to find all the wrong men.

I only realized he was still talking when his hand tightened on mine.

"What?" I said.

"I said: you are no longer just a mortal. You are a potential conduit, and if he ever tracks Doyle down, he'll want to know where you are. He won't just forget you. He'll watch you. He'll wait. And when he thinks the time is right, he'll strike."

"Great," I said, throwing down my piece of Naan. "Now I've got two targets on my back." I crossed my arms over my chest, cupping my elbows.

"Maybe," he said. "But now at least you won't be alone."

I quirked my eyebrow at him. "What's that, now? You think my cat is going to scratch their eyes out?" I watched her curling around on the sideboard, glaring at Maddox. "The only person she seems to hate is you."

He dipped a piece of bread into the sauce and touched it to my lips, poking at the corner until I opened up. I chewed but resisted the urge to close my eyes in raptured delight. He was a really good cook but I wasn't ready to feed his ego.

"She'll warm up to me," he said. "Most females do. It's a curse, actually." He stuffed the edge in. "But she'll have plenty of time to get used to me."

"You're planning on abducting her? I wouldn't advise it. She's pretty particular about the state of her house." I waved the fork to indicate the socks she'd pulled from my drawers and shredded over the living room while I'd been out.

He sent the balls of fabric a dirty look. "No," he said. "Not exactly."

"Then what, exactly, are you saying?"

He dipped his finger into the sauce and tapped me on the nose with it.

"I'm saying I'm your protection. Call me your personal guardian."

I pushed away from the table, scrubbing my nose with the back of my sleeve. When I thought I could articulate exactly what bothered me about that sentence, I realized I was wringing my hands as I sat there. I pulled them down against my hips and held them their while I gave him a careful eye.

"I haven't had a guardian since I left foster care," I said, noting that while my voice was perfectly level, my left hand had begun trembling. "I'm not interested in one now."

I waited for that to sink in and then I picked up my plate, full of sauce and chicken and the delightful aroma of spices, and I carried it to the sink. I dropped the plate on the counter.

I ran through the years I'd spent with Scottie, waiting for the hammer to drop, the years afterward when I expected someone to be recording my every movement. When there was no one there, relief never rested my mind because there was always the next moment, the next corner, the next day.

I was done with all that.

The rest of my life would be on my terms. Whatever that meant, I was going to face it. Starting with the Kindred right behind me.

I spun on my heel, laying my palms out beside me on the counter, aware I was subconsciously making myself bigger. So maybe I had a way to go, but dammit, the buck stopped here.

"I'm a big girl. I refuse to be watched."

"You do naughty things you don't want folks to see?" he said. "Because I'm into that."

Whatever effect he was looking for, he didn't get it. He almost looked chagrined when I spoke up.

"Don't bother with the sexual innuendos," I said dryly. I didn't want to be lulled by that charming facade. "I know your big secret, remember?"

He held my eye and I respected that. He wasn't flinching. In fact, he leaned backward in his chair far enough that it lifted from its front legs and hovered on its balance point.

"How about a proposition, then," he said. "Will you feel better if you think you have a choice?"

I noted he didn't say I had a choice, just that I might feel better thinking I did. I pushed away from the counter.

"A proposition." I crossed one ankle over the other as I watched him get up from the table and close the distance between us. I tracked his progress with my eyes.

"Nothing good ever came from a proposition offered by a virgin."

I stressed the word virgin as though it was dirty.

"Work for me," he said. "I can't promise Absalom will leave you alone, but it will help you network and it will allow me to..." He paused there as his eyes lit on mine before trailing down to my mouth. "...Well," he went on. "It will let me keep an eye on you without lurking in shadows and breaking into your apartment out of fear someone has taken to treating you like a piñata."

So he had been listening. More than that, he had been paying attention. I felt a rush of warmth cascade over the back of my neck. I couldn't speak for the swell of gratitude.

He must have thought I was still hesitant because he added, "And I could use someone at Recollections that has a good sense of property reallocation."

A smile tugged at the corner of my mouth, wanting me to allow it to surface. "You mean a thief," I said. "You're looking for a thief."

He put his finger alongside his nose. "A good thief," he insisted. "The Shadow Bazaar is only one facet of my business. Recollections is my clandestine business inside of it. When Doyle disappeared I set it up as a way to find him and the stone, but it turned into a real money maker. It's the perfect way for a woman such as yourself to start fresh while using the skills your gods gave you."

"Recollections," I mused. "I might be persuaded. What kind of name is that? What would I be stealing, exactly? How would I be paid?"

He grinned broadly and pinched my cheek playfully.

"I guess you'll have to see, Kitten."

-finito-

The excitement isn't over. Fans of the series pick up the Christmas Story, but you can just Keep rooting for Isabella in Soul Merchant, where things get really, really hairy.

About Author

Thea is a NEW YORK TIMES and USA TODAY Bestselling Author. She used to have a black lab at her feet when she wrote, warming up the calves. It can be cold in rural Nova Scotia. Now it's just a cuppa tea keeping her warm.

Whether she's finding ways to lure Isabella Hush into the Shadow Bazaar or throwing the switch on a new monster, her urban fantasy pulses with dark themes and action-packed intrigue. Her characters are always deeply wounded creatures struggling for redemption. The romance is slow-burn but worth it, and the humor just might have a touch of Canadiana.

As a fan of Dannika Dark and Patricia Briggs, she hopes you enjoy slipping into the skin of her characters as much as she enjoy theirs.

Hang out with her on the socials:
Pick up bonuses by joining her email reading group. For more information visit theaatkinson.com

Acknowledgments

Several loyal readers have special places in my writer's heart. Some of them, like Caroline Jenkins and Denise Sherman always take the time to find my little oopsies and sometimes my big ones. An author needs readers like that.

Then there's readers like Crystal Crystal Amason, who isn't just a reader, she's a sponsor, and you don't get more loyal than that. She is the first reader to make me feel like my tales were worth reading. Thank you, Crystal. I hope I can continue to write stories you enjoy.

To my other patrons who prefer to remain anonymous, I thank you. You know who you are.

I really appreciate you all.

-thea-

MORE BY THEA

What are you missing?

By Series

THE IRON KING'S ASSASSIN

ISABELLA HUSH SERIES

COUNTERFEIT PSYCHIC

WITCHES OF ETLANTUM

VAMPIRE ADDICTIONS

REAPERS REDEMPTION

GRAVES FILES

ROGUE HUNTRESS

THETA WAVES

QUEEN OF SKY AND SHADOW

Hale Saint

Mainstream and Stand-alones

One Insular Tahiti

Anomaly

Secret Language of Crows

Throwing Clay Shadows

www.ingramcontent.com/pod-product-compliance
Lightning Source LLC
Chambersburg PA
CBHW031254120726
47906CB00003B/743